Rare Birds

Rare Birds

Kathleen Novak

THE PERMANENT PRESS
Sag Harbor, NY 11963

For information, address:
    The Permanent Press
    4170 Noyac Road
    Sag Harbor, NY 11963
    www.thepermanentpress.com

Library of Congress Cataloging-in-Publication Data
    Novak, Kathleen, author.
        Rare birds / Kathleen Novak.
        Sag Harbor, NY : The Permanent Press, [2107]
        ISBN 978-1-57962-498-9

    PS3614.O9265 R37 2017
    813'.6—dc23   2017007979

Printed in the United States of America

IN MEMORY OF
ANTONIA ANTONELLI
&
JENNIE ANTONELLI NOVAK

THE HISTORY

It began as legend, but after a while it became true. That the whole town had been moved, packed up like a picnic before the rain, meager possessions hoisted into the back of anyone's truck and driven one mile south, an unwanted interruption in their hard-soled lives, simply because they lived on ore, bounteous and deep and none of it their own. And so they rumbled south, some toting whole houses on heavy-duty trailers, gaggles of kids gawking and jeering, but it happened. Mining companies cajoled them with money, built a school with marble steps and crystal chandeliers, a three-story hospital with a high-ceilinged house next door for the nuns. Mining company money moved half the old cemetery, stone by stone, and constructed a city hall with a library and police department in the basement.

By the post World War II years, the legend had taken hold and the town fully settled. One main street became the hub for shops and banks, a movie theater with side balconies like those in the big cities. Bars, cafés. A stately hotel with a lounge and barbershop. This new town had concrete steps and paved roads and churches on every corner. People had an idea that they were all there to stay. They planted gardens and berry patches. They hung chintz curtains and paintings they bought at the new five-and-dime.

Nobody in that northern ore town traipsed in with a pedigree or jewels handed down. They had relations in some Old Country with faces so weathered you could see their every sorrow and triumph in a single toothless smile. So these settlers staked their own, even living so far north on the edge of nothing. On the edge of nowhere, they staked their claim.

And in the center of town, just three blocks from the main street and two blocks from the three-story hospital, a particular neighborhood emerged, with its tidy row of houses and broad elms overhanging the avenues. This enclave was bordered by the town's massive arena on one side and the handsome brick elementary school on the other. It had a church, a grocery, two apartment buildings, a garage apartment, and an abandoned house. At night anyone on those blocks could see every star that ever was. Or so they said.

AUTHOR'S NOTE

Though the events here are fictional,
many of the characters in the book lived—
in a long-ago time, in their faraway place.
Their names are not changed, nor is the
wonder I have always felt for them.

ONE

Monday, June 6, 1960

i.

"Such a sleepy day," said Mrs. Wilke, crossing her thick legs just so on the ottoman. "Such a sleepy summer day." Gertrude did not agree. "Not really," she replied, but Mrs. had already dozed off, the fingers on her left hand twitching in that peculiar way they did. Gertrude had no idea. No matter how long she lived with her older caretaking companion, she never had an idea why Mrs. Wilke's fingers twitched as they did. Or the miniscule nerve in her left eyelid either. Some flaw on that side of things.

For Gertrude, summer erupted. She could hear it rustling and rocking along, every inch of the block a blast of color or noise or movement, the grass hollering and the bugs screeching. Every pale leaf waving about.

She'd already been around some few times. Maybe five or six, her first two before the church janitor mowed, the second few when he was pushing the mower along, the hysteria of green blades flying out behind him, the aroma of grass following her, and then she'd gone again at noon, the quick breath of noon, before the kids came back outside and there she was, Gertrude herself, head in forward motion to see what she could see.

For lunch they'd had their egg salad, Mrs. Wilke's favorite, crusts trimmed, tea with ice, all of that, a dab or two to the mouth with the paper napkins Gertrude loved. Tissue crinkling and twittering, crushed into song. And now Mrs. napping and Gertrude checking the knots on her shoelaces, yanking up the white anklets and off to the block with its twelve houses per side, two apartment buildings, one store, and one church, that one church without a steeple or bell, its sign out there, plain and simple, the Church of Christ, Scientist.

"I never knew," she'd said years ago, when she first came to stay with Mrs. Wilke, first tied on her thick-heeled shoes and launched herself onto the sidewalk. "Christ the scientist, I never knew," she'd said to sturdy Mrs. Wilke standing at the door.

"What dear? You never knew what?"

Gertrude had slapped her scrawny thigh and hooted, "Christ! Did you know he was a scientist?"

"So they say," Mrs. had answered, not particularly interested. And now the grass on the church lawn was cut, trimmed to the sidewalk line and tidy as God's plan, and the snipped grass roaring with sweetness, still alive, hosting bugs, worms, ants, business happening, business transpiring.

She could tell anyone anything about this block. The brick school across the street from the church. The humongous arena

across the street on the other side of the block, her side of
the block, where the circus came once in a blue moon. Skat-
ers all winter. And sports, she guessed. Cars parked up and
down, doors slamming in the silent winter nights, those long
and silent winter nights. Winter slept, that's where Mrs. had it
wrong. Winter slept. Summer roared.

Gertrude waved to the store owner, smoking out on his stoop,
of all things. "How you," she called, hearing her voice tumbling
out, pushing through the cloud of smoke, the singular sound
of herself.

Everyone knew her name. Wouldn't she round the block nearly
a dozen times a day? For five, maybe seven years? Before the
smoker and his wife owned the store, back when the Italian
lady swept up candy wrappers every day. Gertrude could smell
the sausages then, the spices, always something cooking in the
back of the store. Flies buzzing at the screen. Hysterical flies,
Gertrude remembered. She remembered everything.

Mr. McCumber, in his dandy hat, shined shoes. Old Lady
Kirshling with all her grudges. Mrs. Larsen talking, always so
much to say. What time would the mail come? Was it going to
rain? See how little Elise was growing.

Gertrude remembered every house, where everyone belonged,
and when they popped outside, like the girl whose daddy baked
bread. Out she'd come on Gertrude's first round, because the
household awoke early and there she'd be, rumpled little thing,
sticky hair, fat knees.

Possibly, some people laughed when middle-aged, skinny old
Gertrude marched by, the ruckus of a hundred ants warping

her reason, but she didn't think about it. Her brain was full. Mrs. kept her safe, safe enough. She never crossed a street. She remembered things. She understood the thunder in every waking breath.

"How you," she called to Katie Fiore sitting on the curb with Mrs. Larsen's Elise, whose long, perfect braids screamed in discomfort, poor thing, that nervous mother pulling perfect braids, talking and talking. The girls' bare legs dragging in the dirt and the hot, clean summer air making way as Gertrude strode around one more time, her own house quiet, Mrs. in there still thinking it a sleepy day as the afternoon hours budded and burst.

One more time, one more time. Nothing going at the church, Mrs. Kirshling tucked away in her locked house, cranky as a crow that one, the store's shades pulled, a CLOSED sign propped in the window, of all things. And there the girls were again, on the curb, and a new one standing nearby, dirty canvas shoes yowling, but the new girl waved back, a truck of furniture parked nearby. "How you," Gertrude called and made her legs move faster, roaring like the day, like the noisy, busy, cacophonic day.

"That you, Gertie?" Mrs. asked as Gertrude closed the screen door securely behind her. "You back?"

Gertrude ran a glass of water for herself and one for Mrs. Wilke. "A new girl's moving into the white apartment building," she reported, taking two hardy swallows of the water.

"Riff raff," Mrs. answered. She swirled her water in the glass. "Nothing but riff raff in that building."

"She waved at me though," Gertrude had to defend, choosing on the spot not to mention the yowling canvas shoes, caked in dirt. "She waved though," Gertrude repeated and gulped her water without even stopping to breathe.

ii.

Elise's mother, Betty Larsen, spent at least an hour a day trying to make sense out of herself in the mirror. She studied her square face and broad cheekbones, her eyes with so few lashes, her imperfect skin and large mouth, the whole combination of features that did not amount to beauty no matter how she smiled or tipped her chin down or lifted it high and mighty. She might not even be pretty. She was quite sure she was not. "What are you doing, Momma?" Elise occasionally asked, though she seldom got an answer and so wandered off. The girl was a wanderer at heart. A ghost, that's what she was, with hardly ever a word to say.

Betty had given birth to Elise almost seven years earlier, certain it would change her life. Certain that her longtime lover would settle on this beautiful baby. Because unlike her mother, Elise was beautiful. Her father's family spawned these fine-boned girls, graceful, all with mysterious eyes and long aristocratic necks. But the man had not settled. He still came and went, wandering in and out of her days much like Elise wandered in and out of the four rooms in the garage apartment where they lived.

Elise did not call the man Papa or Daddy, but Claus. Betty called herself Mrs. Larsen and wore an inexpensive gold band she bought on a bus trip to Duluth when Elise was just a baby. "That wasn't necessary," Claus told her then. "We'll come around to it." Her face in the mirror every day told her something else however. That she had enough strands of gray to require a box of Miss Clairol once a month and that her mouth was beginning to pucker in perpetual disappointment. Her daughter was already in school, had already finished first grade and so the teachers knew that the girl had only Mrs. Larsen. There was no Mr. Larsen. Mr. Larsen's name was Claus Jacobson and he lived on the other side of town with a tiny, bewildered wife, who had conceived his other three daughters with their regal necks and unfathomable eyes.

Still, Claus came now and then as he always had, parking a block away and walking to her door, where he used his own key to let himself in then hung his hat and suit jacket at the top of the stairs. He didn't call ahead. They never made a plan, which meant that every day she donned a pressed blouse and fussed with her hair and wore the fire-engine-red lipstick that Claus liked. She kept her nails polished and the bathroom spotless, waiting for a guest in a felt hat and perfectly buffed black shoes.

"Hello, Elise," he would say to his youngest daughter, who believed her father had died in the Korean War. Elise would say, "Hello, Claus," because that's what her mother wanted her to say. Then he'd ask her if she'd like to go outside and play, which meant that he expected her to leave for a while. And Elise always did leave. Even in winter. Even in rain. When Claus hung his hat on the hook at the top of the stairs, Elise left the apartment. Betty suspected that her daughter either sat on the curb outside their door or dug her rump into a snow bank and perched there munching chunks of dirty ice.

Elise wasn't allowed to cross the street alone, and she never broke a rule or even challenged one. She'd only cried once in the last several years, because she hadn't been invited to Katie Fiore's birthday party. Elise had stood at the window, watching the girls, all of them two or three years older than she was, and cried so long and feverishly that Betty had finally suggested they walk to Bridgeman's for a milk shake.

But Claus Jacobson never made Elise cry. She appeared to have no reaction to him whatsoever, other than a vague discomfort regarding the nature of his visits. "Why does he come here?" she'd asked Betty, though not nagging, for it was not her nature. "We have business, Elise," Betty had answered. "Because your father is not here, I need a man's opinions."

"You don't want me to hear?" That question had stumped Betty for a minute or two. Elise so seldom talked, that her obvious and insightful question threw Betty off course.

"Well," she'd finally concocted, "some things are better unheard."

Elise had stared at Betty without saying a word, her eyes seeming enlarged with wonder. Clearly, she could not imagine.

But for Betty those things unheard were the very pulse of her life and her reason for being, the large hands traveling her in all directions and the silent, wet mouth, every moment with him unearthly to her, enchanted even, as though this man carried his own electricity, his own quivers of lightning, always more than she thought she could bear. And then it would be over. He'd smile slightly, though not necessarily at her, possibly at the thought of somewhere else he meant to be or merely at his own satisfaction, the sprint completed, the sweat just beginning to evaporate into the rest of time. Then he'd smooth his hair. Then he'd dress and go. From the window Betty would watch him stride toward his car.

"Did Claus say good-bye to you?" she once asked Elise, who shook her head with grave concentration. "Does he ever?" Betty probed, and Elise shook her head again. But that piece of information didn't change the way Betty felt about Claus Jacobson. She didn't think anything ever would.

iii.

The problem for Katie Fiore was knowing too much. For example, she could tell you how many times Gertrude rounded the block on an average summer day and what time Mr. Vernon locked up the store no matter who needed what. She knew her mother's heart was broken and that neither she nor her pop could mend it. She knew that a man driving a blue sedan visited Mrs. Larsen regularly. She knew the teenage boy across the street went into Vernon's at least twice a day and that cross-eyed Godfrey and his wife, who passed her house with an empty basket on their way downtown, always filled it with things they did not pay for.

She didn't want to know everything she knew. Even at nine years old, she would have liked a somewhat different life, where she was distracted by happiness and the full force of childish adventure. She would have preferred to swim lakes like the girls at school whose parents owned cabins. She would have loved to be a figure skater who could shoot the duck without falling over and spin and spin until her short skirt stuck out straight around her.

She might have liked being a sister to someone, but her brothers had died before they were even born. They had names, though. Not Italian names, really, but Catholic at least. Nonna had approved. Then it hadn't mattered because, in both cases, her mother had been rushed to the hospital two months before they were born and come home days later without them. "Seven is unlucky, Kate," she said. "It isn't my number."

"But I was born on that day," Katie answered, when her mother made this observation about the unlucky seven, which she did on the seventh of every month, for example, and when she rolled a seven in Parcheesi and sometimes at seven in the morning or just before *Ed Sullivan* came on at seven Sunday nights. Katie didn't always remind her mother that she'd been born on the seventh, the seventh of October. She didn't always say it, but she thought it every time, so many times she was exhausted thinking it. Seven wasn't her mother's lucky number. "It's not my number, Kate."

Her mother was the only person who called her Kate. She'd stopped calling her Katie when Matthew was almost born. "You're a big girl now," she'd explained, though Katie was just three at the time. And that was another thing Katie knew. She knew her mother had forgotten her daughter's childhood. She talked to Katie as she would any adult and expected restrained, ever polite behavior. "Be seen but not heard," was her mother's philosophy, which meant that Katie moved almost without motion. She read books and sat on the front porch watching. She carved narrow gullies in the sandbox, filled them with water, and saw her rivers flow as they did. She would have liked to have a boat. She would have liked to row a boat down a muddy river and sing, "comin' for to carry me home."

She thought she might be a good piano player perhaps, like Miss Hessler at school, who showed up once a week for an hour, back straight, fingers pounding the old upright she wheeled from room to room, red lips wide open as she sang. Katie believed she could do that, but her parents said they had no money for a piano. They offered the flute as an option, as they could rent one inexpensively through the school. But they had missed the point. With a piano she could play and sing. She could learn the notes of "Don't Fence Me In," and sing all the verses while she plunked out the same melody over and over. Or "The Man On The Flying Trapeze" or "The First Noel." Katie loved so many songs she could hardly list them all. They erupted in her brain every day, tumbling out of her through all her lonely moments. Without skating lessons or a piano or a boat or a brother, she had learned what she could do on her own, and singing was one of those things.

Nonna, her grandma, liked to sing too, but she knew only Italian songs, ardent lyrics she'd learned as a girl tending sheep on a hillside near the Adriatic Sea. The two of them, often left alone by all the busier members of the family, sang for each other and laughed for the joy of it. "*Tutto* funny," Nonna liked to say.

Her Italian grandfather was not so lighthearted. He'd come to America to be a cowboy, rode a horse in Montana, hustled cows, Katie thought, or helped out on a ranch. He moved to this mining town to marry Nonna, who had loved him since childhood. But he didn't work in the mines. He drove a bus back and forth from the oldest part of town to the newest. He was an early settler who, according to Katie's pop, seemed to learn about any real estate opportunity before most anyone else even guessed it. "Your grandpa's a rich man, Katie," her pop had told her. "Shrewd." A short, stocky Italian, Alessandro Abelli had bought land at the right time, put houses on that land, collected rent, and visited the bank weekly. The bank president stopped whatever he was doing when Alessandro walked through the door. "Like Monopoly, Pop," Katie had responded, but he didn't know what she was talking about.

America was another part of Katie's knowing. She really knew America. She knew "This Land Is Your Land" and Monopoly, storybook dolls, *Rin Tin Tin,* and Trixie Belden. Nobody else in her family knew these things. They didn't pay attention. Her pop knew dance band music and some singers like Frank Sinatra, who was Italian too, just like Dean Martin, Perry Como, and Tony Bennett. Her pop played bocce ball with all his relations and all of their extended relations, but he didn't do American sports like baseball or football. He'd joined a bowling league once, but that was the year her mother had lost Patrick, so he quit to stay home and keep her company. That whole long winter they'd played cards in the kitchen until past Katie's bedtime. She could hear their low voices and the occasional clink of ice in their glasses of whiskey.

On the first full day of summer, Katie crossed the street to where Elise Larsen sat on the curb scratching lines in a bit of street dirt. "Claus's here," Elise said without waiting for a question. Katie sat down next to her, nodding to say she understood, which in a way she did.

"There goes Gertrude," Elise pointed out, as the skinny lady in pedal pushers rounded the corner on the other side of the street.

"How you," Gertrude called as she sped by, lickety-split.

"Where's she going again?" Elise asked.

"Nowhere," Katie answered. "She never leaves the block."

"Me either," Elise said.

A green pickup truck had parked across the street in front of the sprawling white apartment building. "Maybe someone's moving in," Elise observed as they watched two men and a girl unloading furniture. The girl stood up in the back of the truck and signaled to Katie and Elise. "Hello there," she shouted, then leapt over the side and ran toward them.

"You live here?" the new girl asked, eyeing the garage apartment behind them.

"She does." Katie thrust her thumb at Elise. "I live across the street."

The girl looked older to Katie, maybe twelve or thirteen, and disheveled. Her tenners had never been washed, her hair went unmanaged, and her clothes didn't quite fit. "My name's Sue Too," she said.

"Two? Like one, two?"

"No, T-O-O, like another Sue." Katie and Elise fell silent thinking about that. "There's always more than one Sue around. But only one Sue Too."

Katie nodded. It made some sense. "I'm Katie Fiore and this is Elise Larsen."

"Well, pleased to meet you. What's crackin'?"

"It's the first day of summer," Katie said. "We're just sitting around."

"Oh sure. Well, we'll be moved in maybe in an hour. Mind if I join you then?"

"Claus's here," Elise ventured.

"Her mom's friend," Katie said.

"He does business," Elise explained.

"Oh sure," Sue Too guffawed. "That's men for you. My dad's the guy over there in the hat. The one in the overalls is my brother-in-law, Joe, but he lives out at the farm with my oldest sister. Anyway."

"How you," Gertrude called to the girls again from across the street, as she marched head first into a nonexistent wind.

"That's Gertrude," Elise said, as all three of them waved. "She's really fast."

"Where's she off to?" Sue Too asked, still watching Gertrude round the other corner and vanish from sight.

"Katie says nowhere." Little Elise's eyebrows rose high on her pretty face.

"That's somethin'," Sue Too said and whistled. "Anyway, see you later. You'll be here later?"

The other two nodded. They were not used to anyone making plans with them. They weren't even sure just what it meant.

"Are we supposed to sit here until she comes back?" Elise asked, clearly concerned.

"I don't know," Katie answered. She'd hit on something she actually did not know.

iv.

After Sue Too galloped off to help her family move into the apartment building across the street, Katie and Elise sat without saying much, watching as the new girl's brother-in-law and father hoisted a sofa, a couple of chairs, bed frames, lamps, and boxes out of their truck. Sue Too had disappeared inside, where Katie assumed she was arranging things in the building's small, shabby rooms.

"Sue Too's interesting," Katie said, thinking that she liked the bright blue of the new girl's eyes and the way her hair had no observable order.

Elise nodded, completely elevated to be whiling the time with Katie Fiore and now maybe an older girl who hadn't ignored her and had a sister on a farm somewhere. It all seemed too good to be true. When the door behind them opened and Claus stepped out, Elise greeted him with unexpected confidence. "Bye, Claus," she said, turning to look right at him from her low spot on the curb. He glanced her way, but continued on in long-legged steps to his blue sedan down the street.

"You like him?" Katie asked.

The little girl's face gave no indication. "He's Claus."

"Does he ever play with you?" Katie was thinking about how her pop always horsed around doing corny things with her, piggyback rides and games, how he'd let her dance on his feet and wear his hats. Silly things her mother would never consider and didn't always approve.

Elise stuck out her lower lip, thinking. "What do you mean anyway?" And when Katie explained, Elise had to concede that, no, Claus had never played with her. "Nobody does really," she added, stating the fact as it was, a bare bit of the truth. "Momma likes him though."

A minute later Mrs. Larsen was at the screen door. "Hi, Katie. Nice to see you. Isn't it nice to see her, Elise? Summer's finally here, isn't it? But we're cool upstairs. Good ventilation, all the windows. Well-built actually, for a garage apartment. Course the fan will help too, when it gets hotter. We don't need a fan today anyway. But it's warm for June." She paused. After initially acknowledging her presence, both girls had turned back to watching the street, which rolled along like a concrete river, its pebbles, ruts, and loose dirt providing an attraction that Elise's mother could not begin to understand.

"Someone's moving in? It looks like someone's moving in over there. Of course, they come and go all the time in that building. Who can keep up with it?"

"There's a new girl," Elise turned around to say. "She's called Sue Too." Elise sounded very proud of this information and, before Mrs. Larsen could react, Katie added, "It's because there's always another Sue."

"Really? What kind of idea is that? There's always another Betty, but you don't see me calling myself Betty Too, do you? Well, she's a girl. Maybe her mother thinks it's cute. Her mother doesn't have another Sue, does she? That would be more than I could take, even for that building. It's always something over there."

"The phone's ringing, Momma," Elise interrupted.

"Oh, it is. All right. Don't leave the block, Elise. Don't let her, Katie. Well, maybe if you stay with her. Elise you can cross the street with Katie. Just one street." She seemed to be saying more as she hurried up the stairs, but the girls could not decipher just what. For a moment the afternoon's silence surrounded them like a balm. Without realizing it, they both sighed deeply.

Then in a crash, Sue Too burst out the front door of the apartment building, jumped the stairs two at a time, and flew over to them, a tightly bagged column of Saltine crackers in her hand. "Housewarming," she said, ripping open the bag and offering it to Katie.

"I can cross the street with Katie," Elise said to their new friend.

"So let's explore. There's a whole basement under our building you know."

Elise frowned, focused on eating her Saltine, baby finger high in the air. "Are we crossing the street?"

"Go big," Sue Too said, shoving three crackers into her mouth at one time.

Katie saw Nonna in the garden working with her tomato plants, knotting strips of old underwear loosely around the burgeoning plants and the stakes that would guide their growth through the summer, too preoccupied to notice the girls on the curb. Katie and Elise stood up, wiped the dirt from the seats of their shorts, and followed Sue Too across the street to the apartment building with its many doors, stairways, levels, and unknowns.

The side door of the building, a low afterthought sort of thing, opened with a creak into a plain basement, dark but clean, surrounded by even smaller doors for storage, each numbered to match an apartment upstairs. "Here's ours," Sue Too cried out, like she'd just won a prize. "Number Seven!" The small, empty storeroom smelled musty.

"My mother would never live in your apartment," Katie commented. "Seven is her unlucky number."

"It's not mine," Sue Too blurted. "For me it's going to be lucky, I can tell." She scanned the basement area, concrete floors, three ground-level windows, laundry tubs, and a coin-operated washer. "Not much though, is it?" Sue Too shrugged at the plainness of it all.

"Well, it's a basement," Katie said, assessing, however, that it had none of the attractions of her own basement, where off-season clothes hung in a slanted closet under the stairs and the pantry shelves were always stocked with enough cans and jars to get her family through another war, if it came to that. In Katie's basement, she had a desk, discarded when an old school was demolished, and her own tiny lamp that allowed her to play there at night if she wanted to pretend she was living alone in the mountains or raising her dolls single-handedly.

"I don't have a basement," Elise put out, frozen in fascination.

"Poor kid," Sue Too said. She continued to roam the room looking for something worth her attention.

"But there's a garage under us," the little girl argued, not really wanting to be a poor kid.

Sue Too had had enough of her apartment building's basement. "Let's get out of here," she said with authority and led Katie and Elise back out into the midafternoon sun, all three of them just a bit more bedraggled than before, as though the dimness of the basement had taken some toll. "Should be something around to explore. Who lives there?" She pointed to the house in front of the garage apartment where Elise lived. Elise lifted her shoulders and dropped them.

"The Saluccis," Katie answered. "They're my grandma's friends," she added to dissuade this new girl from bothering them in any way.

"How about there then?" Sue Too never stopped moving. She wiggled and hopped, tossed her wayward hair, grimaced, and smirked. The two younger girls stood near her, amazed. "Who lives in the old green house?"

Sue Too started in that direction before they could even answer her. Katie took Elise's hand and hurried her back across the street. "Nobody lives there," she called to Sue Too. She tried to remember who used to live there, but no face or name came to mind.

"No kiddin'. An abandoned house right here in front of us."

The three of them huddled at the back fence taking in the small, two-story wooden house, painted a dreary, awful green, like pea soup, and worn to an actual tilt, as though it might soon simply collapse on its side and be done with it.

Sue Too whistled in admiration. "A real abandoned house."

The other two exchanged worried glances. They didn't understand what this new girl thought they were going to do. Break in? "It's somebody's house though," Katie said, using the voice that had known so little childhood. "It's not someplace where we can just barge in."

"Why not? We can try, anyway. No harm in trying, my dad always says." And off she went through the rusty gate and into the overgrown yard. At the back door she turned to Katie and Elise and stuck out her tongue in some funny expression before lifting the padlock and turning the chipped green knob.

All the birds must have been napping and the breezes as well, when Sue Too, with one determined shove, opened the door to the worn green house. "We're in!" she shouted, then slapped her hand over her mouth and signaled the other two to join her.

v.

Betty Larsen almost killed herself trying to answer the telephone, only to find it was nothing, a misdial, a ten-second exchange that left her standing completely alone in her kitchen. Claus would not be back for at least a week, at least seven days, maybe ten or even twelve. He told her his eyesight was failing. "The time will come," he'd said just before he left, "when I won't be able to drive."

"What does that mean?" she'd pushed. "You mean you won't be able to come here?" He was leaning over, carefully tying his dressy black shoes. She stared at the top of his head, the wavy hair mostly gray, the perfectly contoured bones, like a model in the Sears catalog. "I could take care of you, you know."

"I know," he'd said.

"I'm younger. You could rely on me." She didn't whine, because she knew that never worked with Claus. Emotion never worked with Claus. He preferred reason and fact and concrete thinking, as he called it. "You and your wife might be too weak to look after each other. She could live with one of your daughters. And you could live here with me and Elise. You could rely on me," she said again.

"The time will come though." He'd straightened, kissed her politely, and left. That a man could sweat in such passion, then kiss her politely had never seemed natural to Betty. But he was her first, so how was she to know.

Now Elise was off with Katie Fiore and the stupid phone call was over and it was barely three in the afternoon. Too early to cook. Too late for any other plan. She spotted a black streak on her red and white kitchen tiles, tiles she'd polished to a sheen with floor wax. Maybe it was a scuff from the heel of Claus's shoe. Without thinking, she licked her finger and rubbed the mark away, then wished she hadn't. Now there was absolutely no sign that he had been there.

She hated silence. She really hated it. She was sure she always had. Her mother talked all the time and her Auntie Dot, who lived with them back then, also had talked all the time. And since they continually peppered Betty with questions, she learned to talk all the time too. Dot's ex-husband called them magpies and left. Betty's father stayed, but he spent every hour at home reading, reading anything he could take up—flimsy newspapers, cheap periodicals, any kind of mail. Then when Betty was seventeen and half hysterical about not having a date for the school dance, he had slumped over one of his papers and died. She hated silence.

This town wasn't home anyway. The handful of relatives she still had lived nearly 300 miles away near the South Dakota border. She'd come here with a friend, the two of them on a lark, scouting for work and good-looking miners. Then her friend's mother got sick and she went back home. Betty had already met Claus Jacobson, who had come into the drugstore where she worked asking about chocolate assortments for his wife. So there it was. She'd known he was married from the start.

But he was the most handsome man Betty had ever encountered and something, some invisible, thrilling haze, seemed to surround him, as though she'd be singed by his very touch. He didn't even have to try. He was always calm, often aloof, but the magnetic field encircled him all the same and drew her to him. She couldn't help it. She felt superior to every other woman in town because none of them knew him intimately as she did. She felt superior to his wife as well, because the poor little thing was no match for her husband. Betty believed that she was a match. And so she stayed.

She came to town as Betty Larsen, a single woman, but once pregnant, she simply added the Mrs. and moved to a different neighborhood. Almost nobody knew her anyway, except her boss and the clerks at the drugstore. She told them she was marrying a boy from home. If anyone asked, she'd tell them the boy left a week after their wedding day and died in Korea. Lots of husbands had died in Korea. And she quit that job anyway. Claus took care of her.

Now she went downstairs to check the mail, and not seeing the girls around, she panicked. For all the trouble, Elise really was all she had. Her only mail was a new *McCall's* magazine, which she rolled and held on to as she walked the length of the block and across the street, past the Italians' two houses, whole families clustered it always seemed, and found herself at Vernon's Grocery just as Roger Vernon was unlocking the door and propping it open. He removed the CLOSED sign from the front window, lit a cigarette, and nodded vaguely in her direction.

"I thought my daughter might be over this way, but I don't see her around." She stopped without thinking and patted her hair a bit. She'd never met the man before, but she knew Roger Vernon and his wife owned this store. And here he was in front of her, going nowhere, maybe ready for a chat. "Kids," she went on, "who knows what they're ever plotting. Especially when they get together. And now there's a new girl moving in at the apartment building on the corner. They're always moving in and out of that place, which I'm sure you noticed." Once started, Betty couldn't stop herself. One idea just followed the next. Roger Vernon sat down on the bench outside his store and seemed to listen. At least he didn't leave. He smoked and looked up and down the street, but at least he didn't leave. "I'm not always happy with the comings and goings over there, just me and my daughter in the garage apartment. Course we have double locks and the Saluccis in the front house keep an eye out too. So it's not that I worry, but it's nice to know your neighbors. Even if you don't talk with them much. Just to know who goes where." She chuckled and glanced all around. "Well, nice talking with you. Maybe I should come by later and buy some cookies for dessert. My daughter loves the Oreos. Creamy filling and all." She smiled as though they had just shared a wonderful exchange.

As she walked away, she sensed that he was watching her, which made her thankful for good grooming. Even on the spur of the moment, she was sure she looked her best. Nobody could say she didn't.

vi.

For long minutes Katie and Elise waited in the alley holding hands until at last Sue Too popped back out onto the steps of the old house, signaling for the two younger girls to join her inside. Katie felt the palm of Elise's hand get slippery with sweat. "I can't go in there," the little girl said, and with a shudder, she let go of Katie's hand and ran away. Katie watched Sue Too disappear into the porch again before following Elise back out to the street.

Then just as Elise appeared at the end of the alley, her mother came toward her from the avenue. "I'm going to get my bag and go to Vernon's for Oreos," she declared. "For a treat. Oh, there you are Katie. What were you two doing in the alley?" Instinctively, both girls understood that Mrs. Larsen would not wait for an answer, which was true and on she went. "I told Roger Vernon, Mr. Vernon to you of course, how much Elise likes Oreos, right Elise? Creamy filling. I suppose you like them too, Katie. Come with us over to Vernon's, if you want. I'll be back in a minute." She clattered upstairs and the air settled down around them again.

Elise shrugged, almost an apology. "You want an Oreo?"

"That's okay." Katie sat on the curb and Elise joined her. "Maybe I should go check on Sue Too." She kicked at the street pebbles. "Maybe I shouldn't have left her in that house."

"Yeah, maybe."

Katie jumped up. "I'm going back. Tell your mom bye—but don't tell her where I went."

"I won't," Elise muttered. And then Katie was gone and Elise was alone waiting for her mother to take her to Vernon's Grocery for Oreo cookies, which might be fun. But it wouldn't be an afternoon adventure with two older girls.

Katie moved like lightning from the curb to the back door of the decrepit house. It had suddenly occurred to her that Sue Too might be in danger. She clearly did not have good sense. She was what Katie's mother called a flibbertigibbet. Katie could see that already.

"Sue Too," she whispered loudly as she leaned against the door and eased herself into the back porch. The hot stale air took her breath away, scaring her with its very force, as if it had attacked her. "Sue Too?" She called out louder this time as she inched herself across the frightening porch into the kitchen.

"You won't believe it," Sue Too yelled from deeper inside. "It's like a treasure hunt!"

That was not what Katie was thinking as she took in the kitchen, which looked as though somebody had run away in the middle of a sentence. Dishes were stacked haphazardly, a can opener had been left on the counter, a dismantled coffeepot sat in the sink in a heap of grounds, and one cupboard remained open revealing a mix of tin glasses in bright colors.

"Didn't clean up much, did they?" Sue Too appeared in the kitchen doorway. "Looks like our house half the time."

"I got worried," Katie said, not wanting to move farther than where she stood in the kitchen doorway.

Sue Too came close. "Listen, this place is a mystery waiting to be solved. Look at this." She led Katie into the living room and pointed to a large stain on the wood floor. "What do you think?"

"You mean about that?" One room was as bad as the next. Katie could hardly breathe.

"What do you think that is?"

Katie studied the stain, brown and spread across a large patch of the living room floor. "Spilled paint?"

"Oh for Pete's sake." Sue Too lowered her voice. "It's blood. That's what blood looks like on a wood floor."

Katie recoiled. "How do you know that?"

"I spent half my life on a farm, that's how. What you see right there is blood."

"I don't believe you."

"You think somebody just walked in here with a can of reddish brown paint and dumped it?"

Katie didn't have a logical answer. The dry heat and the smell of abandonment made her dizzy—and angry that Sue Too would ruin the summer afternoon in this house of foreboding questions. She saw that the living room contained stacks of newspapers, half-packed boxes of books. She didn't know what it meant. She didn't care what it meant. "All this belongs to someone," she said. "We shouldn't be here."

"The door was left open! Did you think of that? They don't even care, these messy people. They just left everything. Coffee grounds and all this, papers and junk everywhere and they left and you know why? Because someone killed someone, that's why!"

Katie stood covered in sweat. Her eyes had tears in them from all the dust swirling around in the room's stark sunlight. "If somebody killed somebody, then they could come back and kill you. Did you ever think of that?"

"You watch too much television," Sue Too scoffed, but a bit of darkness passed over her.

"You're the one who watches too much television. We can't solve some murder in some house where we don't even belong and where we're going to die of heatstroke anyway." Both of them were shouting.

Sue Too grabbed her arm. "Listen, we can do this. We can solve the mystery and get our names in the paper. Somebody might write a book about us. You gotta think big here. Please give it a try with me anyway." She held on to Katie's arm with both hands and her eyes pleaded.

"You're going to get us both in trouble."

"But you'll try?"

"Tomorrow," Katie said, thinking that this new girl might have a change of heart or someone might lock the door of the old house or she herself might think of a way out of the whole thing.

"Honest?" Sue Too hadn't let go of her yet. "Say honest."

Katie pulled her arm away. "Let's see what happens tomorrow." She moved across the dismal kitchen and porch and back into the fresh air of summer.

"You didn't promise though," Sue Too insisted, one step behind her.

"I can't promise something when I don't know what will happen." Katie felt bolder just being out in the real world again. "I could die in my sleep or something."

"You really do watch too much television," Sue Too said, but she was in happy motion again, bobbing around next to Katie as they made their way down the alley. "Hey, what's your name again? You're my best friend and I don't even know your name." She gave Katie an affectionate punch.

"Katie Fiore."

"Yeah," said Sue Too like she'd known it all along. "See you tomorrow, Kate."

vii.

A half an hour after Betty Larsen had left Roger Vernon smoking outside his store, she returned with her pocketbook and Elise. Two teenage boys sat on the store steps unwrapping handfuls of baseball card bubble gum, their heads bent in excitement, the smell of sugar all around them in an unseen cloud. Just before pulling the door open, Betty threw her shoulders back and grabbed Elise's hand.

"Stick with Momma now," she prompted. "Stick by me." Big-eyed, Elise came behind her into the store, where she'd only been once in her life and that back when she was very little and it smelled of sausages and tomato sauce. The large man smoking behind the counter didn't look up when they stepped inside, even though a bell on the door chimed as they entered. "Back again," Betty announced, doing a half turn in the middle of the store so that her skirt flared out a bit. "It's a warm one, isn't it? For June?" Betty made an effort to enunciate, to sing out in her most pleasant manner, commanding herself to say nothing that could be taken as a complaint, as she'd recently read an article that said men did not like this quality in women. "Course, who doesn't want warm days in June?"

At this Roger Vernon looked up from his sports page to see what was transpiring in front of him. But he didn't greet Betty and barely noticed Elise.

"My daughter loves Oreos," Betty beamed, though she felt she was losing her way in this encounter. "Should we just help

ourselves then?" A row of glass containers on the front counter
held various kinds of cookies—vanilla wafers, molasses, Oreos,
and colored sugar wafers—sold bulk for two cents each or three
for a nickel. Betty reached in the Oreo jar and put six cookies
into one of the small brown bags set out for that purpose. She
twirled one more time before lighting at the wooden counter
where Roger Vernon sat, the cash register towering near him
like an ancient monument.

Setting down the bag of cookies, Betty threw her shoulders
back one more time and handed Roger a dime. "We took six
cookies," she sung out. "Two for now and four for later, right
Elise?" She didn't look her daughter's way when she said this
and Elise, understanding the dynamic perhaps better than her
mother, hid completely behind Betty's full skirt.

At the sight of the gleaming dime on the counter, Roger
Vernon seemed to wake up. His face flushed briefly, a flash of
color that came and went from his full cheeks to the roots of
his dark hair. His eyes settled on Betty, with her one hand on
the counter ready to part with her dime, but his look was not
inviting or interested as she had hoped, her red lipstick and all,
but cutting and angry.

"Big spender," he said. "Keep your goddamned dime."

"Pardon me?"

She was sure she had heard him wrong, and before the moment
could escalate any further, the muscles in Roger's face relaxed,
he pulled the dime toward him, and tossed it into the cash
register drawer, all in one motion, the drawer binging open

and banging shut. "Anything else I can get for you?" His eyes were still fixed on her.

Betty's mind raced in and out of her cupboards, down the shelves of her refrigerator, searching for something. There must be something. "Well, let me take a look," she replied, still trying to keep her smile gracious and lovely, though she knew it was not. But still, the effort. The sweep of skirt. He had to know a lady was in his midst.

With Elise clutching onto her, Betty roamed the store, positioning random items on the counter. Two cans of Campbell's soup, a Betty Crocker marble cake mix, a pink comb for Elise, two oranges she thought might be past their prime. With each item, she'd add a comment. "Now this will be good some rainy day." "You can always bake a cake, right, Elise?" and so on, the girl dragging along back and forth in the small store until, finally in a flourish, Betty told Elise she could take a piece of Double Bubble for an extra treat. Unable to move, Elise let her mother dig into the candy bin, take the gum, and place it next to her other purchases. "Well, now that should do it, Mr. Vernon. Roger," she clarified.

This time he did not meet her eyes. He rang up the groceries, stuck them hither thither into a paper sack, and took Betty's money. Then he went back to reading his newspaper.

"Well, have a nice afternoon," Betty continued. "Don't let the sunshine melt your chocolate candy here." She pointed to the shelf of chocolate bars, but Roger Vernon was not looking and Elise gripped her mother's skirt all the more fiercely. The bell over the door chimed as they walked out to find the two boys still on the steps, now arguing affably and ignoring Betty and Elise as though they did not exist.

Betty held the bag of groceries high against her chest, her mouth frozen in a smile that tried to be bright. "Well," she said to Elise, "you got some Oreos anyway." Outside now she noticed she'd perspired so much inside Vernon's Grocery that the tops of her legs were sticking together. By the time they'd said a polite hello to old Mrs. Abelli out in her yard and climbed the thirty-some stairs to their apartment, Betty felt that she needed to lie down and close her eyes against the world.

For her part, Elise thought only of the two older girls out exploring the neighborhood without her. She sunk sadder than she could have imagined and ate three of the Oreo cookies without asking for permission.

viii.

Gertrude thought she could smell evening. She couldn't really, but in a few hours the moist air of early night would travel in through the screen windows and she'd know it. She'd know what it was and what it meant. "Maybe one more short walk," she said to Mrs. Wilke, as they put away their few dishes from supper. It was always supper. Early and light and never anything the two women called dinner.

"Well don't be long," Mrs. answered and turned on the television set to see what it might bring her, not checking the schedule because it would ruin her surprise. She didn't have many and the television was surely one of them. "Don't be long, Gertie," she called again, when she heard the back-door screen close. She smoothed a wrinkle out of her housedress and sat down to watch the two men behind a news desk tell her what was what.

Gertrude aimed herself west toward the church, as she always did, her direction, the way she liked to navigate. East to west, north to south, west to east and north to home. She'd organized this route the first week she lived with Mrs. Wilke and kept to it ever since. Only once years ago, she'd left the house by the front door and headed directly south, a course which brought everything to her on the wrong side and in the wrong order and left her, at the end, needing to sit down on Mrs. Wilke's cushioned rocker to get her thinking straight again.

Now she measured her landmarks as she went along, a slight breeze in her hair and the grasses tempered for the night. Lying low. Gathering dew. She breathed in to the bottom of herself and lifted her chin into the sweet air. Nobody at Kirshlings'. Nobody at Salvos' or Hockings' or Browns'. Nobody. All inside eating dinner, she supposed, a later kind of meal, maybe lots of meat she was thinking, when she saw that boy who didn't live on her block but on the next, Richard, unwrapping a candy bar on the steps of Vernon's Grocery, a tall homely boy. "How you," she called as she passed, not waiting to hear what he would say and not looking at his face to see how he regarded her. She lowered her chin and marched on past Katie Fiore's, rounded the corner at the Abellis' house, halfway now and still nobody, only Richard, eating that chocolate bar, not saying hello to her, the sound of her thick heels on the pavement reassuring her, rhythmic and substantial. Here comes Gertrude, she kept thinking.

Then a man crossed the street at the far end of the block and started her way, crooked, missing the rhythm, maybe dragging one side, but not dragging, more pulling. She'd never seen him before. Dark-haired, thin, dressed in a suit, nice like going to church but baggy; she could see as she neared that the man's suit was loose, not his, maybe borrowed. He lurched toward her and so her blood lurched too; she could feel it as she walked closer and he walked closer and then his eyes found her face and his tongue hung to the side and she could hear his breath, louder than all the scratching crickets, dark and loose like his clothes, he looked right at her, looked right into her as they passed, one to the east and one to the west, Gertrude forging ahead and the thin man lurching so that it wasn't until she'd reached the corner that she realized she'd never said "how you."

Gertrude walked her last block without seeing any of it, rounded her own corner barely realizing it, and came into Mrs. Wilke's living room with her fright still showing. "Saw a man," she said extra loud over the television voices, enough to startle Mrs. out of her enjoyment. "Who did you see?" Mrs. Wilke asked, but Gertrude heard the edge of irritation there, the edge of one disturbed without cause. The older woman glanced over to see her charge pale and undone. "What, Gertie? What's the matter?"

"You know a man who walks sideways with his tongue out?" She floated the question over the television and over Mrs. Wilke's sigh of nonsense and waited for something to come of it. "You know him?"

Mrs. Wilke frowned back and shook her head. "His tongue out, you say?"

"He breathes with his tongue out." That's what Gertrude had seen and heard, that dark wet breath out there on the sidewalk and the tongue. It wasn't an old Gertie mistake, some old

Gertie exaggeration like the screeching bugs under the churchyard grass. "I passed him."

"Too bad, too bad," Mrs. said and turned back to the newscasters on the screen narrating the politics of the day, Jack Kennedy and Richard Nixon, more to think about than Gertie. "Sit and watch with me here," she said, nodding to the other end of the sofa.

"I saw him," Gertrude had to insist, in case Mrs. wanted to forget. Gertrude would not. She might watch the two men on the screen and drink more water and wash her underarms before bed, tuck into her stiff sheets, and wait for the stars to shoot all over heaven, but she had passed the man with his tongue hanging out and she wasn't going to forget him.

ix.

The gimpy man meandered until the sun began to set. Nobody else passed him as he moved along, eyes wide and watchful. He'd been away and now he was home and he went on without hearing how hard his breath came or how uneven his steps. Like Gertrude he absorbed the cooling air. Unlike Gertrude he did not notice the incessant crickets or the last sweet bird singing somewhere up ahead.

x.

At ten P.M. Roger Vernon shut out the lights and smoked one closing cigarette in the dark store. It was possibly the only time of the day he could stand the place, when his working wife was asleep and the neighborhood locked out for the next nine hours. He could, just then, pretend that the morning would not eventually roll in on him with the same tedious expectations and tasks.

The store was nothing he chose, nothing he ever dreamed. It was his father-in-law's dream. It was the dream of half the Italians in the whole damn town, to sell food and make money. Like the old lady who came before, now swept off to Miami in a whirl of hair color and ease. She'd packed every quarter inch of space with something she could sell—homemade canned goods, homemade donuts, seasoned pork, sausage and salami, noodles, even live chickens from some farm outside of town. She'd kept the store open from six in the morning until almost midnight, never hiring help, using cousins and nephews if she needed them, nobody paid, every penny saved. That's how she made her money. That's why she was off drinking iced cocktails in the sunshine.

He counted almost a dozen neighborhood grocery stores when he came to town, families living in a few rooms behind, like he and Sophia now, squeezed in, and the basement stacked with inventory, the front stoops littered with candy wrappers and the backyards just big enough to hold the clothesline poles. The wooden floorboards in the Vernons' store had been worn to gouges, hard to keep clean if he had an interest in keeping them clean, and carried deep within them the scent of spices and sweets, bubble gum and moonshine from the days when. His wife loved the smell, said it reminded her of her childhood in such stores, places she and her mother went for milk and last-minute supplies, olives, she said, and lemons, sometimes a chocolate bar for the trouble. But Roger never imagined a neighborhood grocery store in his future. Never.

Sophia's old man thought the store would save Roger, give him an income and some place in town, some new connections. But it was a failed plan. A lousy idea. The store saddled Roger with someone else's life and brought in so little cash his wife had to work at a cosmetics counter just to make ends meet. The old Italian's customers realized in a hurry that they weren't going to get homemade anything from the Vernons and hustled off to another Italian grocery just two blocks away. Roger drank much of the beer himself and smoked considerably more cigarettes now that they were right there on the shelf behind him. He closed up at midday to give himself time for lunch and a quick nap and barked at the neighbors if he wasn't in the mood to wait on them. He had no interest in food, didn't know the different brands of cereal or when the next shipment of candy would arrive or why they were out of banana Popsicles. He never sold live chickens. He didn't know how to run a grocery and he had made no effort to learn.

Sophia took it well overall. She was still hoping they'd have children and all her focus stayed on that topic, mapping out her days on a chart she got at the drugstore, needling him at certain times of the month to up her odds. She already had one drawer in their small bedroom stocked with baby clothes she had knit in the neutral infant colors of green, yellow, and ivory. She knew he hated the store, but she pretended he didn't. And her father was such a gentle, generous man, he never complained that they were fumbling, that investing in a store on their behalf had not fulfilled its promise.

Not Sophia, her parents, or Roger were the type to think about what the promise might now be. Sophia prayed for a family and her parents prayed for good health as they grew older and Roger took his life one cigarette at a time. In the silent store late at night he looked out the streaked windows and considered how good a cold beer could taste at the end of a long day.

TWO

Tuesday, June 7, 1960

i.

The next morning Nicky Marodi, hat askew, lunged down the street toward Vernon's Grocery but stopped short in front of the Fiores' house just as Katie came along dragging a hose to water her mother's nasturtiums. He froze when he saw her, and Katie, her dreamy morning interrupted, screamed in fright. Nicky panted a long minute, then walked away as fast as he was able, one foot scraping the concrete, until he reached the corner out of her sight.

Embarrassed that she'd screamed and rattled by the man she'd just seen, Katie watered everything in the front yard, the lilies-of-the-valley and the two mountain ash trees, the lilacs and nasturtiums, even the grass, all the while thinking who the man could be. She'd never seen him before that she remembered and who would forget him? His tongue hung out. Who would forget that?

"Hi." Still jumpy, she jerked her head up to see Godfrey and Edna standing full front, the way they always did when they were passing by, as if presenting themselves, two round people, a matched set.

"Hi," she said back.

"What're you doing?" Godfrey asked. Edna only smiled, her blue eyes large under her straw hat. She wore a dress meant to reveal the tops of her breasts, a swirly, flowery pastel-print dress, and carried a marketing basket draped in cloth.

"I'm watering for my mother," Katie answered.

Godfrey's crossed eyes widened. "You see Kaka Roo?"

"Who?"

"Kaka Roo," Edna repeated and nodded so that her hat bobbed forward. "He's back. Just came by here," she added, then they turned toward downtown, Godfrey chuckling and looking over his shoulder.

Katie set down the hose and ran to the backyard, where she found her mother and Nonna working in the garden. "I saw a man with his tongue out," she said.

Her mother glanced her way. "I heard Nicky Marodi came home. He's a sick man, poor Nicky."

"What's wrong with him? How come I've never seen him before?" Her mother and Nonna went back and forth in Italian, her mother explaining the topic to her grandmother and Katie grabbing onto a word here and there to mark what they were saying. "Nicky Marodi—*un malato—pazzo*." Her mother tapped the side of her head.

"*Che tristezza.*"

"Poor man," her mother translated and bent her head back to the black soil and sprouting plants.

"What's wrong with him?" Katie pressed, just as a loud whistle startled them all.

"Hey, Kate. Ready to go?" Sue Too stood leaning against their iron fence.

"Who on earth is that now?" Katie's mother asked.

"She's the new girl in the apartment building. She moved in yesterday."

"Not the quiet type, is she?" Katie's mother said. Katie stooped down to speak into her mother's ear. "What's the matter with him, Mom?"

Mrs. Fiore met her daughter's eyes. "Nobody knows, Kate. His mind is funny. He can't help it."

"Where's he been? Godfrey and Edna called him some name too. Kaka something."

"They're the ones to be calling names all right. He was in Moose Lake. He's been there for years and who knows why he's back home now. Let me work, Kate. We'll talk some other time. The man is harmless."

From the fence Sue Too let loose another loud, shrill whistle. "What's cookin'?"

Katie ran to meet her. "I was just asking my mom about a man I saw this morning." She realized she didn't want to say the man had terrified her, that his tongue hung out and his eyes were wild. "I guess he was in Moose Lake."

"That's for crazies, you know."

"I know."

"This place is really shaping up. You've got that skinny lady zooming by and our abandoned house over there and now a crazy let loose from the nut house." She rubbed her palms together in glee.

"How was your first night in the apartment?"

"Speaking of nut houses." She shook her head. "Stuff is everywhere. I set up my cot and threw a sheet over it. Maybe we'll fix things up sometime today."

"You don't have a bed?"

"Same thing. Plus, with a cot you can move it around when you want." She made a silly face. "You ready?"

"I can't go with my mother and grandma right there in the garden."

"You're kiddin'. Why not?"

Katie lowered her voice to a near whisper. "We don't belong over there. It's not our house and my mother's strict. She doesn't like me doing dumb things."

Sue Too frowned. "Why is it dumb?"

"I mean unlawful."

"Shoot. It's just an empty house."

"But it's somebody's," Katie argued.

Sue Too looked quickly up and down the street and Katie studied her as she did, the light brown hair going in several directions, the easy nonsense of the way she looked, all apart and yet all together. Sue Too turned back to her with a grin, some kind of victory in her mind. "But whose is it? You don't know. That little girl across the street don't know. So." She'd made her point, some kind of point.

Katie noticed that her mother and grandma had moved farther away to work in the thick rows of raspberry bushes, so she came through the gate to Sue Too's side of the fence and gestured the older girl to follow her. They walked to the corner and around to the front of the green house. "Looks even worse from this angle," Sue Too commented, and it was true. A porch ran the width of the front, sagging low in the middle. The roof on top of the porch sagged and the steps and windowsills beneath the front windows sagged. The house's face of downward angles seemed to look out at the girls and beg relief.

The steps cracked when they walked on them, Sue Too boldly and Katie lingering. But the front door was locked anyway. Just then, the next-door neighbor came out of his house to check his mailbox and saw them. "Nobody home there," he called. He found no mail, but did not go back inside. He stood on his porch until he witnessed them actually leaving the yard. "Take it easy," he said with cheer.

"Let's come back after lunch," Katie suggested. "Maybe that guy next door will be taking a nap or something."

"You're not going to poop out on me here, are you?"

Katie thought she might, but she didn't want to admit it. "No. I'm just hungry is all."

"Shoot," Sue Too said as they moved away from the old house. "I'm always hungry."

The girls went their ways, and the neighbor they'd encountered sat in his house waiting for his wife to come home and make him lunch, and inside the old green house, the sun darted along the walls undisturbed in the dusty living room.

ii.

Gertrude set out with worry. She hadn't gone earlier, as she always did, as she had for all the days and weeks and years before she'd encountered the wild-eyed man. Instead she'd announced, "time for a sponge cake," to Mrs. Wilke that morning. Time for a cake. She'd opened the *Betty Crocker Cookbook*, measured and mixed the three eggs, hot milk, sugar, and salt, talking to herself, listening to herself. One teaspoon vanilla. Careful, Gertie. Hold the spoon flat. Don't spill the vanilla, Gertie, she said and Mrs. said it too, don't spill the vanilla, Gertie. And she did not, though the minutes went by waiting for her to pour that vanilla. And now they had a cake. "How nice," Mrs. Wilke kept saying. "Smells so nice."

More than nice, Gertrude thought sponge cake in the oven smelled like heaven, like the way she could imagine a heaven of all good and no evil, all light and no dark, beyond the scent of new grass or dirt when it rained, beyond all good smells, it would be lemon and vanilla, it would be sweet and warm, but not too warm, just a quiet kind of warm and pale, but not too pale. That's how sponge cake was like heaven.

And now it was baked and cooling and Mrs. had mending to do, and so Gertrude left. Not lickety-split like usual. She left at a guarded pace, looking, listening, barely recognizing the wide world calling out to her as it always did. She made her way so slowly, she thought she'd lose her balance, like a two-wheeler bicycle needing speed. But she had to be ready and she was.

Up ahead she saw the Godfreys lingering at the corner to let her catch up. "How you?" she called and Edna said, "Oh, we're fine, Miss," and Godfrey with those crossed eyes nodded, starting in about new goldfish down at Woolworth's, where she'd never been, and coupons at Red Owl, where she'd also never been. She nodded and kept pressing on, head down, and the couple with their shopping basket followed, Godfrey chattering, whatever he was saying. Better to have company, she thought, strength in numbers and all, so she was happy for the Godfreys. Not happy, maybe. Glad, maybe. Relieved.

They stuck with her the whole next block, Vernon's closed up again of all things, and around the corner and the next whole block, Gertrude telling them about the sponge cake and heaven, which she knew they didn't understand, though Edna kept nodding and Godfrey repeated some of her words just to keep in the game, and that's how they went along until she said, "Bye now," and walked her last block alone hoping she'd see nobody, not even the mailman.

Godfrey and Edna toddled down another block and another until they came to the pink house that was theirs, encircled in willful rosebushes and uncut grass. They walked, telling each other Gertrude's oddness, always on that one block, always in pedal pushers, always wound up. "Going nowhere," Edna said. "Going nowhere," Godfrey said as well, neither of them thinking that the same might also be said of them.

iii.

Edna never wore a brassiere or any underwear if she could help it, though in winter she might layer a cotton slip over a silk one just because. She had no story that anyone knew, only Godfrey, whom she'd rescued from alcohol and despondency years before. He found her beautiful beyond breath. He made her laugh. His crossed eyes took in the world at an angle only he could know. Two moons, two suns, two toasts for breakfast. That was his joke, but it wasn't true. More life looked like a haze, two images juxtaposed in a haze, but she led him along and they made their way and had such great times pinching and prodding, teasing and tweaking. Two fat robins in spring. He adored her. He made her laugh.

Even so, all silliness aside, Godfrey and Edna had a system, well honed and professional. They came into their pink house with a basket full of supplies and treasures they mostly had not purchased, anything from nail polish to canned peaches. It was a clumsy scheme they had worked out over years, an almost clown act of questions and answers repeated, products examined and traded and maybe this and what about that over there, money pulled out and put back, more questions. Edna laughing and showing her loose flesh here and there, her hat obstructing some movements. Godfrey's crossed eyes. The whole act meant to confuse and exhaust the shop clerks in an easy, good-natured manner.

Then in a figurative cloud of dust, they'd leave. And if those clerks and shopkeepers believed they'd been taken for a ride, they almost never said. When they did, the two had an equally befuddling approach to giving the stolen items back. Mistakes happen. Edna thought Godfrey had paid. She'd flutter her hand against her bosom. On they'd go.

They also rotated the stores, never taking from any place more than monthly, but frequenting all of the stores all of the time, cruising through, chatting, browsing, buying maybe one jar of hand cream or a magazine, but taking stock, lowering suspicions, admiring the new goldfish.

Years before, Godfrey had photographed Edna in the nude and sold the photos to men who appreciated that sort of thing. Some people thought he still did this, but they were wrong. When Edna posed now, she did it only for him, one of the many naughty games they liked to play when alone with the shades pulled low. It was surprising actually, the fun they always had together in their own world and outside the main. Most of the time they tended to forget they lived in a mining town, forgot about the iron ore altogether. They never even walked the short mile to the old part of town to see the Hull Rust, fabled to be the largest open ore pit in the world. Possibly, they never even knew it was there.

iv.

Once inside her safe home, Gertrude breathed in and out to hear the sound of herself, to know it was herself who made it around the block without incident, just the Godfreys who walked too slowly, strolling, half the time not even strolling, but inching and stopping and turning and stopping again, all the ants rushing by and the air rushing by as the Godfreys took their time, their own sweet time, Gertrude thought. But they weren't trouble, they were just the Godfreys. Like the low buzz of old flies at the window.

"Time for lunch, Gertie," Mrs. Wilke said, setting out potted ham on toast and peeled carrots, glasses of milk. Gertrude's sponge cake. "How you?" Gertrude called across the table to her caretaker. "I'm fine, Gertie," Mrs. answered, then kept watching Gertrude with her flushed face and restless arms moving about, one button undone on her sleeveless shirt. "You have a nice walk then, Gertie?"

Gertrude looked down at her lunch, breathed in and out again. How could she say her world had changed? At any turn she could encounter the man whose feverish eyes had locked onto hers right on this block, her own very block, as he staggered and pitched toward her. How could she say?

"Gertie?"

"Squawking birds," she lied. "Too many crackpot birds."

"Maybe they'll take a rest this afternoon, Gertie, and you can walk the block in peace." But Gertrude did not look up and agree, as she most always agreed. She kept her eyes on the potted ham. "Maybe," she said to Mrs. Wilke. "Maybe."

v.

On his side of town Claus Jacobson spent more and more time remembering. He kept the curtains closed to protect his eyes and did all the senseless exercises one of his pretty daughters insisted he do, but these things helped little. What helped was remembering how everything looked before, when colors were vivid, when he could drive a car without full concentration and choose a tie without examining it for long minutes to determine its exact pattern. He still dressed for the day and sat at his desk, where he could make out the words, though slowly, work with them, organize his papers and put them into folders. He secured his largest stack of papers with a heavy chunk of hematite from the mine, given to him years earlier by another one of the supervisors. Every time he gripped its rough, substantial surface, he called to mind the man who gave it to him, which was another kind of remembering. Not useful, but factual. A piece of his own life certainly.

Tildy drifted past him on and off all through the day, made him a sandwich at lunchtime and brought him the mail midafternoon, her enormous eyes seeing everything clearly, those wide and bright eyes. He could always find them in any blur. He could always see Tildy's blue eyes. Not dark blue, but bright, Nordic blue. He could always find them. But Tildy could not think straight, had thoughts as clouded as his sight, and so they were a match, the two of them, able to share almost nothing, but holding together after some forty years of marriage and three daughters and day upon day of little to say to one another. They just had so little to say.

He had returned from Betty Larsen's apartment the day before tired of words, as he often was after visiting her. He had an idea, seeing the girl on the curb, that this fourth child of his looked almost identical to his third child. Same look completely. Same braids even, as though Tildy and Betty had known instinctively that the girls' faces should be framed by those tight, orderly braids. Betty had named the girl Elise. He had nothing to do with it. Had nothing to do with her life except for providing Betty with the garage apartment and a monthly amount of cash and helping her along with the administration of life, the paperwork of life, like the vague stacks on the corners of his desk.

He'd calculated that he could walk to Betty's if he could no longer drive. She only lived six blocks away and the blocks were easily navigated down his avenue and across town to her street. Even so, he found himself drawn to her less frequently than before. She expected so much and had so much to say, so many observations and questions and needs. The garbage men came too early, the paperboy too late in the afternoon, new people were always moving into the apartment building across the street, which worried her, and the Italians over there spent too much time in the garden, as if that should matter to her one way or the other. And when would he come back and how long would he stay. In all his remembering, he could not say if Betty had always been this nervous. He tended not to listen to her and to come home relieved that Tildy talked so little.

"Lunch, dear," she announced just now, as she did every day, flustering a bit at the door to his room, a ruffle at the hem of her apron, her hair wispy around her beautiful face and her blue eyes seeing him so clearly. He stretched his long legs and followed her to the kitchen table laid out with two flowered plastic plates of sandwiches and jam glasses filled with milk. Each plate had a pickle. Each place setting had a paper napkin folded at the edge of the plate. Tildy waited until he sat before situating herself across from him then smiled her brightest, belying the confusion she battled within. "Thank you, Tildy," he said, and anyone hearing him say that would know they were becoming old together, would find the inflections of familiarity and dependency, the years of sitting at that Formica kitchen table and finding each other just there.

Certainly nobody hearing him would imagine that he'd kept another woman for a decade, paid her rent and fathered her child. And seeing Claus, reserved and alert, striking in looks and controlled in bearing, nobody would imagine that he was struggling to see and that his heart skipped full beats at odd times, causing him to catch his breath not really knowing just why.

vi.

Out the kitchen window Elise saw Katie Fiore and Sue Too standing by the alley talking. She ran down the stairs to catch them, but they were heading in their own different directions by then. She watched through the screen door as Katie opened the gate into her grandmother's yard, walked through the garden to her own yard, and went inside her house, feeling a nudge of envy that Katie had so much. A dad, a grandma, and a garden too. "Elise," she heard from above. "Elise?"

Upstairs she found her mother sporting a new hairdo of closer cropped waves. "What do you think? It just came over me, this idea. An actress named Liz Taylor does this kind of thing, very chic I think." She pivoted this way and that for Elise, whose wide eyes told her mother nothing, as usual.

But she said, "I think it's nice, Momma," and reached for a puzzle to do while she considered what a girl like Katie Fiore ate for lunch.

Betty had tossed restlessly all night thinking about Claus saying there'll come a time and Roger Vernon's seeming indifference to her even when she spent almost two dollars on food she didn't want. What was the matter with men anyway? She wasn't pretty, she admitted, but she believed in charm and grooming, manners, good cheer. Clearly, something was wrong for both Claus and Roger Vernon to step back from her on the very day she'd made such an effort, her new lipstick, the full summer skirt and open-toed shoes. She just didn't understand. Roger was married, of course, to a really pretty girl. In fact his wife was the one who'd sold Betty the new shade of red lipstick a week before, telling her it was irresistible. Well, she certainly was wrong about that, though Betty did love the color, the way it lit up her face, the possibility of it all. So maybe Roger Vernon was one of those men who kept his eyes on his wife and no one else. But Betty didn't really think so.

Roger had that look she remembered from her younger days, almost a snarl, but not exactly, more an attitude of rebellion and discontent. The look of a man who broke rules, that's what she thought of him, nice wife or not. And she wasn't planning to be untrue to Claus, who was levels of elegance and success above Roger Vernon. Just a bit of interaction, that's what she wanted. Just a reminder of how her life used to be before she knew Claus and had Elise, back when she danced the night away and saw that men enjoyed her even if her face was square. Young men cared less for faces than the rest of the package anyway. That's what she'd always thought. That's what every somewhat plain but shapely girl thought. And most often, the boys proved them right.

She watched Elise carefully place puzzle pieces to make a picture, one tiny piece after another forming something whole and recognizable. That's what Betty longed for—something whole and recognizable. She went into the bathroom and swept up the hair she'd snipped from her head. She went downstairs and shook the bathroom rug, then made peanut butter sandwiches for the two of them. They ate Roger Vernon's soft oranges and finished the Oreos. Elise said little, of course, other than to ask if she could play with Katie Fiore.

"Of course, Elise. But those girls are older. They might not want to be bothered with you."

"I know," Elise answered. That notion was exactly what she'd been sorry about the whole long morning.

"Those Oreos went fast," Betty added. "You want me to go back and get more? I suppose I could pick up a few more of these mushy oranges too, for that matter. Keep them from spoiling completely." She went on with her list, and Elise strategized how she might join the older girls. If asked, neither mother nor daughter would remember just how their disjointed lunch ended. Elise went outside to sit on the curb and wait for an opportunity, and Betty decided to change into a narrow skirt that better showed off the curves of her hips.

vii.

Katie Fiore ate her lunch slowly. She didn't really like polenta, for one thing, and she wanted to figure out a way to avoid that

decaying green house. Her father was working and her grandparents ate lunch at their own house next door, so Katie faced
her mother, who often tended to eat without saying much,
commenting on the food rather than the world around her. "I
would add a pinch more salt next time," her mother said now,
her mind on the taste, her eyes on the ceiling so she could concentrate. "Not much though. But it tastes a little flat to me."
She reached for the saltshaker and poured some into the palm
of her hand, then pinched just a bit on her remaining forkful.
"Better," she said to herself.

"Do you know who used to live in the house next door to the
Saluccis, Mom?"

Her mother squinted in thought. "Let me think. He was a
Lutheran minister and something happened. But I don't
remember what it was. I think it was sudden. I haven't seen
that man around here in maybe a year? Maybe longer." She
stood up, collected the dishes, and carried them to the sink. "I
have to think about this, Kate. Interesting question."

Suddenly, Katie thought about the man who had frightened
her that morning. "Another question, Mom. What is that
man's nickname? That man I saw today with his tongue out.
What do they call him?"

"People can be mean, Kate. Let it go."

"But you know what people call him?" She didn't think Godfrey and Edna were mean. They acted like everyone called
Nicky Marodi by that name, whatever it was.

At this her mother turned her back on Katie to rinse the dishes.
Clearly the subject was closed.

"So you think you could find out about that old house, Mom?" When her mother didn't answer, she added, "It's kind of creepy having an empty house around." But her mother had moved on to her next task.

Outside, Katie saw that Elise was curled into a ball, hugging her knees on the curb. Instead of crossing over to her, though, she disappeared into the raspberry patch to think. Her mother had said something had happened suddenly in that old house. So maybe it was a mystery that they could solve, like Nancy Drew and Trixie Belden did. Lots of young women solved crimes. Girls were clever, even Nonna said that. Girls were thinkers. Maybe Sue Too wasn't exactly a thinker, but she wanted to be, Katie decided. Sue Too was the kind of girl who could benefit from solving a crime.

Katie emerged from the raspberries with the idea that they would sneak back into the old house and investigate. They'd write down every clue they could find, catalog every item strewn about and where it had been left and anything that struck them as odd or unfinished or suspicious. Suddenly she was so excited she was hungry again. She ran back in the house, grabbed a cookie, and scrounged in her bedroom for a notebook left over from school. With that, a pencil, and her snack, she went out to find Sue Too.

"Hi, Katie," little Elise called from her spot on the curb.

Katie waved, but kept going to the apartment building, where she let herself in the front door and tiptoed the halls until she found apartment Number Seven. She knocked several times but got no answer, nor could she hear any sounds coming from the apartment. The hall smelled almost as dank as the basement storeroom did, and Katie started to feel nervous. Obviously Sue Too wasn't home. She wrote a careful note for her new friend to please locate Katie as soon as she returned, as she had important news. She signed her full name, included her family's phone number, and slid the message under the door.

Back on the sidewalk she made her way to where Elise sat and plopped down next to her. Elise eyed the notebook and pencil. "You writing a letter?"

"No, I thought I would record clues in that old house over there. I'm thinking there is a mystery, Elise. Do you know what that is?"

Elise wasn't sure, but she nodded anyway. "You're going in there again?"

"Something's going on and somebody has to figure it out." Katie noticed that she sounded a bit like her mother when she said this.

Elise chewed on one of her cuticles. She wanted to go too, but her mother would not be happy and, Elise was quite sure, she wouldn't really be happy either. But she'd be with Katie, and she'd be figuring it out, as Katie said. They'd both be figuring it out. "I could help," she said at last. "I'm pretty good at figuring."

Katie didn't answer. This was not at all what she wanted. Sue Too had dropped out of sight and Elise thought she could help. She patted Elise on the head. "I'm sure you're good at everything. We'll see, okay?"

"Momma is going to buy more Oreos," Elise added.

"Didn't she buy some yesterday too? Lucky Mr. Vernon, I guess."

Elise pushed her pretty little face so close to Katie's, that she could have kissed her. "Do you like that man?"

"Not really, no."

"He's the bogeyman," Elise said with certainty. "He could get you."

"I think he's just cranky, Elise."

Elise shook her head. Katie might know many things, but Elise knew this. "He could get you. It's the truth."

The two of them sat together pondering this until Betty Larsen clip-clopped down the stairs in her open-toed high heels and straight skirt on her way to Vernon's Grocery. This time she carried a small market basket to indicate she was a serious shopper. She had her money in her pocketbook and a list and a market basket. "You going to buy more Oreos, Momma?" Elise asked.

"I am," Betty said, "but you keep playing with Katie, Elise. Momma doesn't need help today." And off she went, the two girls watching her firm step and determined demeanor.

"Your mom sure likes to shop," Katie commented.

And although Elise had never noticed it before, she answered, "I guess she does."

viii.

Betty was going to make this matter. She was going to make some kind of impression and she wanted it to be good. She had been in Vernon's only twice, however, so she didn't know Roger's afternoon tendency to lock the door and put up the CLOSED sign while he took a rest. When she yanked open the door, setting off the bell above, she was surprised to find Roger Vernon standing near the window holding his sign.

"I'm sorry," she said without thinking. "Are you going some-where? I didn't know." Her eyes darted about the store, but she continued. "We so enjoyed those oranges, ripe as they were, so I thought I might buy a few more. Just in case. And some other supplies. More cookies."

"We're closed," Roger interrupted. He looked directly at her, her bright red mouth and cropped hair, her smile, her expec-tancy. How did so many crazy people gravitate to a single mining town north of nowhere, he thought in a flash. What, for Chrissake, did this woman want?

Betty absorbed his stare, but assigned a whole different mean-ing, which is why she went on as if he had not just told her the store was closed. She straightened and waltzed over to the refrigerated case where the Vernons kept their produce. But just as she reached for a couple of oranges, Roger Vernon boomed, "I said we're closed, lady, don't you understand English?" Betty stopped cold, gripping the fruit, face fixed in terror.

The two of them stood eye to eye thinking surely the other would understand—Betty would leave or Roger would laugh off his rudeness. Betty forgot she was holding fruit, forgot she had a daughter sitting around the corner on a curb wanting more Oreo cookies, might even have forgotten her own name. Roger Vernon's harsh voice had struck her like lightning and for those few moments, she thought, she felt, and remembered nothing.

Finally Roger slammed the CLOSED sign down on the counter, propped open the door, and, in a tone of defeat, said, "Go ahead. Do your shopping." He lit a cigarette and stepped outside. Left alone, Betty began to breathe more evenly and to reestablish herself. She licked her lips and smoothed her skirt. Then with the calm that follows a brief trauma, she shopped. She didn't look at prices or consider recipes, but picked up everything that attracted her in any way, even candy, which she almost never bought. When her stacks of groceries filled the counter, she walked outside to find Roger Vernon pacing and smoking another cigarette. "I'm ready to check out," she said.

He nodded and came toward her, stubbing his cigarette on the concrete, eyes down and away from her. Then he saw all the food she'd piled on the counter. "What are you doing?"

"I bought some groceries," Betty answered.

"You never shopped here before."

Still numb from his earlier outburst, Betty said, "I just discovered how nice it can be to shop so close to home." Then she shrugged and leaned against the counter, letting her weight sink against it. "Someone to talk to for a minute."

"You going to use all this stuff?" He started ringing up her items.

"I'll do my best. Necessity is the mother of invention," she quoted, though she could see that Roger Vernon did not know how that related to his question. "Your wife sold me this lipstick," she ventured, sorry immediately.

"You know Sophia?" He kept tallying her groceries.

"No, but she helped me choose a lipstick. At the cosmetics counter."

Roger nodded, as if that explained something. He was still processing why this woman had stayed and shopped after he'd asked her to leave. "Nineteen fifty," he announced, handing her a receipt with the total of her purchases. He put some of the items into her basket and took out a brown paper bag for the rest. "You'll need help getting these home."

Betty didn't answer. She was reeling from the reality of what she'd just spent and the odds and ends Roger Vernon was packing up for her, not even any meat, eggs, or milk, not the kind of food that would make whole meals, just cans of things and old fruit and cereal boxes. She felt her knees buckle in fear. What had she done?

"You okay?" Roger could see that something was happening to her, peculiar as she was, he could still see that something was wrong. "You want a couple pork chops? They're small, so on the house."

"Oh," Betty regained a bit of herself. "Isn't that nice. I cook a good pork chop, just the right seasoning. A little extra pepper, that's the trick. I cook them very hot too, brown them good, that's the way to cook a pork chop." She tried a wide smile.

"Sure. I'll walk you home with these." Roger put up the CLOSED sign, grabbed Betty's bag of groceries and market basket, and ushered her out into the afternoon sun. "Lead the way," he said, and so she did, one foot in front of the other, a bit of lift to her chin. As they walked the half block, she narrated the neighborhood. Uninterested, as he usually was in anything about this town, he stayed a step behind her without comment, took note of her modest, tidy garage apartment, and set the groceries on her kitchen table. "Sorry I got testy. Nothing meant." With that, he turned and left, barely making a sound on her linoleum-covered stairs.

Heading back to his store, Roger Vernon knew that something had happened there, his outburst, her buying frenzy, the almost twenty bucks in his till to brag about to Sophia when she came home. The lady with the red lips was nuts, he thought, but something had happened. He'd made some money and she'd be back.

Putting away her groceries, Betty also concluded that she was nuts. She'd wanted the store owner to like her, whatever that meant. And now he did. But what earthly good did it do her? Maybe she could drop by for a chat with him now and again. Maybe he'd let her know about specials or something like that. Maybe what. She set the wrapped pork chops onto the refrigerator shelf like they were gold. Hard-won gold. Then she went into the bathroom to assess herself in the mirror, surprised to find that she looked the same as she did when she'd combed her new hairdo and left the apartment an hour before. She shouldn't look the same. After all of that, she didn't think she should look the same.

ix.

When Mrs. Larsen didn't come home and Sue Too didn't return, Katie put her notebook and pencil inside on the garage apartment stairs and walked Elise to the playground behind the arena, which meant crossing two streets and walking another block to get where they were going. Katie pushed Elise on a swing and helped her build a fort in the sandbox, all the while keeping an eye on Sue Too's apartment building down the street. There were few trees on that side of the arena, mostly expanses of concrete where people parked their cars, and vans pulled up to load and unload. Sometimes the lot teemed with sports fans or circus fans or teenagers going to the youth club. But on the second full day of summer vacation, the arena lot stretched out flat and empty. Katie could see all the way to Nonna's back fence.

When Mrs. Larsen came around the corner, tiny in the distance and swishing side to side, with Mr. Vernon behind carrying her groceries, Katie told Elise she could walk her home, though she knew, as she knew these kinds of things, that Elise would have been happier to let Katie push her on the swing until the sun went down. As they neared the garage apartment, the younger girl gripped Katie's hand more tightly. "Should I tell Momma about the two streets?"

"She won't mind, Elise. You're safe with me." They dallied a bit as they walked, so that Mr. Vernon was gone by the time they arrived at the garage apartment. Katie opened the downstairs door, sent Elise up to her mother, and grabbed her notebook.

"Well, there you are," Mrs. Larsen hollered as she appeared at the top of the stairs. "I was beginning to wonder." She was talking too fast, ready to leap to another topic before anyone could stop her. "I bought so many groceries that Mr. Vernon, Roger, had to help me home, and then what? Where to put it all. Things I've never bought before, Elise. Chef Boyardee even. I suppose your mother doesn't buy that, Katie, with all the Italian cooking going on over at your house. I bought Oreos too. Elise?" By this time the little girl had disappeared from sight, as her mother held Katie trapped in their downstairs entry, talking to her nonstop.

Katie continued to nod, her scalp and palms starting to sweat, until at last she interrupted, calling loudly, "Bye, Mrs. Larsen," and closed the screen door behind her. She didn't want to be rude, she never did. But sometimes Mrs. Larsen was so focused on her story, she didn't notice when nobody wanted to hear it.

Without thinking, Katie turned into the alley and, still without thinking, walked to the back fence of the dilapidated house. She opened the old gate and made her way to the door with a mechanical sort of determination, her mind leading her along before her worries could intervene. Everything inside was the same, though with her mother's bit of recall—a Lutheran minister, the sudden departure, maybe something bad that happened—with all that in Katie's mind, she was now thinking the dust and abandonment had meaning.

In her notebook she listed every strewn object in the kitchen: the coffee pot and grounds, the can opener, a teacup on the table, two chairs moved out as though someone had jumped up and forgotten them. The newspapers and books stacked high. She listed them all. Then she noticed the calendar hanging on the door to the porch showing the month of March one year before. The calendar picture for that month of March was of a kitten, longhaired and green-eyed, sitting in a wicker basket and staring off and away. Forlorn, Katie thought, and alone. Too alone.

Her chest felt so heavy, she had to leave. She closed her notebook and slipped back out the porch door, checking the neighbors' yards to make sure nobody saw her. She crossed the street and sat in Nonna's red metal lawn chair under the clotheslines, scanning the quiet street and her grandma's blooming patch of purple pansies in front of her.

"*Come stai?*" she heard her grandma say as she stepped outside to join her. Nonna eased herself into the other metal lawn chair, took Katie's hand and held it. Nobody had such smooth skin as Nonna.

Then Gertrude came by, making her late-afternoon circle of the block. "How you," she called to the two of them, like she always did, seldom slowing, never stopping.

"Good," Katie called back, watching Gertrude's familiar, headlong march into evening. "How about you?" But the breeze muffled her words, and then Gertrude was gone.

"*Sempre in fretta*, Gertrude," Nonna said. "Always in a hurry."

Katie agreed.

The dark mysteries and losses of that old house across the street began to fade in the sweet air. Katie and her grandmother remained side by side in no hurry at all, watching a single white cloud as it moved across the blue summer sky.

x.

Mrs. didn't shove Gertrude out the door that afternoon, but
she almost did. "Such a nice day, Gertie. Such nice sunshine,
Gertie. Come sit in the yard, maybe you'd like a little walk,
maybe once around, Gertie." So Gertrude had headed out for
only the second strange time that day, wishing for her old feeling, her old hardy feeling, calling out, breathing in, the bold
birds in song, bugs busy, all part of a world she knew. That's
what she wanted again and why couldn't she? Why couldn't she
just love that again, the smell of musty bark and dusty dirt?
Summer raving and roaring.

With sweat on her skin, a mist of sweat all over her, Gertrude
passed the Church of Christ, Scientist, new dandelions already
sneaking back, and old lady Kirshling's, the next house, the
next, looking ahead for trouble. Vernon's door open, music
playing of all things, no kids on the stoop. Then there was Katie
Fiore and her grandmother sitting outside in those red chairs.
"How you," she called, giving a side wave, hearing Katie's voice
coming back at her. And onward, past the apartment building
and around to the last block, the last stretch, the arena looming
silent to her right where it was meant to be, no trouble yet,
almost home and no trouble, past Mrs. Kerns's, the next house,
and there he was, coming around from that wrong direction
she never took, coming her way, coming her way, listing to the
side, the tongue, the eyes.

And Gertrude did what she'd never done, what she thought
she'd never do, she crossed the street to get away from him,
midblock and almost home, she crossed the street and then
she did something else, without looking his way, she yelled
"How you," loud enough for him to hear over his own large

breathing, and in a second, a small hungry awful second, she heard him say "Hi" back, his voice blurred by bad breathing, raspy, dark, and then he said it again. "Hi."

Gertrude never slowed, she never ever slowed, but she turned her head and saw his wild eyes the way she remembered, and the crazy man also smiled and lurched on, crooked and relentless, he smiled and lurched on.

She made a wide circle, walking an arc back across the street to her own house as the man with his tongue and his smile dragged along the other way.

"Well, that didn't take long, Gertie," Mrs. Wilke said, still out in the yard, the fence high and safe around her. "Such a nice day to be out, sleepy old summer, right, Gertie? Should we have another piece of your sponge cake?" Mrs. Wilke sighed the pleasure of someone who knew no imminent fear and whose lawn had been mowed for the week and who had fresh cake waiting on the table inside.

"I'll cut the cake," Gertrude offered and opened the door to the serene kitchen, almost dark in the late afternoon and cool, the aroma of heaven still present. She cut two slices of the cake and settled them onto plates the way she knew and found two forks and her favorite paper napkins, then stood alone to survey what she'd done that day, all herself, made the cake and cut it too. A little air rippled the curtains, a small tune in its folds, the pure air, the clean breeze. The man said "Hi" and smiled. His tongue must hang out for some reason she couldn't imagine. That's what Gertrude determined, though she thought she could imagine pretty much anything.

THREE

WEDNESDAY, THURSDAY, & FRIDAY
JUNE 8, 9, & 10, 1960

i.

Rain started in the late night and went on for two days, turning the green grass greener, forcing ants to run for cover, and making easy baths for all the early summer birds. In those two rainy days Sue Too's family did not return to settle their apartment and Katie Fiore's mother and grandmother did not venture into the garden. It was a time to catch up on indoor projects, to sew an apron out of a worn dress and clean out the pantry. Betty Larsen had the idea to make a cherry pie with the canned filling she bought from Vernon's Grocery. She let Elise help roll the dough and sprinkle sugar on the scraps to bake like cookies. Katie read another Trixie Belden mystery, her brain circling the possibilities of the old house across the street.

Godfrey and Edna were undaunted by the weather. They'd conducted their regular rounds in snowstorms and heat waves. On the second day of rain, they headed out underneath their favorite stolen umbrellas and roamed the downtown, easily pilfering a pair of socks at Penney's, a dried salami at Leo's Market, and two bars of soap at the drugstore. They also legitimately purchased butter from Leo and a pair of silky pink panties on sale at Penney's. Godfrey chattered mindlessly to the bored store clerks, and Edna giggled like a girl as she tucked what she needed into her cloth-covered basket. Even so, they came home tired from the effort and wet to the bone from the chilling June rain.

Gertrude ignored the rain altogether. For all the hours since she'd seen the crooked man smile her way, she could only wonder about him and that tongue and that lurch and the particular fact that he traveled her block. He was a fellow traveler, Gertrude thought, and so she walked the block on her old schedule, the way she did before she was afraid. She tied a pleated rain scarf under her chin, enduring its phony crinkle, as if it were a tissue or a fading leaf, instead of ridiculous clear plastic covering her head. She buckled into her raincoat and walked around in the morning and in the late morning and after lunch, twice actually that time, and before supper and right after supper, until Mrs. Wilke had to say, "Please sit, Gertie, and take a rest." By then her feet were chapped red from the rub of wet shoes, and she had to give up. She thought she'd see the man again. She thought for sure he'd be interested in the wet tranquility of the rainy day. But he was not. Or she missed him. He didn't live on her block, so he lived on some other block and maybe that's where he walked.

The second day of rain, she still did not see him. She collapsed at last into Mrs. Wilke's flowered armchair to air her sore toes. The sponge cake had gone stale by then, and Gertrude's anticipation had dulled. She went to bed before nine and never moved again all night.

Nicky Marodi had forgotten her anyway. He'd been happy for her sideways greeting, her head bent into wherever she thought she was going, and he'd stored it with the few treasures of life as he now knew it. But after an hour or two, he was certain that he'd dreamed up that skinny odd girl in her short pants and high shoes. Her "How you" faded off into the incessant pulse of rain on the roof those two days. There was something to his memory of her though. Just what, he could not conclude.

ii.

Nicky grew up on these blocks, rode a broken bike his Uncle Freddo gave him, went to the brick school with its wooden desks in rows, papers with lines, letters that curved every time in the same way, the g always a g, the h always an h. He was good at school. He kept to the order of school and took to the information it presented—who sailed around the Cape of Good Hope, how coral formed at the bottom of the sea, when to use a plural verb. He knew these blocks then, the store with the Italian lady who yelled to pick up your wrappers, always agitated, the skin under her arms wiggling and her hairnet loose. He saw the store now, but it wasn't the Italian lady's store, some man smoking inside, wrappers everywhere, nobody picking up wrappers.

He had pictures in his mind of what these blocks used to be, though he was struggling to find that again, as though the earth had lurched in its orbit, as he did when he walked, jiggling the neighborhood off-kilter, different encounters at every turn, alarm on faces. Years ago, people had welcomed the handsome Nicky Marodi with brightness in his eyes and a million ideas bouncing around in his young and feverish mind. That was all before the confusion began, when the letter g could become the letter h, when he saw the windows take shape and his mother's front door reach out to swallow him.

He had one whole story as young Nicky Marodi. Now he had another story as a man who frightened people. He didn't think he was dangerous, but for years he'd been confined to a hospital that reminded him of a kingdom, a place away from other places with locks and bars and uniformed staff and its own laundry and its own bakery and its own electrical power, everything its own. The sick screamed. He probably screamed too. He was sure he did, but it wasn't an exact sureness, it wasn't a detailed sureness. It was an elusive picture, like the elusive picture he had of a skinny lady in short pants. A foggy recollection of a place he'd been for so long he now had gray hairs he could see in the mirror and an ache for everything he'd never known and maybe never would.

Nicky Marodi had been diagnosed as a schizophrenic when he was eighteen, just before he was to go into the army and fight for world freedom and peace, both notions that he ascribed to at the time, grand notions he wanted to defend. But as the months before he graduated from high school became more disordered, his mind taking nightmarish leaps and his dreams hovering on horror, his mother took him to see Dr. Murray, who referred them to another doctor in Duluth, who told his mother this news and, in perfect medical English, tried to explain to the Italian woman that her son would not simply recover. There was no medicine that would return him to the self he was just one year before. They took the train home together, holding hands as they sat side by side, Nicky working to keep himself in check and his mother whispering the rosary without any beads.

They worked and prayed like that for the next five years, as the war ended and the victorious returned, as the world trudged on, not necessarily peaceful or altogether free. The neighborhood around them grew more intolerant of Nicky and his unusual ways, his jerky movements and wild eyes, his lack of control over his tongue and his weird, often incomprehensible outbursts. The kinder people, like the Abellis for example, shook their heads in pity and made an effort to say hello. But others, especially the newcomers to the blocks he walked and the older boys and girls who had lost their childhoods to the Depression and the war, were not so kind. Groups of them took to chasing and mocking him. Someone came up with the name Kaka Roo, which the boys called out even if he was a block away. He couldn't escape the cruelty. And the worse it got, the worse he became.

When he was twenty-five, his mother committed him to the Moose Lake State Hospital for the mentally ill. That's where he had been for more than a decade. He didn't think of it that way. A decade had no meaning for Nicky. Life was a day full of minutes that may or may not go his way. He'd been home for one week. So far he had slept through the long nights. So far he had avoided groups of boys coming his way. That's all the meaning he held right now. Full minutes. Long rests. His mother made him wear a scapular blessed by the monsignor. "Please, Nicky," she said. "Don't ever take it off."

iii.

The rain stopped in the night and the air smelled like new life. Nicky left his mother's house to walk and almost immediately met Godfrey and Edna strolling toward town. Godfrey parked himself some feet in front of Nicky like an old friend. "Nice

day, don't you think?" Godfrey said. "Very fresh." Edna stood
slightly off to the side, nodding to affirm what her husband
had just said, her wide-brimmed hat rocking about on her
head. "You going for a morning walk?"

He didn't look their way, but beyond them to where he wanted
to go, where he thought he was going before they'd appeared.
"I am," he said, his tongue blocking clear diction, "going to
walk." He wasn't sure how he was supposed to go around these
two people and so he stayed where he was, put his hands in
the pockets of his suit jacket and dug them deep. "Bye," he
added, thinking that it might get them all moving again. "See
you later."

The lady turned and waddled away, her hips bouncing, her
dress swaying, her hat bobbing. It was the first funny thing he'd
noticed in some time, and so he tried to smile, let the muscles in his face pull his mouth outward and upward, watching
as the man joined his wife and they both walked toward the
corner of that block. That's when Godfrey turned and waved.
"Have a good day, Kaka Roo," he said, still waving, his wife
still bouncing and bobbing, the new sun still shining.

Nicky didn't move; he couldn't. The name had come back to
tell him he wasn't new like the day or the June buds or the
baby birds in their nests. He wanted to be new. For a moment
he considered the blocks ahead of him after a hard rain, the
free steps of his feet on open pavement, the air and large movement. Instead he turned and went his way home to sit on an
old wooden chair his mother had left leaning against the house.
It was a defeat. Even so, he angled his face up to the sky and
let it touch him any way it would.

He did not know that Gertrude, on her own block and in her own way, had been looking for him all through the rains and was now making her fourth determined lap. She barely noticed anyone or anything and identified no particular creatures calling to her, but tromped on and on, alert to find him, maybe befriend him, understand why his tongue wouldn't stay inside his mouth, that tongue and all the wet breath around it.

Though everywhere the day sparkled, refreshed and beautiful, none of it could distract her. Not the droplets hanging onto the green, green grass or the dewy faces of Mrs. Abelli's purple pansies, or the clean swept sky itself. And she didn't want to see Godfrey and Edna again, yet there they were blocking her way, his suspenders and bad eyes, her fluff and hat. "How you," Gertrude said, but flat, without exuberance, her mind zooming about as she considered how to get by them, cross between them, roar around them.

"You see Kaka Roo?" Godfrey asked her.

"We just saw him," Edna added. "He's out walking too."

"You see him?" Godfrey probed again.

Gertrude had no idea what they were talking about or whom. She shook her head and bolted right between them, gleeful almost in her victory, the Godfreys now behind her and the sidewalk ahead, all hers again.

"He's a walker too," she heard Godfrey call after her. "Kaka Roo," he repeated and Gertrude, far gone in her tall strides, took in the name and shivered. Maybe, she thought, she needed a sweater. Maybe the rain had left a chill.

iv.

Sitting on her curb, Elise saw Gertrude go around and around and the funny couple pass by on the other side of the street and Sue Too's family's green truck arrive with more to unload into their apartment. She watched as Sue Too ambled out and over to Katie's yard and the two of them came toward Elise, said hello to her, and walked into the alley, where Elise knew they would unlatch the gate to the old empty house and disappear inside. They hadn't invited her, but they'd greeted her, their energy crackling as they went by, moving quickly, on their mission, whatever it was. Elise had no idea what they hoped to get out of that house.

While she sat taking in the neighborhood, her mother was doing laundry and hanging the clothes on the line to dry. Betty Larsen went back and forth from their washing machine in the garage to the lines behind the Saluccis' house, tossing comments to Elise who made patterns in the street dirt and worked on not having to pee, which she did, but feared leaving her post. Just in case the older girls needed her.

When they finally came out of the alley, their energy and voices were subdued and the dusty heat of the house was still with them. "Hi, Elise," Katie said, "you still here?"

"Did you solve a mystery?" Elise asked, standing to meet them.

"Something," Sue Too said, shaking her head. "Wanna tell her?"

Katie flipped open her notebook of clues and settled herself on the rough boulevard grass, and Elise did the same, still wishing she could escape to the bathroom without disturbing the moment. But it was only a wish, and she stayed, settling next to Katie with her back straight and her legs very crossed. Sue Too plopped down on the curb grumbling, "You guys ever sit in chairs around here?"

"We think the man who lived in that house killed his wife," Katie announced with authority, though her voice stayed barely above a whisper. "He had to. All the clues point to it."

Sue Too picked up the story. "We think there's blood and we think he was a church nut—Katie's mom said he was a minister or something—and he left in a hurry probably taking her body with him."

"In his car," Katie added. "The car is missing."

Sue Too stopped her. "Well it's not exactly missing if we don't know they even had one."

"Everyone does," Katie answered.

"We don't," Elise said.

"That's because your mom doesn't drive," Katie dismissed. Most women they knew didn't drive. Katie's mother certainly didn't and Mrs. Larsen didn't either. Katie turned a page in her notebook. "Anyway," she went on, "there's all kinds of stuff just left in a hurry, messy stuff and coffee grounds, so we think he killed her right after breakfast."

"Plus there's a thousand newspapers," Sue Too threw in. "These people never met a newspaper they didn't save. You'd think the whole place would go up in flames."

Elise's eyes widened at this. "Really?" She was trying to understand how coffee grounds and newspapers pointed to someone's
murder. Of course, Sue Too had said something about blood too.

"But I don't think those newspapers mean anything," Sue Too
interrupted.

Katie sat up straight. "Of course they do. Somebody saved
them for a reason."

"I think the minister saved those newspapers," Sue Too said.
"He was a reader, all those boxes of books around. The guy
would read anything."

Elise hoped they'd come to some kind of agreement soon, so
she could run upstairs and pee without missing any of the mystery. Then her mother banged through the screen door with a
basket of wet clothes. "You girls look like you could use some
Kool-Aid," she said the very second she saw them, and continued on about the pretty day after the rain, her loads of laundry,
and the breeze she was depending on to dry her clothes quickly.
Elise saw the look of alarm that Katie signaled to Sue Too, and
they were up and off before Elise could dream of a way to keep
them there. Calling bye, they crossed to Sue Too's building and
disappeared inside.

"Well, that was fast, wasn't it? Not everyone likes Kool-Aid, I
guess," Mrs. Larsen commented, but her daughter had already
scampered upstairs to pee, overcome with crushing disappointment that she was alone again.

After using the bathroom, Elise looked out the window at the
top of the garage apartment stairs, the window that faced the

old green house. "What if one of those houses caught on fire?" Elise asked her mother busy in the kitchen. "Would we catch on fire too?"

"Of course not," her mother answered. "Fire can't jump across the whole yard." Elise pulled out a puzzle to take her mind off the sagging green house with its old newspapers and dead people and mystery. She became too absorbed to notice that her mother had come from the kitchen to the same window, where she stood a long while assessing the probability of house flames leaping from one roof to another to her own.

v.

Katie marveled at the chaos in Sue Too's apartment. In some ways it was worse than their mystery house. There, the order had been disassembled. Here, in this beat-up apartment, Sue Too's family had fashioned no order whatsoever. The boxes and grocery bags of stuff had been left everywhere, so that the girls had to watch every step they took not to crush an alarm clock or break some dish. "At least we have chairs," Sue Too said as they sat side by side at the table near the kitchen window.

"Where are your parents?"

"Back to the farm for another load." She looked around at the clutter. "Maybe it won't work out. I mean living in town. We're kind of big barn people, if you know what I mean."

Katie did not know what Sue Too meant, but she didn't ask.

"We don't stay put much. I mean, we did before, when I was a kid like Elise. We had our own farm then and my sisters were around. But then my dad came down with some kind of condition and he couldn't do the work. So we had to move."

"You must have liked the farm," Katie offered, watching her friend's face get a little dreamy with the thought of it all.

"Yeah. Anyway, now Shirley's on a farm, that's my older sister. And Diane, my other sister, lives in Bemidji. And me, Mom, and Dad go from place to place."

"What about school though?" Katie couldn't imagine the kind of life Sue Too was describing, the lack of a foundation, like living in a house with no basement just waiting for a tornado to come and blow you away.

"I go to school wherever we are. So I started out at the school by Findlayson near our farm, but then we went to Bovey because my mom's cousin lives there, and then I was in Bemidji with my sister one year, fifth grade. I really hated fifth grade. Then last year we were with Shirley, so I went back to Findlayson. Now I'm here." She shrugged. None of this was her idea; that was clear.

"Our high school is the best. You'll love it."

"Really?"

"It has marble steps and walls painted by artists. You know with pictures of miners."

"I'll have to give it a try, I guess. If we last the summer." Both girls sat in silence surveying the state of the apartment, wondering, each in her own way, how the family's life would take shape there. "I don't think we have curtains," Sue Too concluded.

"My mom sews ours," Katie said.

"You're kiddin'? That's something."

"I think we should read through the newspapers in that old house to see what we can find."

"You're as crazy as they are. What do you think you're going to find?" Sue Too didn't care what Katie answered. Nothing they found would be worth the anguish of reading a million dusty newspapers.

"They saved them for a reason." Katie opened her notebook and read, "Six piles of newspapers, two feet high each."

"You're giving me a heart attack," Sue Too said. Then in a flash she bounced up and rummaged through her family's things to pull out a faded plastic plant that might once have had flowers attached to its stems. "So why do you think my mother keeps saving this?" Katie had no idea. Her mother wouldn't have let such a thing into her house in the first place.

"No reason, that's why. Some people just save stuff. That's just what they do. Like those crazies over there saving newspapers. Maybe they thought they'd use them some day. That's what my mom always says. You never know, she says." Sue Too dropped the plastic plant on the floor. "I bet most of the stuff people keep they don't have any reason why." She sat back down on her chair. "And I'm not spending my summer reading leftover newspapers." She stared out the window. "What's with that couple down there? They go about two steps a century."

Katie glanced down. "It's Godfrey and Edna. All they do is go downtown and back every day, so they're never in a hurry."

"I guess not."

"They shoplift."

"You're kiddin'. Those two? Don't they get caught?" She burst out laughing and couldn't stop, which made Katie laugh too, both of them snorting and hooting as they watched Godfrey and Edna toddle slowly down Twenty-Fourth Street, Edna carrying her covered basket filled with who knew what.

But when Katie left Sue Too's apartment a little while later, she wasn't so light. Sue Too did not live in a normal place with a normal family. They had unpacked almost nothing and continued to go back out to her sister's farm to get more. Already Sue Too wasn't sure they'd make it through the summer before they'd pick up and move on again. Maybe their mystery would not be solved. Maybe Katie would have to return to hours of reading and singing and riding her bike around town by herself. Not that she'd be unhappy necessarily. But then, maybe she would be.

vi.

Mrs. made egg salad, but Gertrude ate mindlessly, not enjoying the squeeze of mayo out from between the bread or the crinkle of the paper napkin. Nothing. She frowned and ate all right, but her mind kept going around and around the block searching. She hadn't made him up, though Mrs. didn't know him, but no wonder. The older woman never left the yard, her very own, left to her by her husband who put up the gate and fence before he died, just to have a bit of privacy, as Mrs. said, a place where one could sit without stockings now and again and who was to know. But now all this backyard business made Gertrude angry, because Mrs. Wilke couldn't help her find the man.

"You're in such a snit, Gertie," Mrs. remarked as she cleared their two plates after a wholly silent and sullen lunch. "You always liked those chips before," she said, but Gertrude barely heard her, only her voice, some words. Nothing to help Gertrude though, who downed a whole glass of water from the tap before she headed for the door, ready to try again. She passed Christ the scientist. Earth orbiting the sun, she remembered that bit of science. Something about the moon too, what did that orbit? The earth maybe. Or it sat there waiting for the earth to come on by like Gertrude on her block.

Now there were boys by the Vernons', of all things. Stealing gum or what, but she didn't slow, she never slowed, which was almost a rule, almost science for her to keep moving, keep orbiting. "How you," she called not knowing any of them.

Then she heard "Where's the fire, lady" and "Hey, Cuckoo Bird." She heard giant rough laughs like bulldozers mowing down trees. "Hey, Cuckoo Bird." She walked faster thinking harder about science and Christ and what the moon was up to, until she nearly collided with Mrs. Larsen crossing her way, all words and lipstick. "How you," Gertrude said to be polite and Mrs. Larsen answered something about Oreos as Gertrude kept going, bounding forward, full thrust, while the entire world

around her jostled and jeered, not just physically, but audibly
and horribly, such that not any bitty bird song could make its
way through and such that the speck of a figure leaning or perhaps lurching two blocks down could not stop Gertrude from
charging straight home to the fence and the gate that latched
and closed her inside Mrs. Wilke's tender spot of green.

Still panting she sat in the lawn chair and breathed and breathed
and tried to bring back the scent of the green, green grass after
rain. Only then did she know what she'd seen as she'd rounded
that last corner. She'd seen him. He was real. She'd known he
was real and now he was just a block away, dragging along, hat
on his head. She'd seen him. Mrs. Wilke called to her, "Feeling better now, Gertie," as she came slowly outside carrying
two glasses of lemonade on ice, striped straws poking high like
batons in a parade. "Gertie?" Deep in her lawn chair Gertrude
sat measuring the yes and no of roaring one more time around
the block to see the gimpy man and his tongue. Yes, because
she'd say some words this time and maybe he would too and
that would be the start of something. No, because she'd get all
snagged in boys by Vernon's Grocery and forget what to say to
anyone. Or worse, those boys would yell at the man and she
wouldn't be able to stop them.

"Gertie?" Mrs. Wilke handed her a glass of lemonade, which
she slurped so fast, Mrs. had to comment about manners.

"I should try," Gertrude said suddenly, loud and hard as if Mrs.
had argued the point, when of course Mrs. had done no such
thing, nor would she, as she settled down with her lemonade
and wiggled out of her shoes. By that time Gertrude was on
her way again, passing the front of Christ the scientist church
once more, where the new grass was near wild to be cut again,
all its bugs zigging and zagging below.

vii.

Betty Larsen relaxed her steps as she walked by the boys in front of Vernon's Grocery. She would have denied it if asked, but there it was, the sway of a somewhat available woman among males. Not that she would have accepted any notion of her availability either. She had Claus after all. And a daughter. The boys, all teenagers, huddled in some other absorption that had nothing to do with Betty. She entered the store completely unseen.

"Good afternoon," she sung out as she strode inside, but no one was there to hear her. Roger Vernon had stepped into the back apartment for a minute and, unlike the other small-storekeepers in town, did not come barreling out the minute he heard the bell ring over the door. "Hello?"

Puzzled, Betty stood still and listened to the store creak quietly around her, wondering now why she had come. She'd spent too much money last time and had barely used any of the canned goods she'd bought. But two rainy days in the garage apartment watching Elise put together puzzles and play with a doll had left Betty itching just to have some kind of conversation, even with sullen Roger Vernon. He was good-looking at least. She liked the smell of the store, actually, whatever it was. Ice cream or wafer cookies, maybe. Old wood and tobacco.

"How you doing?" Roger said, coming back, wiping his hands on a towel.

"Oh, I'm fine." Betty smiled broadly, then noticed his towel. "Cleaning up a bit? No end to that is there?" She wanted to launch into the whole topic of cleaning, products and techniques and all, but when Roger tossed the towel on the counter and lit a cigarette, she decided against it. "Back for a few things," she said instead. "No end to that either."

Roger Vernon watched her with detached curiosity, still wondering what she was up to. She had stacked two bags of cookies on the counter and was flouncing about, when they were both startled by a ball hitting the front window. "Goddamned kids." Roger's rage sent him flying out the door. "What the hell are you guys doing out here? Buy your candy or smokes and go home."

Two of the boys laughed, and a third said, "It was nothing, Mister. Just a slipup. Nothing broke." He looked like he wanted to laugh too but was containing himself. The boys didn't leave and Roger didn't go back inside and then there was Gertrude coming like a human bullet down the sidewalk toward them, terrified but resolute. "Jeesuz, there's that Cuckoo Bird again," the same boy said loud enough so that they turned her way, and she kept coming, not even breathing, poor Gertrude, marching through the fray.

"How you," she said, almost shouting as she stormed by, looking only straight ahead, the very air rumbling around her.

Through the store window, Betty Larsen watched as the moment accelerated and Gertrude hurried past, the boys laughing and Roger Vernon glowering at the whole fiasco in front of his store. "Go home," he yelled again, but too late to save Gertrude. "I don't want you guys hanging out here, you understand?" He stood taller and wider than any of them and in a last gesture moved toward them and bellowed, "Scram!"

Still laughing, the boys dispersed in two directions. Roger waited until they were well off the block before he went back inside to face Betty Larsen, who stood silent and appalled, holding her wallet against her chest like a shield. "Who are those boys?"

"No idea," Roger answered. "Never saw them before."

"Gertrude's slow, you know," Betty said.

"That her name?" Roger went behind the counter and lit another cigarette. "You want a beer or anything? Calm your nerves?"

"Her name is Gertrude Wilke. Well, Wilke's the name of her caretaker. She's no trouble."

Roger Vernon shrugged. "Boys," he said.

Betty felt too distressed to know what that meant. She liked Gertrude. She should have run out to protect her; she should have done something. "I think I'll come back later," she said, forgetting her groceries on the counter and leaving the store. Outside, she walked quickly to Mrs. Wilke's house. She peeked over the fence to see the older woman sound asleep in one of the lawn chairs, shoes off and mouth open, and Gertrude sprawled in the other chair holding her hands over her eyes.

"Gertrude?" Betty asked softly. "You're all right now, aren't you?"

Gertrude slid her hands down and pressed her palms together. "They didn't get him, anyway," she said.

"Who Gertrude?"

"The man with the tongue."

Betty nodded as if she knew what Gertrude was talking about. "Well, you're all right now," she repeated, still nodding, and Gertrude nodded too. "Tell Mrs. Wilke hi," Betty added. Then without thinking or planning it, Betty said, "You're everyone's friend, Gertrude. Don't forget how we think about you." With one more nod, she left the two in their lawn chairs and walked home, uncontrollable tears running down her face, ruining her makeup and even the side curls of her hairdo. Only when she stepped into her own vestibule did she think about the groceries she'd left stacked on Roger Vernon's counter.

viii.

Nicky Marodi had spotted those boys in front of the grocery store that didn't belong to the Italian lady anymore. With a certain and deliberate lurch, he'd altered his route farther south and then west to make sure he wouldn't encounter them even if their circle broke apart. He'd be ahead and off their track.

He'd spent the morning recovering from the round little man calling him Kaka Roo and spent lunch in his mother's yard watching her pull dandelions, some that she discarded and some, the light green and tender ones, that she kept to cook. All the while he had let the sun come his way, mild and easy like June itself and leaned against the worn wood of his mother's house.

He would have liked knowing that someone, even an oddball in pedal pushers, thought enough to look for him in the neighborhood and brave the pack of boys just in case she'd find Nicky at the other end of her trouble. He would have liked hearing her "How you," too loud for the air it traveled, but well meaning. Nicky had many things to say to someone, but he didn't dare try just yet. He liked the summer air and his mother nearby. He liked his dressy clothes, the backyard, being home.

ix.

In the early afternoon Claus Jacobson took a short walk down his street to test out this type of mobility, this simple act of getting from one place to another without driving a car, but he did it with some reluctance, even arrogance, as if a man like him could never be separated from his car. He loved cars. He'd been just a boy when Henry Ford rolled out his Model T and in only a few years half the men in town had one. Ford made millions of them in his Detroit assembly plant with its moving belts of parts, and Claus loved those cars the moment he spotted one coming down First Avenue, the new driver honking and waving to him like a visiting king. There were cars before the Model T and cars after the Model T, but Claus never forgot that one on First Avenue with the black fenders that gleamed.

He bought his own car when he was sixteen, a sturdy Ford that had been crashed into a tree by a driver who lost control out on Highway 169. Embarrassed and ready to show off a newer model, the owner sold it to Claus for a few bucks down and monthly payments over a year. A gentlemen's agreement, he'd said. Claus had dropped out of school that year to work as a janitor at the mine, so he'd paid off his first car without trouble and immediately coveted his next, the Oldsmobile that he bought when he was nineteen and drove for ten years.

Boys went out on their own early back when. Parents couldn't support full-sized boys able to work and eating three hardy meals every day of the week. His parents had come to America in 1894, part of the first rush of immigrants migrating across country to the mining ranges of Northern Minnesota. They traveled from Sweden, many weeks on the boat, took a dirty open-car train to the Midwest, and found themselves in country so raw and untamed that his young mother sat in the dirt and cried.

They thought they'd come to a land of dreams, and maybe it was eventually, but when his parents arrived, they faced hardscrabble lives they didn't imagine in the sturdy, scrubbed houses of their childhoods. But they'd put down roots for him and his three brothers. Three girl babies were buried in the old cemetery north of town, done in by fevers and the mysterious curses of that era. When babies died, only their mothers grieved them. The rest of the world charged on into the new century, the newly founded territory, the rigors of living that did not end.

After walking at an even pace for three blocks, Claus found himself working harder to breathe. He turned abruptly for home, not worried but puzzled. How odd to be so tired. He'd always prided himself on his youthful energy, on a strength and vitality that allowed him to maintain a relationship with a woman almost half his age. With each block it seemed his breath became heavier, as if too dense to pass easily through him. He did not slow down, however. In fact, Claus forced himself to take larger strides, one hand swinging wide to help move him along and the other held protectively to his chest.

x.

Roger Vernon sat in the silent store for longer than his usual afternoon break. He drank two beers and stared nearly motionless out at the street with its steady line of cars driving to town, home from town, and home from the mining shops north of town as the day shifts ended. He didn't know those men who mined the ore. Most of them had grown up in town and moved from high school into mining with maybe a four-year break to go overseas during the war. They had their lifelong friends, taverns where they gathered, wives who met for coffee, stories that went back decades.

Roger had applied for a job in the mines when he married Sophia, but they weren't hiring then and he had no trade to offer. "You could be an electrician," his wife had suggested for some reason. But trades didn't interest him. He'd never had any particular interest; one thing in life had just followed the next. He'd been just young enough to avoid one war and just old enough to avoid the next. The thing about those boys outside his store was that he'd been one of them. He'd loved any kind of joke on the adult world. Maybe that's what had thrown him off. He knew those boys better than he knew that goony walker speeding by a million times a day or the lady coming in now to buy Oreos all the time. This neighborhood, he did not know. The immigrants with their gardens and card games and lights out by ten. They were strangers to him, like his father-in-law was a stranger to him, content with a lawn groomed better than Roger groomed himself for god's sake. These people worked and worked and worked. They never stopped until the sun hung low, and then they hauled out their decks of cards and worked at making an extra two bits off a pair of queens.

He understood the boys out there laughing to high heaven over every peculiarity. Why the hell not? There was no harm in it really, even the calls out to this Gertrude who hiked on through them anyway. No harm was meant, just a good laugh and a way to feel important when you were young and dumb and had no importance whatsoever anywhere. It was tough to want to be somebody and know you weren't. So you smoked. You snapped wads of gum in your jaw, drank beers you popped open with one hand, slouched like a panther, coveted girls, and lashed out at the rest.

Roger wasn't that way anymore. He had Sophia, bless her, and this goddamned store he hated, but which nonetheless had his name on the sign over the door. He liked sports on the radio and television. That was something. He liked taking Sophia to the Howard Café for gin and steak on some Saturday nights after they closed the store. He wasn't an angry kid anymore. A little angry maybe, stuck behind the counter all day, but not like those boys in front of the store. He was long gone from that time of his life.

So he had pulled his 185 pounds into play, loomed over them, and shooed them away. They'd be back though. He would have been back. If he were one of those boys, he could have hardly waited to come back.

But the image of that Gertrude blasting through them all nagged him. People like her should stay home. Stay out of trouble. What the hell was he supposed to do about her? It was a public sidewalk after all. If every goofball wanted to walk by, he couldn't stop them. And the boys at least bought cigarettes and chewing gum. Business was business, his father-in-law liked to say. Though he was another one who knew nothing about business.

Roger unlocked the door in the late afternoon, just before Sophia returned from work, tired of being on her feet all day, but happy to see him, as she usually was. She brought him out a sandwich to eat while he minded the store and sat on the stool next to him. "What happened today?" she asked.

"Nothing much."

"Did Betty Larsen come back for more groceries?"

"She swung by," he said.

"What did she buy this time?" Sophia was still excited about the twenty dollars their neighbor had spent a few days before.

"I can't remember," he said, not looking to see the disappointment register on her pretty face.

"Oh well," she sighed. "Maybe tomorrow."

FOUR

SATURDAY, JUNE 11, 1960

i.

Katie spent long minutes considering everything they'd discovered in the abandoned house, all the daily items left behind, things half-packed, the coffee pot not even washed. She'd learned from books that nothing was ever quite what it seemed. Complications tripped up plans, and mysteries lurked beneath perfectly ordinary situations. Maybe the stain on the floor was blood. Maybe the minister who read religious books about God, Jesus, and the Bible, would, deep down in his conflicted heart, be capable of murdering someone. But the more she thought about it, the less she believed it.

She sat this Saturday afternoon in her childhood sandbox, bare toes dug into the sand, singing a Perry Como song she'd been hearing on the radio, and waiting for Sue Too, who eventually showed up toting another row of Saltine crackers. "Want one?" she asked, shoving the package toward Katie.

"No thanks. I'm just thinking about what happened over there."

"Blood on the floor. That's what I'm telling you."

"But why would a minister murder someone?"

"Geez, Kate. Why would anyone murder anyone? For love maybe. Or money." Sue Too stuffed a handful of crackers into her mouth. "Or maybe some kind of secret." This idea appealed to her. "Okay, so let's say this minister had something shady in his past. Something like a scandal. Maybe he used to be a thief. And then he puts that behind him and becomes a minister until, wham, a guy from the past shows up and tells his wife. And his wife threatens him." She spread her hands wide in conclusion. "So the minister kills her."

Katie didn't want to laugh, but she found this idea ridiculous. "I don't know."

"It could happen, Kate."

"Maybe. I do think people kill for love though," Katie offered.

"People do anything for love. My sisters, you can't believe. Changed their hair color, Shirley knit socks for one guy, and he left anyway."

Katie shook her head. "I don't mean that. I mean how people love the wrong person or they aren't loved back."

Sue Too stared at her. "Did you see that on television?"

"I don't know. I hear stories. My mom and pop talk about people, old stories, things that happened. One of my mom's aunts had to marry a man who paid money for her. It was all arranged. She didn't even want to marry him. She wanted to be a nurse."

"How much did he pay?"

Clearly Sue Too was missing the point. She didn't feel the misery that Katie could imagine in this situation, going through life with someone you didn't choose. Maybe even someone you didn't like. Or someone who smelled bad. "I'm just saying," Katie said, not answering Sue Too's question.

Her friend ate the rest of the Saltines and crumpled the bag, smashing it one way and another until it was completely flat. "So much for that," she said and glanced around in that busy way she had, always ready to hop off to the next thing. "You want to go back in?"

"What are we going to do?"

Sue Too thought about that. "Well, did we go through everything upstairs?"

"Pretty much. Enough to know a woman lived there. I wrote it all down in my notebook. Gloves and lipsticks, handkerchiefs. They had perfume on them, you know."

"I miss my sisters' lipsticks," Sue Too said out of the blue. "I don't care if I ever wear lipstick in my life, but I liked kind of messing around with them."

"At least you have sisters. My mom had two boys, and they both died."

"You're kiddin'? Two brothers died?"

"Well, they never lived actually." She tried to explain about her mother and the unlucky seventh month.

"That's tough." Sue Too kicked off her dirty tenners and stuck her feet into the sand next to Katie's. "I could be your sister, like unofficial."

Katie looked at her eager new friend. "Well," she said, "we could be something anyway. We could be a team. We could be a club if you want."

"Oh, man, that's a great idea. I've never been in a club. That's even better than sisters. You don't wear lipstick anyway."

"Maybe a detective club."

"Oh, man," Sue Too said again. "That's the best. So we need a name, right?"

Katie searched Sue Too's face for an idea. "We could just call it a secret club."

"So it would be a secret?"

"Don't you think? Nobody knows what we're doing anyway."

"So will we have a secret code or a handshake or something?"

"We can do whatever we want. It's our club." Then Katie remembered little Elise always sitting on the curb outside her garage apartment. "But we should tell Elise at least. She's all by herself."

"Poor kid. You don't have a sister, but that poor kid don't even have a dad."

"I know." Katie couldn't imagine what she'd do in life without her pop's good humor. "Let's go tell her she can be part of our secret club."

"Then we're not going in to explore again?"

"Maybe we can just work on the club today and go over our clues. Stuff like that," Katie said, happy for a plan that did not include going back into the old house. They brushed off the sand and, still barefoot, hustled through the Abellis' garden and across the street to find Elise.

ii.

Betty heard the girls talking to Elise outside, the giggles and occasional squeals of excitement. She remembered those conversations with girlfriends, the exaggerated reactions just to maximize the moment, the delicious drama of making large gestures and loud noises. She'd never seen Elise that way, but if Katie Fiore squealed, Betty was sure Elise would too. That's how it was with girls. Whatever one did, they all did.

Betty always liked being a little girl, in spite of her mother's opinions and her father's detached exhaustion. Maybe she was just one of those people who was meant to be silly and dramatic, even frivolous. She liked being in love and feeling pretty, even though she wasn't. Feeling pretty and being pretty were two different animals. Anyone with the right attitude, the right outfit, and a flattering shade of lipstick could certainly feel pretty. She'd proven this to herself forever. She liked primping and dressing, all of it, right down to straightening the seam on her wispy nylon stockings. She liked having this garage apartment too, all charming with swag curtains and polished floors, the sun coming in one way and then another as the day moved reliably from morning to late afternoon.

But she didn't like the silence of loneliness, the weeklong stretches between Claus's visits, the lack of company. She didn't have a yard where she could sit comfortably waiting for a neighbor to pass, say hello, maybe chat. Out her kitchen window she often saw old Mrs. Abelli sitting in her red lawn chair, and it seemed someone always stopped to talk to her, leaning on the fence, yakking away in Italian. These people came all the way from another country and still had more friends than Betty.

After the shock of the boys chiding Gertrude the day before, Betty had felt listless and worn out. She'd spent hours on her bed today not even caring about her flattened hair. She'd have to think about dinner soon, some kind of dinner. Maybe open a couple of the stupid cans of food she'd bought at Vernon's Grocery. Baked beans or something. She didn't remember what she'd bought, only that she'd bought too much and that it hadn't mattered. Roger Vernon was not the kind of man who went out of his way to be friendly. Not to her. Not to Gertrude either. To him they were just part of the landscape, like that half-dead tree out on his boulevard. To him Betty and Gertrude were just objects in his sight line. He didn't hear Gertrude's, "How you." Betty was certain he didn't. And he certainly didn't notice Betty's new hairdo. She and Gertrude were misfits, stories the other neighbors told to one another, hardly real.

"Momma." Elise leaned over her mother, her breath hot on Betty's face. "I'm in a secret club, Momma." Betty opened her eyes to see Elise, her face flushed with excitement, her eyes bright. "Can I go to Katie's house across the street, Momma?" She hovered so near that the moisture in her breath touched Betty's skin.

Betty nodded in response. For once in Elise's life, her mother had nothing to say.

"Don't tell anyone, Momma. About the secret." And in a second, Elise was gone, taking her warm, wet breath with her and her dusty smell of the curb and early summer. Better than a flower, that smell. Better than Evening in Paris, Betty thought, and sat up on her bed. Unconsciously she moved her hair this way and that. She worked her curls and tucked in her blouse and walked in her stocking feet to the telephone, where she dialed Claus's number from memory even though she had never actually used it before. She listened to it ringing on the other end without caring if Claus's wife answered.

"Hello?"

"Is Claus home, Mrs. Jacobson? It's Betty Larsen calling."

"Oh my. Oh." Betty heard some clatter on the other end, the phone banging against something, a table or phone stand. She'd never been in their house to know. And then footsteps. And then Claus.

"Betty? Is something wrong?" The deep clarity of his voice did not fit the airiness of her garage apartment, with the sun through two windows and the dusty smell of Elise still with her.

"I'd like to see you tomorrow," she said, a simple request, but one she had never made before.

The line fell quiet. Instead of rushing in to chatter it away, she breathed back at him and waited. She wanted to go to bed that night thinking about seeing him, looking forward to seeing him. That was all she wanted.

"I'll see what I can do," he answered and hung up the phone.

On her end, however, Betty did not immediately hang up the phone. She held on to it and leaned against her refrigerator. Claus should not have said that to her. It was the wrong thing to say. In a kind of energized trance, she tied on her apron and started pulling things out of her refrigerator and cupboards so that by the time Elise returned from her secret club at suppertime, her mother had cooked a spicy hash with "a medley" of cooked vegetables. She'd baked a marble cake and frosted it with chocolate. And after they ate and cleaned up the dishes and pans, Betty sat down at the table with her daughter to tackle the toughest puzzle they could find on the shelf.

iii.

When Claus hung up, he too stood still by the phone. Betty should not have called him at home. It wasn't an emergency. The child wasn't sick. Betty wasn't injured. Her call signaled a trouble Claus did not want, a nagging reminder that he'd created another reality for himself, an enjoyment that now chose to be more. His feet felt very cold, in spite of the summer afternoon and the streaks of sun wavering on the living room carpet. His hands felt cold too. "Tildy?"

"I'm here," he heard her say from the arched doorway between their small living room and even smaller dining room. "Is there a problem?"

Claus turned in Tildy's direction, with the stark light behind her and her blue eyes, his hand still on the telephone receiver. She knew about Betty Larsen, of course, though he preferred to assume she did not. It had been a long time. A habit for all of them. "No," he answered, but did not move. The phone seemed to ground him to the floor, the house he'd bought with his own money, the house where they'd raised three daughters who now had their own houses all over town, like planets to the sun, different sizes, different elements, hot and cold, porches or not, their own children sucking thumbs and pouting, tumbling around on floors like this one in his house, which just then held him and did not let him go.

"Claus?"

"No problem," he reassured, though he was not looking at Tildy when he said it. He was still standing by the phone thinking that problems were the things in life a man could fix, like rotting front steps or a tooth that needed pulling. Betty Larsen and her daughter were not a problem. They were a trouble, an aching, begging, sad, sad trouble, and he'd brought it on himself, and he could not make it go away. Troubles followed a man. Like his bad eyes and short breath. Like the look of Tildy there in the archway knowing that he was not hers alone and had not been for much of their married life.

A crow called to another crow outside the window, loud enough to break the moment. Tildy scuttled off to see what was what and Claus, unconsciously, removed his hand from the phone and walked to his favorite chair in the living room. If he visited Betty the next day, would she be encouraged to startle him with such calls more often? Or, if he did not visit, would she be prompted to call again immediately, demanding to know why? The crows outside continued to caw. They had troubles of their own, he supposed.

iv.

Elise could hardly fall asleep that night. In one day, just one sunny summer day, she'd been admitted into Katie Fiore's club and learned a secret handshake and had cake right out of the oven for dessert and basked in her mother's undivided attention right up until it was time to go to bed. She'd listened to Katie and Sue Too reviewing their clues until they were in a tizzy about this murdering minister. Sue Too was certain he'd be coming back and, if he did, they were going to be ready and catch him and bring him to justice and get their pictures in the newspaper. Sue Too thought big like that. Elise could tell that Katie was not so sure how all this would happen. He's not a butterfly, Katie had argued, though Elise did not actually understand what Katie meant by that.

Still, Katie Fiore was the smartest person Elise had ever met, even if she was kind of bossy. Some people had to be bossy or everyone else wouldn't know what to do all of the time. Katie kept a whole notebook of clues from that awful green house. Elise's favorite clue was the coffee grounds left in the kitchen sink. Her mother would never do that, even if she were about to murder someone. Even if someone were stabbing her to death, Elise's mother would stagger to the kitchen to clean up those coffee grounds before she fell dead on the floor.

Closing her eyes in bed, Elise could just see those coffee grounds, dumped and forgotten forever. Her mother had pulled her bedroom shade, but left space at the bottom for air, and through the open window Elise heard the summer night happening. Neighborhood dogs barked at night and cars roared down Third Avenue. Many blocks away she thought she heard a siren and boys laughing like they did in front of Vernon's Grocery, that low and knowing laughter that made Elise scoot down farther under the sheets.

She loved summer now. She had everything now, even a secret handshake, which she had promised not to tell anyone, ever. And she wouldn't either.

v.

The boys came back to Vernon's Grocery that night, not caring that they had been chased away just hours before. These boys had no names as far as the neighborhood knew. They weren't Richard across the street from Vernon's or any of the boys Richard sometimes hung around with—Bobby and Red and Jack and Johnny. Richard's crowd lived within a block of Vernon's and harassed Mrs. Kirshling down on the corner because they knew they could get a rise out of her. She'd pound the sidewalk with her broom and yell, never having enough sense to just go inside and ignore them. Richard and his crowd knew the neighbors and the neighbors knew them. Mostly they didn't cluster. Some of them played ball in the summer or were playground helpers or the like. They thought Gertrude was funny, but they never called her names. Anyway, they were used to her. They'd watched her circle the block maybe a thousand times in their lives.

At nine thirty, Roger had just opened his second beer and was idly straightening the shelves, thinking about some gossip Sophia had told him, these busybody stories women passed around when they were bored. So and so out dancing at the VFW with somebody's husband. Some mother of five suddenly buying magenta lipstick. Sophia chatted about such things with no more ill will than when she reported on her father's garden or the blouse she saw in the window of Feldman's Department Store. Sophia just didn't see the cracks in the road. She remained sweetly unguarded. That was all he was thinking when he heard the pack of boys approaching, loud guffaws and low currents of conspiracy. There were four of them, but only two came inside the store.

"You sell beer, mister?" the shorter one said, all full of himself.

"You're the right age, I got beer," Roger answered, keeping himself cool, not about to be outmaneuvered. "You got an ID tells me you're the right age?"

The boy grinned like a son of a gun. "One of us here got whatever you need." He went outside and brought back a big mutt of a guy with yellow hair combed away from his face so slick that Roger could see the lines of the comb. The big boy's shoulders hunched, hiding his neck.

"I wanna buy beer," he boomed, took out a frayed wallet some relative had pawned off on him, and pulled out an ID that told Roger his name was William Mackey, age twenty-one. While William waited for Roger to approve him, his small cocky buddy grabbed two six-packs out of the cooler and handed them to William, who then set them on the counter with a five-dollar bill.

Roger studied the big guy. Maybe he was twenty-one and maybe he wasn't. Roger nodded slowly, moving the two packs of beer closer to him, side by side on the counter. "Says here you live in Kelly Lake, William."

"We call him Mack," the shorter boy said, his grin showing white. "'Cause he's a big old Mack truck, right man?"

William Mackey nodded, shifting from one foot to another, but he didn't look up and meet Roger eye to eye. "Yeah, Kelly Lake," he repeated.

"Pretty far for a guy your age to come for beer," Roger said, then gave up on the situation. To hell with it. He rang the sale and handed Mack his change, keeping one eye on the boy who did the talking. "And what's your name?" he asked as he slid the beer toward them.

"Hawk."

"He don't miss nothing," Mack said. "He's the Hawk."

"I'm sure he is."

Outside the sun had slipped away in those few minutes the boys had been in the store. Under the lights, Roger watched them open the bottles and start to drink, right there on his boulevard, wanting him to follow and confront them again or wanting him to know they meant to mark his store as their territory. Or both. He wondered how they'd react if he sauntered out with his own half-full bottle and joined them. He sure as hell knew more raunchy jokes than they did. Chuckling over that notion, he flipped all the switches inside and out and locked the door. In the shadows he waited, listening to the four boys as they drank and meandered off in the direction of First Avenue and the Saturday night action.

Sophia was awake in bed reading a movie magazine, tucked halfway under the covers in a lacy type nightgown, a peachy gauzy thing. Roger always thought she'd look like a million in black, with her red hair. But it wasn't her style. "Elvis is coming home," she reported without glancing up. One of the headlines on the cover of her magazine said, What Liz Can Tell You About Making Love.

"Good magazine, eh?"

"Well, it's Elvis. You kind of look like him, Rog, did you know that?"

He rolled in next to her. "And that's why you married me?"

"I didn't even know Elvis when I met you." She put down her magazine and turned out the light. "But you do kind of look like him."

vi.

Gertrude had been sitting for hours with her ankles pressed together and her hands folded in her lap. "Are you waiting for the queen to visit, Gertie?" Mrs. Wilke had asked more than once, but Gertrude only shook her head in answer. Of course she wasn't waiting for the queen. The country didn't have a queen, anyone knew that, even Cuckoo Bird Gertie. That's what Gertrude was thinking. Cuckoo Bird, Gertie. Cuckoo Bird, Gertie. She felt a wiggly lump of anguish making its way

up her throat, but she didn't cry. It wasn't like her to cry. Lots
of things could make you cry. If it came to that, a person could
be crying all the time.

She sat up straight in Mrs. Wilke's wingback chair, her eyes
steady on the corner of the living room, the wall painted pale
green, even the baseboards, all pale green down to the flowered
carpet. She sat straight and let the boys' words pulse through
her again and again. Their laughter too. The whole way they
had taken her block away that day, made it treacherous for
her to venture out, thrown the mirror of truth up just as she
marched by, determined to find the gimpy man again and not
thinking how she looked, head forward, following her destiny,
as she believed she was, owning her block the way she thought
she did, everyone knowing her as Gertrude and not Cuckoo
Bird.

"Should I make popcorn, Gertie?" Mrs. Wilke was taking a
break between her television shows, the mysteries and Westerns
she watched with her full concentration, though they weren't
real, as she explained often to Gertrude, they weren't like the
news. The news was real, which Mrs. Wilke preferred. But Gertrude wasn't interested in popcorn. She was interested in her
block, in having her block back. She sat dreaming of her block,
as if it were a country she'd lost, a place she'd had to abandon
through no fault of her own. She didn't hear Mrs. Wilke pop-
ping away out in the kitchen or smell the hot oil in the pan,
so lost was she in the block outside.

Maybe, she began to think, she could have just her side of
the block back. Her own side, where there was no grocery or
church or Mrs. Kirshling with her angry broom. On Gertrude's
side of the block there were only houses, and she knew the

people in those houses, the Dominichettis, the Lamores, Mrs. Kern. She didn't know the people in the apartment buildings, but she'd never really seen them outside. People in apartment buildings stayed indoors, she thought. She could go up and down her side of the block, breaking her routine and upsetting her flow, but claiming something of her own.

Without a word to Mrs. Wilke, she stood up and bounded out. She propelled herself in high gear south down Fourth Avenue, and when she reached the far corner by the apartment building, she turned abruptly on her heel and roared back. She did this three times and on the third trip, just as she was about to make her turn, she saw the man she wanted to see, one block farther south, hat on his head, turning into a yard on the other side of the street, a yard bordered by bushes almost as tall as he was, so that within seconds he disappeared from her view. She stopped, struck by her discovery. That's where he lived. On the next block. Right there, where the hedge rose high and the red roof angled above it. Right there.

Gertrude made a round, sloppy sort of turn and walked home almost at a stroll, faster than the Godfreys, but not marching this time because her path home took her away from the man, not toward him. Anyway, now she knew where he was, and this side of the block was hers again.

Coming in the house she announced, "I'm home," with such gusto that Mrs. Wilke gave a laugh.

"Well, so you are, Gertie. And you're happy again, I see."

"Ready for some popcorn," Gertrude replied, and fixed herself on the sofa next to Mrs. Wilke and what was left of the bowl of popcorn. She scooped a mouthful then leaned toward the stupid television set and its show of pretend people.

Nicky had seen Gertrude too, hard to miss, like a skinny locomotive coming his way. He could have walked farther to the corner opposite her corner, but he didn't. He turned into his yard instead. He had an idea that he'd keep seeing her, that she'd stay on that block over there, that one dangerous block with the grocery store and the busy street, places he used to know easily. Back when he was Nicky Marodi. Before he was Kaka Roo.

His mother had never bought a television set. She was alone in the house and did not understand English well enough to struggle with what was being said. She liked her knitting. She liked embroidering full linen tablecloths and crocheting baby slippers for the church bazaar. She'd listen to Caruso or one of the two Italian opera recordings Nicky had given her back when. *La Bohème* was still her favorite. Listening to *La Bohème* gave her a chance to weep without believing she should not. Listening to the lovers sing, Mrs. Marodi lost herself in sorrow. Sometimes she sang with them. She didn't need television.

So Nicky came into the cramped living room where his mother sat in her corner of the maroon velvet sofa that was decorated like all her furniture, in perfectly starched doilies. He found her finishing the darkest green leaf on a tablecloth that lay in folds all around her like the skirt of a ballroom dress. He took off his hat and jacket and sat next to her, close enough so that his elbow lightly bumped her own.

Neither of them spoke. They never had to.

vii.

The boys didn't own cars. They didn't have girls. The cocky one called Hawk was waiting to turn sixteen and drop out of school. He had ideas for his future. Not plans, but ideas. He saw himself running something, some kind of something with trains or construction or liquor. He saw himself at a steel desk, two phones ringing at one time and a secretary who liked to screw at lunchtime. He saw men scurrying to make things happen every time he came into a room. That was Hawk's idea.

After they left Vernon's Grocery, the boys followed him down First Avenue to the old neighborhoods on the far side of downtown, where they raided gardens and rocked cars, all Hawk's notions of a good time. This early in summer there were no tomatoes to steal, so they yanked the plants out, ripped leaves, wreaked enough havoc to tell the world they'd been there. Crossing the railroad tracks, they threw their empty beer bottles at the side of a warehouse, watched the glass shatter, and laughed.

Even so, Hawk did not feel satisfied. He never felt satisfied, and that is what drove him forward and nurtured his cruelty. Where others might hold back, picturing their grandmas' gardens at home, maybe, or fearing the cops out looking for guys just like them, Hawk felt such a moment's pleasure in destruction, that he only wanted more.

"We've gotta go back to that store," he told the boys. "They didn't see enough of us. Right, Mack?"

The big kid called Mack nodded, though his heart wasn't in it. The man at Vernon's knew Mack's real name now and where he lived. He was as large as Mack, and he wasn't too dumb. He could be trouble. "Sure, Hawk," he said. But an hour later he hopped on the town bus to Kelly Lake with a sense of relief that the night was over.

By midnight everyone but Hawk had drifted home, leaving him to walk on alone. He headed north again to the darkness of the Hull Rust pit and through the abandoned cemetery where the early settlers were buried, half of them children who had died in droves of everything unseen, from illnesses and accidents to the spirits of crows outside their windows.

He'd heard the stories. His old man's first three siblings lay under this dirt somewhere. He didn't know where. When the town moved south a mile to dig prime ore under the old neighborhoods, half this cemetery had been left to grass and sinking tombstones, and he didn't come from the kind of family that kept track of babies' graves. The dead were dead. Half the living were too, from what he'd observed.

He passed the town's park, the playground and picnic pavilion, and stayed on Third Avenue, a magnet pulled by force to Vernon's Grocery, where he propped himself against a tree on the other side of the street and lit a cigarette. The sign had been turned off and all the lights as well. These neighborhood groceries weren't much, one-story boxes with concrete stoops and a window or two. He considered what it would be like to own a store that sold two-bit items hour after hour, day after day, chunks of bubble gum and kids' candy, single bottles of milk, and six packs of beer to boys too young to drink. No wonder the guy got surly.

There was something about this grocery guy that challenged Hawk, though he couldn't quite name it. Some look on Vernon's face, maybe. Some look that Hawk didn't like. Then again, maybe he did. He stood across from the store long enough to smoke two cigarettes. He had to walk another mile home, and the whole way he met no other person. He strolled like a prince beneath the shadowed trees, taking the deep, full breaths of one who believes he controls everything that his eyes can see.

viii.

When school ended not even a week earlier, Katie had held no particular hopes for this summer. She expected it to unfold as other summers had, a series of long days that she struggled to fill with books and home chores and playing games with the few girls from school whose parents did not have lake cabins and who, by and large, were humdrum company anyway. But then Sue Too showed up. And the mystery happened. And so she found herself that day at the center of admiration and adventure.

"Wow, Kate, you got a great setup here," Sue Too gushed about her bedroom and everything in her bedroom, her own desk with a globe and her own chair under the window, just a chair bought with Green Stamps, but Sue Too couldn't tell. She sat in that chair and surveyed all of Katie's belongings with appreciation, even the starched white dresser cloth with its lacy trim. "Kate lives like a queen here, heh, Elise?"

Elise had circled the small room again and again, touching the books in Katie's little bookcase and spinning the globe. "You get to have a closet," she said, enthralled, then went inside and closed the door. She stayed in there so long that Sue Too got worried.

"Hey, kid. What're you doing in the dark?"

"I'm here," Elise answered, though she still did not open the door.

"Come on out," Katie finally had to say. "You can sit at my desk, Elise."

"I like the way it smells in here," came the muffled reply.

"It's my pop's clothes. He keeps his jackets in there."

"They smell good," Elise repeated, taking one last full breath before Katie led her out.

All afternoon the three of them worked on code names they could never tell and a handshake they could never share. Sue Too popped off with one kooky notion after another, so that they almost never stopped laughing except when they practiced their handshake, a somber activity that required depth and concentration. Katie's mother brought in cookies she'd just made, warm from the oven and dripping with white frosting.

"What do you call these?" Elise asked, as she took a delicate bite. "I've never seen these before."

"They're called Cry Babies. Because the frosting looks like tears."

"Looks like delicious to me," Sue Too muttered and ate three more.

It was all so unlikely. A farm girl who couldn't remember to call her Katie and little Elise from the garage apartment. "Seems like you had a good day," her mother said after Katie had walked Elise home. "How old is that girl from the apartment building?"

"I never asked," Katie said, surprised that she hadn't. "I'd say thirteen. Or maybe twelve."

"Hmmmm."

Katie could tell that her mother thought Sue Too might be too old for her. Too much a teenager. "She's the youngest in her family, you know, Mom."

For a minute her mother said nothing. She stared off in some private thought, a burdened thought, surely, for at the end she took a deep breath and held it almost too long. "Well, you had fun." Then she bent her head to her crocheting.

"Did you ask anybody about that minister, the one who lived in the old green house over there?"

Mrs. Fiore shook her head. "I forgot to ask." She looked up to see Katie waiting as if for important news. "Tomorrow," she said.

"But who will you ask? Who would know?"

"Aunt Carmella will know."

Aunt Carmella was the relative who hadn't wanted to marry her husband. Alessandro Abelli's brother Giorgio had come from Italy and put up the money for her. And Carmella's parents went along with the plan. "Sold like slavery," she'd heard her mother say on the telephone to someone. Katie wasn't supposed to know this terrible story, but she liked knowing. It didn't make her dislike Uncle Giorgio though. He was old country, Pop had said. And though Carmella never seemed happy, she didn't seem unhappy to Katie either. She had three children, a set of the *Encyclopedia Britannica*, and a piano. "How come she'll know?"

Katie's mother kept to her crocheting. "I'll ask her. She'll know."

Katie continued to watch her mother, the precise moves of the crochet needles, the pull of yarn, shades of yellow and gold, hands relaxed and in control. Her mother had moved beyond the topic of the minister in the dilapidated house. She might even have moved beyond Katie herself, forgotten that her one and only child sat wrapped around a velveteen throw pillow waiting for more conversation, for more information about Aunt Carmella's uncanny knowledge of the neighborhood or even for information about herself, her day, her thoughts deep in the tunnel of her concentration, anything really. Katie waited for anything.

Her brain full of mystery and the memory of a happy day, Katie did not read or flip through magazines or ask to watch television later. She sat hugging the pillow and watching her mother's impassive face and rhythmic hands. She sat waiting for a sign that her mother might be happy too.

ix.

Every Saturday night Katie's grandparents played canasta with their relatives from Montelago, Italy, a village small enough that they all could remember everyone else's front doors, the ironwork or wooden carving, the tiled entries and stone walls.

When Alessandro Abelli had traveled to America so many years before, he'd left a trail for the others to follow, one by one, on steamers, then trains, across the Atlantic and halfway across the new country, then north to where the mines boomed. Now here they were, established citizens, property owners whose children went to school, whose wives no longer had to work as domestics, and whose basements held barrels of wine they made every September of grapes shipped by truck from California.

Nobody from home was excluded from their interest. They all knew Freddie drank too much, but that was Freddie. His wife, Lizzie, shrugged, not in the old-country way with one shoulder up and the other down, but in this American way, both shoulders to the ears. All of them relied on one another, the Abellis and Freddie and Lizzie, Alessandro's brother Giorgio, even his brother's wife, Carmella, with her modern ideas. They helped turn each others' gardens and pour their concrete driveways, fix wiring or plumbing, paint doors and windows, haul bricks or fencing or whatever was needed. This was something they brought with them across the Atlantic, this sense of belonging to one another, by blood and history, by habit and fact. They almost never discussed Montelago. Even now in their fifties, sixties, and seventies, they looked at what lay before them, not what they had left behind.

"Joe Monte's building onto his house," Freddie said, in Italian of course.

"He's got money?" Freddie's Uncle Angelo asked.

"It's always money," Katie's grandmother clucked and stood up from the table to bring over a plate of castagnole she'd make that afternoon for her relatives, none of whom quite had her heart or skill for cooking. "*Sempre soldi*," she repeated.

"You know Nicky Marodi's back?" Lizzie asked Mrs. Abelli, who nodded and shrugged the old-country way, one shoulder only, her head bent to meet it.

"What can you do?" Mrs. Abelli said. "Poor man. He used to be so smart."

"*Genio*," Alessandro said. "See?" He picked up a castagnole and ate it without finishing his thought, though the others waited to hear what he might say. Alessandro Abelli was the undisputed head of the family, the man who'd arrived in America first and amassed money the others couldn't fathom. He owned four houses, all the corner lots, and, though he never had much to say, everyone who knew him was always ready to listen. Wiping the honey from the castagnole off his fingers, he looked around the kitchen table and said, "You hava good luck. You hava bad."

His wife shuffled the cards, and they went back to their game. The kitchen where they sat was spotless, the curtains at the window handmade and pressed. Outside in the garden, rows of vegetables lined up evenly, the dirt between the rows free of weeds, the climbing plants already staked once to keep them upright. The iron posts in the fence had been cemented into the ground in careful circles. This was their respectability, this godly, hard-earned order. Mrs. Abelli never crossed the hallway from her bedroom to the rest of the house without having twisted her hair into a bun, secured it with tortoise-shell hairpins, and dressed completely right down to the handkerchief folded over the belt of her dress.

"You discard now, Freddie," Mrs. Abelli said, because her nephew so easily lost focus on the game. Lizzie laughed and did her American shrug again. Freddie rubbed the top of his hairless head as if that would help him figure out what to do. A June bug banged against the window screen, and Alessandro poured more of his own wine.

"Mama, you talk to Mrs. Marodi?" he asked his wife.

She played her turn before she answered that she did. She liked Elisabetta Marodi. Alessandro gestured to the bottle of his homemade wine on the table and, as an afterthought, at the plate of castagnole. Mrs. Abelli always kept her wide brown eyes open to the world around her, which she registered in a mind as fine and tightly strung as a Stradivarius violin. In another era, Mrs. Abelli could have run the finances for an entire country. Or kept the order of a small state. One look from her said many words in any language. In this way, she answered her husband that she would bring wine and pastries to their neighbor.

"Why does Joe Monte need a bigger house?" Freddie asked, but none of his relations sitting around the table bothered to answer him.

x.

Tildy didn't go to bed when Claus did. Once he left the room, she began her nightly puttering, her half-confused moving of things from one place to another, switching decorative pillows around and her cat figurines, which she collected in place of the real cats that Claus never wanted in the house. He didn't notice these minor adjustments, especially now that his eyesight had dimmed, and so she felt the freedom to do as she pleased, shuffle things about, make her very old possessions look different.

Tonight she decided to rearrange some of the furniture, shift the angles of the chairs to the sofa so that the persons sitting in those chairs could not help but see one another, so that if she looked up even for a split second, she would know the exact expression on Claus's face in the chair across from her. She tested this theory, hopping like a robin from one chair to the other then making adjustments until she got it right. She'd turned on only one light, and flitted in and out of the glow in a determined sort of contentment. The rest of the house slept, the summer air moving through, windows open, the scent of cut grass hovering.

Happy with her outcome, Tildy sat in the chair that was known to be hers and leaned back satisfied. She liked the house when Claus slept. He was close, but he could not disturb her. He was hers more then than ever. Though subdued and sometimes befuddled, Tildy's wisdom ran deep in the very corpuscles of her blood and the very constant beat of her heart. She'd raised beautiful daughters. Her garden flowers flourished every summer from the early tulips to the midseason sweet peas and all through the zinnias and late roses of fall. She knew how to bring things about, to allow them to blossom. In her own way she knew herself to be beautiful as well. At least she knew the memory of beauty, as she knew the memory of love. At night, alone, all of this came back to her and she gathered it up like a bouquet of her own life, striking in color even if the many stems might twist and bend. Not all flowers could withstand the rain or wind or even the glaring light of day.

In this reverie, she thought she heard an unfamiliar sound and sat still to listen for more. When she was sure she was not imagining it, she followed the sound out of the living room and down the short hallway to the bedroom where Claus slept. Except that he was not asleep, but up and bent over. "I'm sick," he said, "I'm going to be sick."

"I'll get you a towel," Tildy answered, already on the run to the bathroom. "I'm coming, Claus," she hollered in the darkness, forgetting in her panic to turn on a light. "I'm coming."

By the time she'd returned he had slid to the floor and was leaning against the bed, clutching his stomach, moaning low like an animal dying, Tildy thought. Was he an animal dying? For a second she couldn't react, but stood in Claus's bedroom doorway watching her husband of forty-some years gasp and moan. She flew to the phone and wailed for an ambulance to be sent fast. "He might be dying," she added, then felt embarrassed at the possibility that she was overstating. He was Claus, after all. He was stalwart and sure and not even old really.

Realizing that she still held the towel, she hurried back to the bedroom to give it to him, walked to him on her toes, and laid the towel across his lap. "An ambulance is coming, Claus. Don't worry, you'll be fine. Should I turn on the lamp? Will that help?" When he didn't answer, she repeated, "You'll be fine, Claus." She wanted him to look at her, to acknowledge that she was at his side and working to save him, but he focused only on his pain, a pain that seemed to grow more and more intense, as though he had turned inside out right there on the floor in front of her.

She didn't turn on a light. She forgot. But if she had, she would have seen that his skin had turned almost gray and so pale that blue veins had become visible on the sides of his head. If she'd turned on a light, she would have been certain that Claus was dying before her eyes. She didn't see this, though, and when the ambulance attendants came to take him away, they asked her to wait outside the room, then scuttled by her too quickly for her to notice how bad he looked. They'd asked her to sign papers, but they didn't invite her to ride along with them to the hospital, or if they did, she must have said no, because the ambulance sped off down the dark avenue, its lights flashing, while Tildy watched from her front yard until the bright blink of red was out of her sight.

Even then she didn't go back inside. She stayed in that one position on the grass she'd mowed herself just the day before. Gradually she noticed the arched shadows of the boulevard trees and the immense stillness surrounding her. She buttoned the top button of her housedress and went in to telephone her oldest daughter.

She didn't hurry. She needed a little time to find some feeling. In the living room, she adjusted the chairs' angles one more time before dialing Grace's number. It was after midnight now. Something bad had happened and all Tildy could muster was a concern that Claus had no change of clothing. He probably wasn't even wearing his watch. It was all too large to feel. That was the problem. It was just too large to feel.

As the ambulance attendants pushed Claus's gurney into the glare of the hospital emergency room, his blurry eyes settled on the lit sign above the door. EXIT, it said. How odd he thought briefly. He was coming in an exit.

FIVE

Sunday, June 12, 1960

i.

The Immaculate Conception Church, or the Italian Church as it was commonly called, offered a first Mass at six thirty every morning. Father Giuseppe Stefanelli, a small brusque man with a keen eye, knew his regulars by sight, even if he made little effort to learn their names. This June Sunday, a profusion of pink roses decorated the altar, left from a wedding the day before, an extravagance Father Giuseppe merely tolerated. He preferred simple weddings with the couple's parents, the witnesses, and no pomp whatsoever. As if all these roses would send the newly married off with more luck than anyone else.

He looked out to see Mrs. Marodi and her cockeyed son sitting in the last pew. Just in case he needed to escape, Father supposed. He had not been at the parish when Mrs. Marodi's son was committed, and so he had no recollection of the handsome altar boy, the star confirmation student, or the industrious church helper that Nicky used to be before his troubles began. Father Giuseppe kept an eye out through the short Mass with an added prayer to the Good Lord that there be no outbursts or lack of control.

Mrs. Marodi understood this, as did Nicky in his own way. His life outside of Moose Lake State Hospital balanced on a thread. Nobody knew when he would fall into inappropriate behavior, though Nicky himself had the idea that he was fine. This was his town, his neighborhood; he was back and could be someone again. He had his spasms, yes, he knew this. But he hadn't quite assessed his physical presence, the way others saw him, with his lurching and lopsided face, the panting and wild eyes. Nicky didn't think about that.

He looked outward, gripping to reality. Roses on the altar, vases and vases of pink roses. The short priest up there with his wire glasses and green robe, his loud voice calling *Kyrie eleison, Christe eleison.* Next to him Nicky could hear his mother whispering, *dona nobis pacem.* Grant us peace. Grant us peace. She'd folded her bony strong hands one into the other as she prayed. He really loved his mother's hands, the way they worked with such agility, cutting the pasta, twisting the pastry dough, arranging things for him, buttoning and mending and sewing things for him, the way her hands snapped peas and cleaned lettuce, the quick skill and ease of her movements. Now her hands folded one into the other like a sculpture, like a beautiful, mottled sculpture. He focused on that. *Pater et Filius et Spiritus Sanctus.* He focused on that.

After Mass, one of the busy ladies of the parish cornered Father Giuseppe to talk about the pancake breakfast coming up in a few weeks, rattling in an Italian dialect so different from his own that he had no idea what she was saying. "Speaka Inglese," he said to her, disinterested anyway. Beyond his captor he saw Mrs. Marodi and her son slowly leaving, keeping to the side aisle, heads down and together.

Father Giuseppe was not one who thought a disease of the mind reflected the devil's work, but he mistrusted crazy people anyway. Education did not necessarily diminish fear. Spiritual wisdom did not necessarily embrace oddity. So Father reflected. He may be able to save souls, however, and even crazy people had souls.

"Speaka Inglese," he barked again at the lady in front of him, whose name he did not recall. Was Nicky Marodi any more deranged than half these parish ladies were? He had to wonder.

ii.

The first birds woke her up, out there chirruping madly. Gertrude groped for her glasses to look at her clock. Not even six. Barely past night. Even so, she yanked up her shades to let all the sun shine in and pulled on her clothes, tidied her hair, and went downstairs to see what she might put together for breakfast. Not cereal. Mrs. didn't allow cereal, all boxed and unnatural, flakes and shapes and sugar. Toast, she decided. Gertrude made herself toast with butter and jelly, poured some milk, and sat to think.

No boys would be around this early. Vernon's Grocery wasn't even open this early. Who would know if she walked her whole block again? Who would even care? She toasted a second slice of bread, but was almost too excited to finish eating it. She tied on her shoes, unlocked the back door, and stepped out to a fresh day, a Gertie day, all her own.

She set course in her habitual direction, passing the wild and
raucous lawns, the glistening dewy dew, holding to it all as
a lost love returned to her, a treasure laid out for her. Not
even the baker's sticky little girl was up and out, and so none
of the morning's air had been disturbed until Gertrude came
through, moving more slowly to keep the sunny serenity. I'm
back, she said, the words formed distinctly, but only in her
mind, because she knew the ants could hear her think, and
the grass and dandelions, every boulevard tree, not to mention
the birds chattering, they could all hear her and urged her on.

She rounded the third corner by the white apartment building when she saw her man, crooked and lurching, coming her
way across the street with an older woman at his side, heading
home, Gertrude calculated, to the house on the next block
with the bushes and red roof. She could hardly keep herself in
one piece, in one connected body with arms and legs attached.
"How you," she yelled out, though they were still too far away
to hear her. She wasn't going to risk her chance. "How you,"
she called even louder than before and watched as the older
woman stopped walking to say something to the man and then
they both stopped, turned, and stared at her.

Gertrude kept going in their direction, too beside herself to
know what she should do. She didn't want to cross over to
where they stood and she didn't want to stop and stare back
or, worse, roar right by them before the man spoke to her, and
so she slowed and slowed and took shorter steps, little Godfrey steps that were not at all her usual large, eager Gertrude
steps, and she hollered across one more time, "How you," and
waved with one whole long arm and all her fingers flapping,
and when she did that, the man waved back and bolted her

way, leaving the old woman standing watch on the other side of the street.

"I'm Nicky Marodi," the man said, more frightening up close, because that tongue hung out and his eyes kept moving, like candles flickering, steady but not steady at all. His voice came out low and dark, not morning or June, but late night in winter when the winds groaned. And if he smiled, she wasn't sure due to all that motion, eyes, and tongue and all, but he might have smiled. "Hi," he added, "hi to you, lady."

She answered, "I'm Gertrude, I live there." She pointed up the street to Mrs. Wilke's white house. "Gertrude," she said again before registering that he'd just told her his name was Nicky Something, Nicky Something and she'd already forgotten. "How you, Nicky?"

"I'm fine," he said, like a gentleman, and turned abruptly to go back to the older woman waiting. Then the woman said, "Hello," loud enough but quiet too, peaceful like the morning, whoever she was, with her nice little blue hat and shawl.

Stunned, Gertrude forgot to move again, forgot to propel herself back into orbit. "Bye then," she shouted, a bit late, but they heard her anyway and both waved one last time, like passengers on a ship pulling out of harbor, lumbering forward slow but sure. If she'd heard the ship's farewell bleating, she would have been no more dumbfounded than she was watching Nicky Something and the old woman in her hat as they walked toward home.

"Gertie," Mrs. Wilke said, making morning coffee, "you're up with the birds."

"The Cuckoo Birds, you mean," Gertrude answered and slapped her skinny thigh and laughed to happy high heaven.

"Well, what's got into you lately, I cannot say." Mrs. Wilke filled the coffee pot with water, set it on a burner, and turned the heat on high.

"I cannot say either," Gertrude answered, and sat down to listen for the coffee's frenzied boil.

iii.

Now Elise had to tell her mother that as part of her membership in a secret club, she would be expected to help her friends sort clues in that terrible green house. She couldn't not tell her mother, and she couldn't not go into the green house. Tucked under her sheet this Sunday morning in June, she saw no way to accomplish both of her objectives. She heard an early church bell ringing, her mother busying about in the kitchen, one of those scary neighborhood dogs barking somewhere. She'd have to join the day soon, something she'd been so excited about the night before when she was giddy with the club's secrets. But now, now she was back to being a six-year-old girl in a large world. Now she had to face the problem of the terrible green house.

"Momma." She appeared in the kitchen, her seersucker nightie trailing. "I have to do something."

Betty had just folded back the Sunday paper's crossword puzzle and was considering number one across: a planet with rings. Was it Jupiter or Saturn? "What, Elise?"

"I have to help Katie Fiore today, Momma."

If Betty hadn't been so preoccupied, she would have noticed her daughter digging her thumbnail into the skin of her arm. "Well, I'm sure that's fine, Elise," she said. "Have you studied planets in school yet?"

Elise shook her head.

"Never mind. You get dressed and I'll make pancakes."

When they sat down to eat, Elise was certain her mother would want to pry further into why Katie needed Elise's help or what kind of help she needed, but that was not what happened at all. Betty had a topic of her own, and that topic was Claus Jacobson.

"You know, Elise, Claus is a good friend to me and the reason I stayed in this town away from everyone in my family. Because he's my benefactor. That's the term. You might see it in a crossword puzzle someday. It means he looks after us, which is nice, but he isn't getting any younger, Elise, and neither am I. Momma's in her thirties now, you know, so I have to keep an eye on the future. And so I'm thinking Claus needs to visit more often. Maybe have dinner with us once in a while. He'd like my swiss steak, that's what I'm thinking. He could get to know you, too, Elise, now that all his daughters are grown."

She went on. "I read an article in *McCall's* that said women need to ask, ask, ask. Men aren't mind readers, after all. That's what the article said. Women need to ask for what they want. Like a new car or help folding laundry, though god forbid any man would be caught dead doing that. I would never ask that. And I don't drive, so that's out too."

She stopped to chew a fork full of pancakes, leaving the kitchen hushed in her wake. "These are so good, aren't they, Elise? I added extra vanilla, can you taste? That's what I mean. I have a knack for this homemaking business. No one can say that I don't." She went on to describe the many things she would be able to do for Claus, just as she did them for Elise, and Claus's need for such care. She paused only for hardy bites of her breakfast.

Through all of this Elise nodded, wide-eyed, as if she were actually listening to her mother or even understood Betty's point. Did she want Claus to live with them, Elise wondered. Her mother never said where she thought he would fit. He was a tall man. He had very large feet. Mostly Elise enjoyed her pancakes soaked in Aunt Jemima syrup and felt relieved that her mother appeared unconcerned about Elise helping Katie Fiore. After they ate, they did the dishes together, and when that was done, Elise said, "I'm going to sit outside, Momma."

But by then her mother had hung up her apron and was back trying to figure out the planets in the crossword puzzle. Because she was a child, Elise did not notice her mother's nervous anticipation, the way Betty fidgeted waiting for Claus, her proximity to the telephone, or the intentional order to every curl of her hair.

As soon as Elise went outside, Betty popped out of her chair to go study herself in the mirror, to rehearse particular facial reactions she might have when Claus arrived later that day. She redid her lipstick, all smeared from eating. She added one more subtle sweep of rouge, then met her own eyes and watched herself. Her face looked better since she'd cut her hair. The bounce of the curls neutralized her square chin, she decided, and put the focus on her eyes. With a well-sharpened eye pencil, she had shaped her eyebrows the way she'd noticed that Roger Vernon's wife did hers—thin and arched. It certainly worked for her. Roger Vernon's redheaded, Italian wife could pass for a movie star. But there she was married to a shopkeeper.

Outside Elise stood at the corner of their garage apartment and leaned around into the alley. She'd never looked closely before, assuming it was off-limits, a place of dusty pebbles, weed-like flowers, and tin garbage cans. She'd watched countless cars wheel out of that alley and onto Twenty-Fourth Street. She'd even seen a boy smoking a cigarette right behind her garage apartment. But she'd never ventured into the alley except that time with Katie and Sue Too before they were a club. She hadn't liked it. The sun beat down too hot on her head. Sun in the alley could eat you up, like a fiery dragon, like an orange tiger.

iv.

The secret club did not convene until after lunch. Because it was Sunday, the Fiore family called it dinner and gathered for a full meal before anyone was released. So it was after one when Katie and Sue Too headed over to Elise, who by this time had been monkeying around on her curb for more than an hour, scribbling in the dirt with a stick and imagining all the things that might happen next.

"I've had enough of unpacking, I'll tell you that," Sue Too remarked as they crossed the street. "There's nowhere to put things anyway, and then my mother thinks, oh, we should go get that cupboard out at Shirley's and then we all argue about where that would go."

Elise got up from the curb so excited that she forgot to brush the dirt off her butt. "Do we do the handshake now?" she asked, running through the specific moves in her brain. But Katie shook her head as the older two kept walking right into the alley, leaving Elise to hurry along after them, frightened as she was and not wanting them to know.

The blast of heat and dust in the old house hit the girls as it had before, but they pushed through it without saying any-thing and proceeded directly into the cluttered living room and situated themselves on the stacks of newspapers. "Now we'll do the handshake," Katie said. Whatever varied experiences they'd had—Katie in her small Italian family, Sue Too with all her chaotic relatives, and Elise alone in the garage apartment with her mother—none of them had ever known the rare gravity of a secret triumvirate, this meeting of dedicated minds closed around a large and grown-up mystery. At the conclusion of their handshake, they remained in a tight circle next to the brown blotch on the floor that may or may not be blood. "Let us begin," Katie said. She opened her notebook and again read them all her findings, just to clarify their direction.

Elise was assigned to examine the kitchen cupboards. "What am I looking for again?" she asked as Katie brought a chair over for her to stand on.

"Funny things. Things that don't belong or don't make sense. Maybe a book stuck in with the dishes or a map or souvenir or something."

Sue Too clattered upstairs to study the bedroom dresser and closet again, and Katie stayed in the living room paging through the books in the boxes and on the floor. For ten minutes the old house was silent, the three girls lost in the thrill of the hunt. But then Sue Too called down, "I'm dying of heat up here," and started coughing uncontrollably. "The dust, help, the dust is killing me." She pounded downstairs and sat on the bottom step. "I have no idea what you think I'm going to find in some dead lady's slip drawer."

"Slips," Elise said out in the kitchen and giggled at her own joke, a silly, warbling giggle that they had never heard from her before. A few seconds later she stood in the doorway, hands flat and full of trinkets. "Clues," she said. In the center of the living room Elise set down a book of matches from the Hotel Duluth, a plastic fish that said Lake Kabetogama, a red plastic squirt gun, and a photo of a young couple grinning out of time in front of a small cabin.

Katie asked, "Is this them?"

"They look too happy to kill each other, if you ask me," Sue Too said, studying the photo over Katie's shoulder. "Look at them. They're probably on a honeymoon."

"You think they squirted each other?" Elise asked, but her friends were deep into speculation about the tiny images of the thin, blond man and happy, blonde girl. Pine trees towered over them on both sides of the log cabin, a cozy spot with smoke curling out of the chimney, and though the photo was not in color, the secret club saw color, all the colors of the woods in fall and the bold sky above.

"Is it a clue?" Elise asked of the photo; then both she and Sue Too turned to see what Katie would say.

Katie kept her eyes on the photo. "They look so normal."

Elise tapped her older friend on the shoulder. "Was it a good clue, Katie?"

Katie nodded, full of doubt that the happy couple could possibly have been caught up in a violent crime. "Maybe he didn't kill her. Maybe they had some emergency," she offered, "and had to leave in a hurry."

"And never came back?" Sue Too couldn't believe it. "You can't just leave your stuff in a house like this. When you stop living somewhere, you have to pack up and go. I've done that enough times to know, you can't just leave your clothes and dishes any which way."

"Why is the door left open?" Katie's dark expression and tense voice gave Elise a shiver.

"What do you mean?" Sue Too asked. "He killed her and who locks a door after murdering his wife?"

"But look at that calendar in the kitchen. It's from a year ago. So why wouldn't someone have locked the door for them?" Katie's eyes moved from Elise to Sue Too, almost in accusation. "Don't you think that's strange?" To Katie, it was enormously and obviously strange.

This new query made Elise nervous. "Can we go now?" She picked up the squirt gun and plastic fish and began to back up toward the kitchen.

Sue Too gave an exaggerated shrug. "All right, Elise. I'm dying in here anyway."

Without a word, Katie slipped the photo into the pocket of her yellow shorts and followed her friends out of the kitchen and across the slanting, cluttered porch. "Don't go until the coast is clear," she hissed at them, catching Sue Too from slamming outside in her usual noisy way. "Elise, poke your head out and see if anyone's around."

Elise did this only because she would do anything for Katie Fiore. "Nobody," Elise whispered, her voice wet and fuzzy.

At that they crept through the yard, opened the gate, their heads bent low and out of sight. Back in the alley, they ran pell-mell to the front of Elise's garage apartment. "Let's go sit on Sue Too's steps," Katie said, not wanting to deal with Mrs. Larsen just then or anyone in her own family either.

"That picture don't mean he didn't kill her, you know," Sue Too said as she sunk onto the top step of her building.

"I don't know what to think," Katie answered.

They fell silent considering what to do next. Only then did Katie notice that Elise held the bright red squirt gun and plastic fish in her hands. "Why do you have those, Elise?"

Elise looked down at her own clenched fists. "Because they're clues."

v.

When Claus arrived, Betty did not want to look like she was just sitting around waiting for him. She also did not want to be in the middle of some big project like baking cookies or cleaning out the refrigerator. She didn't like him to see her mending, because it was so menial, and she certainly wasn't about to clean and get herself all dusty. Most of the time she had no idea when he'd show up and so had to proceed looking as nice as she could, while still getting her work done. This time she planned to ask him about spending more time with her, like the *McCall's* article had encouraged, and that made her feel extra alert and on edge.

She'd almost forgotten that he'd said only that he would try, that he'd see what he could do. She'd busied that whole response out of her mind as she made Elise an elaborate dinner the night before and played with her and planned what she might wear today. By the time she woke up that morning, she'd blocked out any notion that Claus wouldn't come to see her. She kept vigil while pretending she was not. She changed her shirt from the crisp white sleeveless cotton that seemed right when she first woke up to a black knit with short sleeves that she didn't usually wear in summer, especially not on a Sunday. But the mirror affirmed her choice. The black deepened her coloring, so that her hair and eyes seemed to shine more.

Betty finally decided to make her own greeting cards. She found two bundles of old cards in her stocking drawer, which she set on the table with scissors, glue, and the colored construction paper she kept around for Elise. She cut out images that she liked from the old cards and placed them artistically on the colored papers to create new cards. This turned out to be so much more fun than she'd expected, that she was able to lose several hours. While she worked, she played a Peggy Lee album and drank three cups of coffee, forgetting to check on Elise or to panic that Claus had not yet arrived.

Midafternoon she rinsed her coffee cup, touched up her lip-stick, and stretched out on her bed for a short rest, still believing that Claus would come. She'd never asked him before, and she had so much on her mind to tell him, about poor Gertrude and the rough boys and Elise's new friends and to coax him, too, to come more frequently and stay longer and maybe do a puzzle or listen to Peggy Lee or even Pat Boone, whatever he liked.

She needed him now. Elise was already in school and busy and the rest of life stared back at Betty with hard eyes these days. She needed Claus, and so she was certain that he would do the things she asked, as though her need could conjure action and there he'd be at her door or, better yet, taking the steep steps up to the apartment with a suitcase in his hand and his sedan parked in the garage below.

These pleasant thoughts lulled her into a casual sleep, a catnap as her mother used to say. She adjusted the pillow so that she wouldn't crush her hair and kept her sandals on to be ready whenever she heard Claus coming through the door.

Three blocks away, Claus lay barely conscious, breathing in an oxygen tent and thinking the haphazard, hallucinatory thoughts of the very ill. His childhood self skipping rocks on a lake, his first daughter asking him to play marbles, men from his office laughing in shirtsleeves and Claus laughing with them, the hospital Exit sign, a pale blue wall and pale blue eyes and an unnaturally pale summer sky.

"Is it going to rain?" he gasped to no one in particular. "I washed the car," he gasped again. "I just washed the car."

Tildy sat in the corner of his room trying not to jump to conclusions. Things happen, she told herself, because that's what her daughters all had said that morning in-between their fits of tears and challenges to God. The doctor told them that Claus had had a heart attack. He shouldn't do anything that taxed or upset him. He should take life easy and walk the neighborhood and not drink very much alcohol.

"He already does those things," their oldest daughter, Grace, had refuted. "How can that help?"

The young but weary Dr. Milton had adjusted his wire-rimmed eyeglasses to focus on Tildy. "I'm sure you take good care of him," the doctor had said. "That's all you can do." He'd squeezed her hand, which made her feel better. His touch was warm, almost hot, and sure and kind. She wished he could hold her hand all day and the next. But the doctor left and then her weeping daughters left, and Claus breathed on in his tent.

"Your car will be fine," Tildy answered, though she wasn't quite loud enough for him to hear her. "Don't worry."

vi.

The secret club sat on the apartment building steps staring out at the neighborhood. Old Mr. McCumber passed by dressed up as he always was, a summer fedora squarely on his head, his tie knotted over his starched white shirt with sleeves secured by cuff links. "That's quite the game you girls have going for you." He chortled knowingly. "Just let those boys try and stop you, eh?"

"Hi," Katie said. "Have a nice walk, Mr. McCumber." He lightly touched the brim of his hat and moved along slowly toward Third Avenue. "He lives in the apartment building next to you," Katie explained to Sue Too.

"What was he talking about?"

"Just anything. He gets mixed up sometimes." At that they fell silent again.

Elise could feel her friends' restlessness, their dissatisfaction over the way this mystery was unfolding, but personally Elise could hardly have been happier. She was with the older girls, they were out of the scary house, she was sitting across the street high up on Sue Too's apartment steps instead of on her crummy old curb, and she had a red squirt gun and a plastic fish that neither Katie or Sue Too seemed to care about. Maybe she'd end up keeping them and finding a way to play with them. Maybe she'd hide them in her room as mementos of the secret club.

"What now?" Sue Too asked for the fifth or sixth time since they'd parked themselves on the steps of her building. "If nobody got murdered, what is there to solve? What kind of mystery is it?"

Hoping with all her heart that their club would not fall apart already, Elise said quickly, "What if it's a people mystery? Because we don't know why they left."

Katie bobbed up and down. "Exactly, exactly. You're very smart, Elise."

This bothered Sue Too. She knew she wasn't ever the smartest girl around. But Elise was barely out of kindergarten. How could she say something so smart? What difference did it make if two people left their lousy old house for a year? If she couldn't solve a mystery and get her picture in the paper, what was the point? These girls didn't think big enough. They'd never looked out over whole acres of pasture. They didn't care about the wide expanse. "I got to go to the bathroom," she said and left them so quickly, she stopped Katie in midsentence.

"Oh well," Katie concluded, "maybe it's not a real mystery."

"But you have clues," Elise reminded her, though her voice wavered.

"I would like to know why they left in such a big hurry. Not even doing the dishes," Katie said, staring off in thought. "I would just like to know."

Inside her family's apartment, Sue Too made herself a peanut butter sandwich and then another. She might not fit in here. She might be expecting too much, that two younger girls would be as much fun as she needed them to be. It seemed like they might be. But this notion of people being a mystery did not make sense to her. In fact, it worried her. If she was going to start thinking about people being mysteries and why they left coffee grounds in the sink or why they read one kind of book instead of another or any kind of book at all for that matter or forgot to lock the door for a year, then where would it end? Every person on the planet was a whole mess of why this and why that. Why did her mother not mind all this clutter?

Why did Diane marry that stick-in-the-mud Bill? Why was she herself hungry all the time? She didn't want to think about it. Thinking like that would make you more crazy than half the people on their block.

She slapped together two more peanut butter sandwiches to bring out to Kate and Elise, but her heart was not in it.

vii.

Gertrude had never considered that anything was wrong with her. She didn't know what kinds of lives others lived and so never thought to compare her own. For a long time, years ago, she had lived with a woman who said she was Gertrude's mother's sister, an awfully long, loose connection in Gertrude's mind, since she couldn't remember having a mother or any other relative. This loose connection wanted Gertrude to call her Miss Leona, always Miss Leona across the dinner table with its lace cloth and heavy legs carved like animal heads that might snatch you in their four mouths and many teeth. Gertrude hated that table. She didn't care to eat on that table, so she picked and nibbled and was sent to her room upstairs where Miss Leona's flowered draperies hung to the floor, blocking the day and the night and all the frenzied storms and everything Getrude might have loved if she could. This loose connection kept Gertrude at home with only that room where she paced and paced and listened for sounds outside and creaks in her floorboards.

When Miss Leona died, someone found Mrs. Wilke for her, a widow with an extra bedroom and lawn chairs, a widow who made egg salad and lemonade and let Gertrude walk outside to her heart's content. Nobody had ever pointed to a difference in her, though she had an idea she might not be the same as others. She'd never been a girl on a porch step or a girl on a bike or a girl playing big games in a churchyard like the one on her block. She thought she'd remember if she'd ever been a girl like that.

Still she didn't think anything was wrong exactly. Since she met Mrs. Wilke so many years ago, almost everything was right really, except for the television set and those boys by Vernon's maybe. Almost everything, until now, until this very day when Nicky Something told her his name and his mother in her hat waved and they walked away to their house with bushes on a block that Gertrude could see plain as day from the front of Mrs. Wilke's. That was how close. That's where he was. She could round the block and when she got to that corner by the apartment building with the flat roof—like a chicken coop, Mrs. said—on that corner she could glance over, even with one eye, her right eye just traveling over, and there would be the untrimmed hedge with the red roof poking up and somewhere in all of that Nicky and his tongue and wild eyes and his voice like a gurgle in the basement pipes.

Nicky gave Gertrude the notion that there may be something wrong with her, something old and awful and truly wrong, because for no reason at all she longed to see him again and again. His sideways walk and noisy breath scared her as much as ever, and still she longed. As soon as Mrs. Wilke settled in for her forty winks with the living room blinds letting in only so much light, Gertrude started walking her block again and again, her mind always on that third corner, that clear view, that moment when she was nearer to Nicky Something than at any other time.

viii.

The girls still sat on the steps and Gertrude continued circling the block when Mrs. Abelli took off her apron, put on her hat, and headed out to bring castagnole and a bottle of wine to Elisabetta Marodi. Slowly, as was her way, she carried her parcels and watched her step, waved to her granddaughter, and kept going. At the Marodi front door, she knocked and waited, not wanting to think about the overgrown yard and rotting wood steps. You see, she wanted to tell the world, this is what it comes to with no relations other than one poor son who's lost his mind. No paint. No mending. No trimming or new steps or weeds pulled.

"*Come stai*," she called through the screen when Nicky's mother appeared, a beautiful woman even in her misfortunes, beautiful skin and thick hair not all gray. "Alessandro sends his wine, because it is the best," Mrs. Abelli joked. "*E il migliore.*"

"Every man's wine is the best," Mrs. Marodi agreed. She covered her mouth in delight at the castagnole and shook her head. "*Grazie,* Mrs.—sit, sit."

Mrs. Abelli chose a rose-colored velvet chair and sunk into it with pleasure. The inside of the Marodi house was cared for the way a house should be, clean and polished, with curtains that matched the pretty rose velvet furniture and light, lace-trimmed cloths on the tables. Mrs. Marodi had picked a bouquet of lilacs and the scent hovered, light and reminiscent. "*Bella casa,*" Mrs. Abelli said, but Mrs. Marodi had ducked into the kitchen to bring them each a glass of limoncello.

"I make it," she said, handing Mrs. Abelli a glass. "*E il migliore,* the best," she added and they both laughed.

Mrs. Abelli relaxed further in her chair. "*Bene, bene.*" The two women sipped and regarded one another with ease. "How's your boy?" Mrs. Abelli asked after a time, but that too had ease, a question mothers asked no matter what the circumstances.

"My Nicky's a good person, poor Nicky. He sits in the yard, always a tie." She took a full breath of air. "We see. We see who leaves him be and how we go along."

"He stays home?"

Elisabetta shrugged. "He walks, goes out. He's a man, you know. So he goes." Both women concentrated on the sweet limoncello. "We see."

Mrs. Abelli also shrugged. "How's your garden?"

"You come look." Mrs. Marodi walked her guest through her spotless kitchen to the back door and the wild back lawn and the perfect garden in the middle of it. Like most Italian gardens in town, Mrs. Marodi's displayed even rows of hardy plants, beans and tomatoes secured with posts, cucumbers set to climb against wire, all in order. Nicky sat on the wooden chair with his head leaning on the house, his hat half covering his eyes.

The two mothers laughed to see him, which felt like some kind of blessing to Mrs. Marodi, who regarded her son for that minute as one more lazy young man stretching out in the afternoon sun.

"*Come un gatto,*" Mrs. Abelli teased. "Like a cat."

Under his hat Nicky heard the lilt of their voices and knew his mother was happy, so he remained still and let the ladies laugh at him. Their voices trailed off as they left the backyard, still talking about this and that, and before Mrs. Abelli finished saying good-bye, Nicky had fallen asleep again.

ix.

At six P.M. Betty Larsen gave up. Claus wasn't coming. He never came after dinner. She'd waited all day and now it was clear that he wasn't coming. She boiled hot dogs, heated a can of beans from Vernon's store, and sat down with Elise to eat, even though her stomach churned with absolute anger at the daylong snub she'd endured.

"What were you girls doing on those steps all afternoon?"

"Sitting."

"Well, that was obvious, Elise, but why? Why not play or something? How can young girls sit all afternoon like three old ladies with nothing better to do?" She shoveled a forkful of beans into her mouth without even realizing she'd done it.

"Katie likes to think, and Sue Too kept getting food to eat." As Elise said this, her eyes followed her mother's abrupt moves. "Be careful not to spill, Momma."

"Don't worry about me. What's that girl's name again?"

"Sue Too."

"Good grief." Then Betty ate without saying anything more for long enough to ease her daughter's concerns. But just because she wasn't talking did not mean that her mind wasn't dodging every which way looking for solutions to her predicament. Finally she pushed her plate away and crossed her arms in front of her chest.

"What?" Elise asked, seeing that something big was coming, like one of those clunky street sweepers rolling down Twenty-Fourth Street or the garbage truck growling in the alley every Wednesday. "What, Momma?"

Without answering, Betty sprung up, went to the phone, and dialed. Her foot tapped on the red and white linoleum, but she didn't speak. She slammed the phone receiver back in place and dialed again. When nothing happened at the other end this second time, she quit trying.

"Elise, would you like to go visiting with me in the morning?"

"Visiting?"

"Would you like to see where Claus lives?"

Elise thought her mother asked the question with troubling fierceness, the same way she'd eaten her beans and dialed the number and slammed the phone. Elise had no desire to see where Claus lived. "Would we go in his house?"

Betty hadn't actually thought that far. "Well, if he invites us in, I suppose." She'd lost some of her punch. "I don't know, Elise. I just thought you might like to see where he lives and we could knock on the door and say hello and find out if he's alive or dead, for heaven's sake."

Elise poked at her remaining beans.

"You could show Momma some enthusiasm, you know. Anyway, we'll dress up a bit and walk over in the morning." At that her mind moved on to what they should wear to enhance the visit, how they should present themselves at Claus Jacobson's door. Subdued, she decided. They'd dress subdued. But not too subdued. She didn't want to look like they were collecting for some church charity or orphanage. Casual subdued. Summery and modest.

She washed the dishes and left Elise to entertain herself. She had no interest in doing puzzles with Elise tonight. As if all of life weren't some godforsaken puzzle anyway.

x.

The boy called Hawk hated Sundays. He had trouble gathering his buddies on Sundays and trouble getting beer on Sundays. The guys he knew, even big old Mack, had noon dinners on Sundays and families that listened to ball games together, which left Hawk sitting on a discarded sofa out in the garage, breathing in leftover gasoline fumes from his old man's banged-up Chevy. This Sunday he'd worked on walking a rubber band with his fingers, just a stupid show-off business that he knew would impress the guys sometime.

His mother had left early for her breakfast shift at the hotel and his old man would sleep until it was time to have his first drink. So here he was on a Sunday morning, alone in the garage. Out of cigarettes. Out of sorts. His mother said he was born with a chip on his shoulder. That he got up on the wrong side of the bed. That he dreamed in color. She loved that one—he dreamed in color. "What the hell does that mean?" he'd yelled back at her a hundred times or more. Then she'd yell back, "You know damn well," and wave her arms wide like that was supposed to explain something. Anyway, he didn't dream in color. He dreamed in black-and-white, in leather and smoke, in night and spotlight. White heat. Black flame.

You couldn't take a guy like him, christen him Daryl John Hay, and expect anything good to come of it. You couldn't scream at, swat, and shove a guy like him against every goddamned wall in the house and think he was going to dream some ordinary dream. It wasn't going to happen.

Here's what was going to happen. A guy like that was going to grow up to be Hawk, to swoop down and swallow his prey whole, to scan the landscape with sharp dark eyes, not missing an opportunity, not forgiving a single heartbeat. Even in this two-bit town, he could make a mark before flying off high and away to his real life. To the life he imagined in all of his black-and-white dreams.

SIX

MONDAY, JUNE 13, 1960

i.

On Monday, Gertrude woke up before the morning light. She sat dressed in her pedal pushers and blouse waiting for day like a hungry owl waits for night. She pictured the house down Fourth Avenue and the man who lived there, his brown hat and suit coat, his weird walk and eyes that bounced from place to place, the man who had crossed the street to say his name to her, as if she mattered.

The day before she had rounded her block so many times that she developed a blister on her left big toe. She'd quit waving at Katie and her friends or anyone else to concentrate on her speed as she got closer each time to that one corner where she could see Nicky's hedge out of the corner of her eye, without stopping or turning her head, just her right eye looking his way until she had to head north and start the whole long maneuver all over again.

"You got some kind of bee in your bonnet today, Gertie," Mrs. Wilke had said when they sat at the table for supper, then she talked Gertrude into watching *Ed Sullivan* with her. Still agitated, still wanting one more chance at glimpsing Nicky before the sun went down, Gertrude perched on the sofa next to Mrs. reluctantly, plotting how long she'd have to stay before she could bound back out the door. But then she got caught up in that talking Italian mouse and her muscles relaxed into the cushions and the day came to a close.

Even so, she'd gone to bed not ready to let go of that day, when something significant had happened to her. She slept in spurts and in between she stared at the ceiling with this horrid new feeling of want throbbing within her, worse than being a Cuckoo Bird, way worse, because this was something inside of herself, this reaching and hoping, this wanting. It was inside. It was her own and it was asking and she did not think she could walk far enough or fast enough to satisfy the question.

ii.

His nurses had removed the oxygen tent so that Claus Jacobson was able to breathe the antiseptic hospital air on his own, able to see the room around him, and have a shave and a morning glass of orange juice. For the moment, his daughters and Tildy had not yet arrived with all their large eyes upon him, and so he rested and listened to the hub of hospital activity on his ward. He supposed his heart attack meant that he would not live as long as he'd always imagined, whatever he'd imagined. That he'd live so long it would seem like forever. That the end was a mere speck in the distance, barely there, possibly not there at all. He supposed that was no longer the case, but he didn't know what exactly was the case.

Dr. Milton had lived across the street from the Jacobsons when he was a new resident in town. Claus once lent him his lawnmower. But shortly after, the doctor had moved to a newer part of town, where the lots were bigger and the wide picture windows had views and double garages were attached to the houses. "How you feeling today, Claus?" the doctor asked, striding into the room, crisp and loud, honing in on Claus with intense concern. "You look better than you did yesterday morning."

Claus nodded and waited.

"So your ticker took a hit Saturday night, Claus. These things, there's not much we can do once the heart's been damaged. Like any muscle, we can't repair them like we can bones."

"I should have broken my leg," Claus said with such seriousness, the doctor wasn't sure he'd meant it as a joke or not.

"You're in good shape overall, Claus. Not overweight. Retired. Healthy wife to look after you. Family around. They say you don't drink more than a scotch or two a week. So all that's in your favor." While the doctor looked down at his notes, Claus considered this phrase, *in your favor.*

"You mean I'll live longer or not really, but I'll feel better while I live? This favor. What does it mean this favor?"

Dr. Milton looked puzzled. "When a man your age has a heart attack of this magnitude, he most likely will not live to be one hundred. But given all those elements in your favor, as I mentioned, you will enjoy a normal life, maybe less active, but normal for many years." He stood up and clapped Claus on the shoulder. "You'll be fine. Meanwhile, take it easy here for a few more days so we can monitor you. I'll stop by again tomorrow."

Claus watched Dr. Milton go, thinking that he would like to change places with him and step out in confidence to meet the next patient, knowing that every visit put money in his bank account and that at the end of the day he could play a robust game of tennis or golf or whatever the doctor liked and go home to eat and drink whatever he wanted and still have energy left when he jumped into bed with his wife. Doc Milton didn't have to worry about living a less active life or how many years before he dropped or what to do in this so-called less active life until he did drop.

He felt tired again. Just breakfast and the doctor's visit had tired him out. He wondered how much he weighed. Lying there in the sunny, bare room he felt as heavy as one of those diesel trucks loading tons of ore out of the mines, tires grinding slowly up the makeshift roads, burdened to the brim.

iii.

Betty dressed in a dark skirt and the crisp white blouse she'd abandoned the day before. She made Elise wear a dress too, a yellow dotted swiss that she'd splurged on at Feldman's. Immediately after breakfast, the two paraded downstairs and out to the street, where they walked straight west four blocks, turned south, and went another block and a half to a white frame house bordered by an array of pink and red tulips that Betty tried not to see.

"Claus lives in a nice house, doesn't he, Momma?" Betty tried not to hear that either.

At the door she smoothed her hair and rang the bell. At barely ten in the morning, Claus's neighborhood was so still, Betty and Elise could hear themselves breathing. No girls sat on steps or played in yards. No Italians tended large gardens, nobody rounded the block, or talked over fences or made themselves visible in any way.

"Shhh," Betty hissed at Elise, a reflex only, because her daughter stood beside her as still as a statue. Betty tried the bell again and knocked, as a new panic rushed over her. "Hello?" she called into an open window. "Claus? Hello, Tildy?" When she didn't get an answer, she backed away from the house, dragging Elise with her.

"Who's Tildy?" Elise whispered, but her mother, stunned at another plan foiled, stood staring back at the house. "Momma?"

"What, Elise, what? Stay still while Momma thinks."

"You looking for the Jacobsons?" Betty turned to the woman coming her way from across the street. "I seen you knocking over here. He got sick the other night, you know. Took him away in the ambulance around ten, maybe eleven. After eleven maybe. Lights flashing."

Betty blinked. "Claus?"

"Yeah, Jacobson. Guess he lived through it though. So that's where you'll find them two now. Over at the hospital."

"Well, thank you," Betty said, gathering herself together. "Thank you for letting me know."

"Cute little girl there. What's your name, Sweetie?"

By now, Elise's eyes were saucers as big as the moon. She couldn't even talk.

"Her name is Elise," Betty answered and tugged Elise's arm to go. "Thank you," Betty said again and fluttered a wave and tried not to faint as she walked away from the neighbor, the Jacobson house, and her whole idea of demanding Claus's attentions.

"I'll tell 'em you come by," the neighbor called.

"You do that," Betty muttered. "You just do that very thing."

All the way home she considered going straight to the hospital to see Claus and barging right into that cozy family gathering around poor, sick Claus, but that notion subsided to a great fear, even terror. Claus took care of them. Without Claus she'd need a different life. She'd need to find a job. She dragged Elise along so quickly that before Betty knew it they were across from Vernon's store and just steps from their garage apartment.

"Let's stop at the store, Elise. Let's see what kind of ripe fruit Roger Vernon's selling off to the world today."

Elise didn't answer her mother, and when she got smack in front of Katie Fiore's house, she broke loose from Betty's grip and ran through the Fiore gate. "I got to see Katie for a minute," she called and followed the Fiore's side path to the backyard, where she sat on the steps as if she belonged there. She didn't think to peek through the kitchen screen or knock. She just wanted a minute to think, like Katie liked to do. The trip to Claus's house had given her some kind of stomachache. Not like throwing up really, but almost like that. She didn't know why. Lots of people weren't always home when you came to visit. But her mother had yanked her all about and held her hand too hard and hurried away from Claus's house as if it were on fire or something. As if it were abandoned and creepy like the mystery house down the alley.

The screen behind her slammed and there was Katie. "You're all dressed up, Elise."

"We went to visit Claus."

"Really? That's such a cute dress on you."

"I guess he went to the hospital, some neighbor said. No one was home, and we called in a window to him and a Tildy."

"Really," Katie had to say again. Her little friend looked so distressed. "Do you want one of those Cry Baby cookies?"

Elise finally met Katie's eyes. "You mean with the frosting tears?" Her round, sad eyes glimmered.

While Katie went in to get the cookies, Elise watched Mrs. Fiore pass by from the side door of the house with a basket of washed clothes. She set the basket on the grass and started hanging in snappy, precise order, just the way Elise's mother did. She'd already hung the white sheets, one next to another flapping merrily in the light breeze and was now adding the towels.

"Here you go," Katie said as she placed a small plate on the back steps between them. "They're not as good as when they're fresh, but I still like them."

"Me too," Elise replied and gave herself over to the moist molasses cookies with their frosting that cried like tears.

iv.

Roger Vernon was stacking the meat in his cooler, when Betty Larsen came in the door full force. "How you doing?" he said, barely looking her way.

Betty paced the small store. "Do you need any store clerks here?" she blurted.

"Just a minute." Roger finished his task, wiped his hands, and went to his safe spot behind the counter. "You want a job here?"

The question repelled Betty. "Of course not. Of course not," she repeated. "Just seems like there's a lot to do." She trailed off, her eyes moving from the shelves that weren't full to the cooler that wasn't full to the candy jars that also needed filling. "Seems like you could have more to sell in here."

"I'd say we need more people to buy what we sell in order to have more to sell."

"The old Italian made her own sausages."

"Good for her."

"Not that I shopped here then anyway," Betty rambled, not knowing where she was in this conversation let alone where she was going. "But empty spaces don't look good in a store. In general."

Roger pulled his cigarettes out of his pocket. What was it about this woman? He never knew what the hell she was up to. "Want one?" he asked.

"Does your wife smoke?"

Roger had to laugh. "You know, sometimes she does. Now you want one?"

Betty did want one. In her mind she could see herself nonchalantly lighting a cigarette and exhaling the smoke with her chin tilted toward the sky and her eyelids lowered like Lauren Bacall. But she said, "No, thank you," then reversed her answer immediately. "Well, maybe I can buy a package for myself. Whatever you have there." She opened her purse as Roger set a pack of Old Golds on the counter for her. Then she added two Hershey bars and another marble cake mix. These decisions empowered her to say, "If you ever do need help here, let me know. I'd have a knack for running a store." She pursed her lips as if challenging him to disagree.

"I'll bet you have a knack for all sorts of things," Roger said, and immediately hearing the unintended implication, he added, "Efficient and all," and looked away.

She took her small sack of items, but she stayed in front of him with more to say. "Does your wife like her job selling makeup?"

"I guess she does." He'd never really asked, but Sophia was the type of person who liked just about everything in her life, except being poor. She liked it when it rained and she liked it when the sun scorched the backyard grass and she liked it when they were buried in snow. That's how she was, Sophia. Naturally pleased.

"Maybe I should talk to her," Betty said more to herself than to Roger. "I think I'd have a knack for selling makeup."

This time Roger said nothing in reply.

After Betty left, he lit another cigarette and surveyed the store. It did look tired, he had to admit. But so was he. To hell with it.

v.

Betty had no idea how to smoke a cigarette. Smoking never seemed like a polite thing for women to do, unless you were a movie star and even then, it was daring and brazen. Not polite. But the past twenty-four hours had diminished Betty's desire to be polite at all levels. She was tired of being alone, sick of taking the brunt, and scared to death about her future. Back in the airy comfort of her apartment, she kicked off her shoes, pulled her stockings off, poured herself a cup of cold coffee, and opened the package of Old Golds.

It took her a few tries to figure out that she needed to inhale just as she put the match to the tobacco, and then the sting of hot smoke so startled her that she choked. It was one more attack on her spirit, and for a minute she wanted to smash the whole pack with her tired, bare foot.

But she liked holding the smoldering thing, its smoke rising in a tiny cloud above her. She really liked that. And when it had burned to the almost end, she enjoyed stubbing it out into the one ashtray she owned and seeing the butt stained with her own shade of lipstick. That brought enough pleasure for her to light another, stopping short of the deep inhale and posing again with the cigarette held in gracious repose between her two fingers. This time she took small, shallow intakes every once in a while to get the knack of holding it in her mouth. It wasn't all as automatic as she'd expected. She'd certainly seen enough people smoking in her day to think it would all happen like some involuntary reflex. She never thought she'd have to coordinate so many small movements to smoke a cigarette.

On her fourth try, she felt she had it down, though by then the room had become so smoky, her eyes began to water.

"Momma's on fire," she heard Elise yell from the bottom of the stairs and then the footsteps of Elise and Katie Fiore came clunking up to the apartment. Seeing Betty, barefoot in a cloud of smelly smoke, the two girls stopped short and stared at her.

"Want a chocolate bar?" Betty asked, tossing her head in the direction of the two Hershey bars on the table. "Never mind me. Just conducting a little experiment." She scooped her nylon stockings off the floor and hopped up to empty the ashtray. "Nothing you girls ever want to do, I'll tell you that right now." She smoothed her hair and met their gaze. "So," she said, "should I make lunch?"

vi.

Rounding the block for the eighth or ninth time that morning, Gertrude was the only one to see Sue Too's family take off in their green truck. She called "how you" to the girl, saw the wary wrinkles on the mother's face and the frayed hat on the dad's head. From the truck window, Sue Too waved back and watched Gertrude's wide turn at the corner, wishing for the simplicity of living on just one block like the skinny lady roaring past.

Now they were on their way to see her sister Diane in Bemidji, because the bedrooms there needed painting and her parents wanted to help. Their own apartment remained in unpacked disorder, so Sue Too did not understand this excursion at all. They'd have to sit in the truck for more than two hours to get there then sleep on sofa cushions just to paint walls in someone else's house. As if Sue Too had no life of her own. As if she weren't a crucial element in a secret detective club.

Without her constant prodding, she figured her friend Kate would return to building roads in that sandbox or something. The secret club needed her in order to forge ahead with daring. Nobody ever got famous in a sandbox. Nobody ever got famous in a truck lumbering to Bemidji either.

Her mom had packed liverwurst sandwiches to eat as they drove, along with a thermos of coffee. Sue Too pressed her face against the truck window and watched as they passed by grazing cows, rickety barns, and cattails along the road's edge. She thought about the abandoned house, letting her mind play out scenes of love and disaster. She let the blond minister and his pretty wife argue, the wife throw a book of prayer at her husband's head, the minister dump out the coffee grounds in anger, the wife push him away, and the minister push her back so hard her head smacked into the kitchen doorframe. Hurt, she staggered into the living room, where she collapsed on the floor in the exact spot where the girls found the brown stain. In Sue Too's imaginings the wife's blood gushed all over the floor. Maybe she screamed or maybe she was too weak and stunned. The minister shook her to revive her, horrified at what he'd done. Then he ran for a blanket upstairs. Or a small rug. He rolled his wife up, carried her to his car, locked her in the trunk, and drove away without looking back.

Sue Too ate a second sandwich. Why didn't he look back? She didn't think people ever left whole houses forever. She turned to her parents, who were absorbed in listening to the radio.

"You guys ever hear of people leaving a house without taking their stuff?"

"Well, I don't know," her mother answered, just to be sociable.

"Lucky stiff, if anyone did," her dad said without taking his eyes off the crooked, two-lane road.

vii.

Katie Fiore had also pondered the abandoned house all Sunday night and all Monday morning. It wasn't that she needed to make sense of it exactly, but the chaos held messages, indications of what had happened to two pretty people in a slanted old house. Like voices she could almost hear. Trouble she could almost identify.

After running upstairs to the Larsens' apartment when Elise thought her mother was on fire, Katie had stayed miserably through Mrs. Larsen's lunch. She saw Elise sneaking quick peeks at her every minute to see if Katie was going to bolt as Mrs. Larsen talked on and on, the way she did, from one topic to the next: who invented the sandwich, the wonder of Woolworth's, the empty shelves over at Vernon's Grocery. The girls each ate four Oreos for dessert before Katie finally said, "I got to go check something at home." She pushed back her chair and moved toward the stairway determined to make it all the way to the bottom and out the door. "Thank you for lunch, Mrs. Larsen. Bye," she called and kept going, knowing that if she showed any hesitation, Mrs. Larsen would launch into another topic and Elise's sad eyes would pin her there for another hour at least.

"Bye-bye, Katie," she heard Elise say behind her.

She came through the back door at home to find her mother
having coffee with her Aunt Carmella who smiled at her gra-
ciously. Aunt Carmella had a particular gentility, an educated
poise. For a woman who'd been forced to marry a man she
didn't choose, Aunt Carmella remained remarkably calm.
Almost transcendent.

"Tell her," Katie's mother prompted Carmella. "She's been
hounding me about this for a week."

Aunt Carmella turned to Katie and said, "A Lutheran minister
lived in that house on Fourth Avenue. Very handsome, they
say. I met his wife at sewing circle." She took a sip of her coffee
as if she'd finished the story.

"So what happened?" Katie tried not to sound too interested,
too urgent or demanding. But she already knew more than
what her aunt had just offered. "I mean, it looks empty now,
the house does."

Aunt Carmella nodded. "Well, of course. He fell apart, you
see." She stopped again, as if all this made perfect sense.

"Fell apart?"

"He had a nervous breakdown, Kate," her mother translated.
"Aunt Carmella says he became hysterical and his family
had to take him away someplace. Down by Rochester, right,
Carmella?"

"Lovely man, they say. Who could know? Poor girl went with
him, trying to make the best of it, I suppose." Aunt Carmella
sighed. She knew much about making the best of it.

Katie sat down between them at the table, stunned at this news. "So he's crazy?"

Her mother rolled her eyes, and Aunt Carmella sighed again. "I wouldn't say that. Not like Nicky Marodi. Not like that. Maybe an overly sensitive type." She turned to Katie's mother to say, "I heard he was supposed to be moving to a church in Duluth. Then he had this breakdown."

"Things happen," Katie's mother said, thinking about her lost baby boys and the anguish she still felt for them. Years back she thought she might have a breakdown too.

The two women drank their cups of coffee, while Katie considered the comparison between a minister whose nerves gave way and the wild looking man on the street whose tongue hung out. One was crazy and the other only sensitive? How did people know these things? The state of the dilapidated house seemed crazy enough to her.

"So they were planning to move?" Katie asked her aunt.

"That's what they say." Aunt Carmella finished her coffee. "You know the church owns that awful house, and I hear they haven't touched a thing in there since the minister and his wife left. It's all just the same, can you imagine?"

"Did he bleed?" Katie blurted.

"Bleed?" Her aunt looked surprised. "Why would he bleed?"

Katie slumped in her chair.

"As if having a breakdown wasn't enough," her mother countered.

"And probably losing his job too," Aunt Carmella added, then stood and organized herself before leaving. "Stop by someday, Katie. Tell me about what you're reading this summer."

Katie's mother went outside with Aunt Carmella, but Katie stayed at the table in a trance. There had been no murder. The stain on the floor was who knows what. The books were half-packed because the young minister and his wife thought they were moving on to a new position in Duluth, where the fog horns sounded on cloudy days and the waves of Lake Superior crashed against the rocky shore. They'd left coffee grounds and chaos because he'd become hysterical. Katie could not imagine this. She could not picture a nervous breakdown. Did he cry and thrash about? Scream? Could he explain what was happening to him when he broke down?

No wonder she'd heard the house talking to her. The kitten in its basket on the calendar and the folded hankies in the chest of drawers, the dusty air whispering. The minister and his wife had left their story unfinished. It wasn't a fluke that Sue Too had dragged them into that old place. It was some kind of destiny, some kind of plan. These people needed her.

viii.

The Marodis' overgrown backyard was a paradise, a *paradiso*. The wire fence on the north side leaned with the weight of grapevines that Nicky's family had planted decades ago in some dream of the Old Country, some idea of fertility and wine now bent and sagging. But lush in its way. The wire fence to the south stood strong next to his mother's rows of tomatoes, beans, and peppers, all small and promising. The wooden chair against the house stayed in sunshine until midafternoon, where on most days he stretched out protected and unseen, a man in a clean shirt and nice hat anyway.

He'd spent all Sunday there after Mass and all that morning helping his mother hang their sheets on lines pulled across the wildest growth of the yard, weeds up to her ankles, dandelions cheerfully tall and scattered about. They'd had leftover cutlets for lunch and a half glass of wine each to wash it down, and now he stood by the door deciding to leave and walk, something he always had to weigh for some minutes, remembering scenes, vague harsh scenes that he might have imagined, but didn't think he did. His mother blessed herself three times whenever he walked out, so that was a caution to him too.

But if he avoided people when he walked, if he looked out at the houses on both sides of the street and measured his safety and angled his hat forward enough, he felt free and almost normal.

Thinking this, he left the yard, choosing to turn right onto the sidewalk in the direction of the arena and the skinny lady's block, realizing immediately that this was a mistake, because the round couple with the basket were rolling right at him like two bowling balls down a wooden alley. "Kaka Roo," the man yelled, louder than the afternoon required and beaming at him. "There's Kaka Roo, Edna. Nice fellow."

Nicky lurched toward them until he was so close he could see the man's eyes, inside out as they were, and Nicky screamed his own terror and turned and galloped his weird walk back into his yard and around to the silent backyard where he focused on one golden dandelion and kept focusing on it until he had just about lost the vision of Godfrey's crossed eyes. He'd never been that close before. He'd never known those eyes.

Seeing her son back so soon and unharmed, Mrs. Marodi whispered her thanks to Mary Mother of God and went outside to sit with him.

On the sidewalk Edna giggled and pinched her husband's nose. "You scared him away, Tooty," she said. "You scared away Kaka Roo."

In turn, Godfrey pinched her backside, glancing around to see if anyone was watching. Through the thin cotton dress he could feel her plump flesh, no layers between, just flesh and, impulsively, he stuck his tongue deep into her ear. "You just wait," he whispered, and without discussion they picked up their pace in a desire to get home.

ix.

A man had mowed the churchyard again, but Gertrude forgot to listen. She didn't hear the bugs in the grass or the pale rustle of summer leaves either. Her wanting held her prisoner as she rounded her block again and again, not able to call to people or see them half the time. She couldn't understand why the man Nicky didn't appear, why he didn't long to see her too. They were both walkers after all. So what could have happened to him?

She'd had such an unsatisfying day, all the hours leading to nothing. At lunchtime Mrs. Wilke studied her as if she were some rare bird blown in on the wind. "Gertie?" she kept asking until Gertrude looked up from her frowning and met her eyes. "You sick?"

But Gertrude couldn't answer. The air felt too thick for words. Lucky she could make out what Mrs. was saying. Sick. Of course she was sick. Her toe hurt and she could barely hear. The summer kept raging without her and where was she? Missing in a fog. Gertrude bent her head and covered her ears, and because she was still chewing on a carrot, the inside of her head exploded with such a racket, she thought she'd cry.

Now, at the end of the long and unsatisfying afternoon, she came to Mrs. sitting in the shadowed living room taking a sip of her sherry and asked, "Is this the only block I get?"

"You get?" Mrs. Wilke blinked.

"Do I get to go on other blocks?"

Gertrude loomed close and agitated, her blouse wrinkled by the day's exertion, her face damp and her eyes bouncing around behind her spectacles. Mrs. set her glass of sherry on the table beside her chair. Gertrude's question wasn't easy. Beyond this block people might not know her or make allowances or leave her to walk along in peace. And Mrs. Wilke was responsible. She herself hardly knew the people on other blocks.

"Why?" the older woman asked. "I thought you loved our block here, what with the church and store, the apartment buildings, and all the nice neighbors you know."

Gertrude didn't answer or budge. Her breathing came louder and her fingers curled into a fist. "One more block," she said.

"Can you tell me why, Gertie?"

When Gertrude didn't answer, Mrs. Wilke asked, "Which one block?"

Gertrude pointed south. "Kitty corner," she said.

"You want to walk on the block kitty corner on Twenty-Fourth Street?"

Gertrude nodded, but still no other part of her moved at all.

"Just a little ways on that block or all around the block?" Mrs. leaned forward trying to understand.

"Just to the hedge where there's a red roof."

Mrs. Wilke went out so seldom that she had no idea how far Gertrude would have to go to get to the hedge and red roof.

"Not far," Gertrude added. She walked away into the kitchen and thumped back in big steps. "Just two times this far. Or three. Just that far. To the hedge."

"Maybe I should walk with you," Mrs. Wilke offered, dreading it even as she said the words.

But Gertrude didn't like this idea. "It's not far," she said. "Just to the hedge and back."

Mrs. Wilke took up her glass of sherry and drank it in one swallow. "All right, Gertie. You go and come back and tell me right away. Come back and report how it went for you." She slowly pulled herself out of the chair. "I'll make a tuna salad and when you come back, we'll eat and talk about it. How's that sound?"

Gertrude didn't wait to answer. Hearing "All right, Gertie," she pivoted toward the door on her way to the best thing that had happened all day, out the door and around the block the long way, her way she decided, for the luck of it she'd go her way, past the mowed churchyard and Mrs. Kirshling's, then the store, Abellis' garden, no girls on the curb, but the sun still lingering in the June sky and past the apartment building to the corner where she could see the hedge.

She stopped. She looked in every direction for cars. She looked again, stepped off the curb and crossed on the diagonal to Nicky's block, where instantly the air shifted to a lighter, sweeter breeze, so much lighter. No wonder he stayed home all of the time, she thought, no wonder. Nobody on her block had a red roof.

At the hedge she stopped again to take in the overgrown yard and the tied-back curtains at the windows, windows that were open wide so that Gertrude caught the aroma of tomatoes traveling on the light, sweet air. Then grinning with a great happy secret within her, she turned and walked home. She found Mrs. Wilke still chopping onions and celery for the tuna salad, the tuna's fishy smell filling the room.

"How was it, Gertie?"

Gertrude sat at the kitchen table and eased out of her shoes to wiggle her toes. "That's the best block," she answered. "They cook tomatoes."

"How nice," Mrs. answered. "How very nice."

x.

The sun hung on past eight, past eight thirty, almost to nine before it began to slide away from them. Gertrude and Mrs.

Wilke sat side by side on the sofa watching a silly show, each thinking that the day had been a success and there they were together in the quiet light. A half block away Nicky Marodi, not knowing he'd been the object of Gertrude's success, carefully dried his mother's gilded-edged dishes, bought one by one over a year with grocery store coupons when he was away and now stacked like the king's ransom in their kitchen cupboard. He'd already nearly forgotten his encounter with the cross-eyed man, though the sense of fear remained, enough to keep him home that night with only the dream of walking freely from one block to another.

From his hospital bed Claus listened to the low hum of his daughters talking, catching references to him that buzzed now and then through the room, pesky but inconsequential. Tildy had gone home to sleep. One of their granddaughters was staying with her until Claus returned in four or five days when Dr. Milton had told them he could go. The surprise of his new reality had not completely settled in on Claus. His one question—what do I do now—went unasked, because he didn't think he wanted to know the answer.

Of course, Betty understood none of this. Her lousy Sunday waiting for Claus had turned into an even more lousy Monday walking to his house only to find him off in the hospital. Late in the afternoon, she'd taken Elise by the hand and headed downtown, walking strategically past the hospital on their way to Bridgeman's, where they split a large hamburger, coleslaw, and potato chips along with a chocolate malt mounded in whipped cream and topped with a cherry. This exercise at least distracted her and cleared her mind again.

The Woolworth's store sat across the alley from the hospital, a juxtaposition that took on some kind of meaning in Betty's mind, places that might impact her future, if not one of them then the other. On the way home she walked so slowly past first Woolworth's and then the hospital that Elise took up a hopping dance so she wouldn't collapse in slow-moving boredom.

Elise hadn't liked the day either. Everything had come to nothing. Claus wasn't home. She never found out who Tildy was. Katie wouldn't do the club without Sue Too and had never returned after their silent lunch together. The afternoon had dragged on and on. She'd watched Katie's mother and grandmother take their clean clothes off their lines and fold them. She'd seen Gertrude zoom by all afternoon, but even Gertrude didn't acknowledge Elise sitting on the curb.

Finally, at Bridgeman's she could smell ice cream and eat chips and a pickle, not to mention the creamy cold malted that reminded her how good life could be. Even on a bad day.

Just past midnight the rain began, a torrential, unrelenting June rain that pounded on their roofs and windows. Mrs. Wilke, Betty Larsen, Katie's mother, and Nonna all jumped up to close windows and wipe the sills, then returned to their beds. But Betty tossed from one side to the other for the rest of the night, thinking with each restless turn that she would need to get work. She would need to move on from Claus and his bad health and bad eyesight and unwillingness to claim her. The rain was a sign, like a baptism, she thought. Like what's his name in the Bible, getting cleansed and getting on with some blessed new life.

SEVEN

Tuesday, June 14, 1960

i.

Betty woke up renewed and determined. She put on a dress she thought of as sensible, a dress with no gathers or kick pleats. She couldn't remember why she'd ever bought this simple green dress in the first place. Maybe when she worked at the drugstore or right after Elise was born and she thought she might soon be Claus's wife. It was a wife kind of dress for certain. She buttoned herself into it, realized the closet had creased noticeable wrinkles in the skirt, and so took it off to iron it.

Elise came out of her bedroom just as her mother, in a slip and nylon stockings, stood ironing her dress. "Are we going visiting again, Momma?"

"Momma's going downtown for business, Elise. So here's what I need you to do. Eat your cereal there. I cut the banana for you, and then you can play all morning right here. Okay? You don't even have to get dressed," she added, when she saw her daughter's face clouding. "You can just loaf around, like a lady of leisure, like a princess. I pulled out the watercolors for you in case you feel artistic." She kept looking up from her ironing to see some spark on Elise's face, but the child only watched and listened. Betty didn't have the foggiest idea what was going on in her daughter's mind half the time. "Eat the rest of the Oreos if you want." Betty beamed her encouragement.

Elise only sighed, seeing ahead of her another lonesome day without mystery or secrets, dark basements, or exciting friends. "What if Katie Fiore comes over?"

Betty folded the ironing board with a loud smack. "Oh, let her in, Elise, if you must. I can't see what harm can come of that. She's probably off doing other things anyway. But I do not want you outside while I'm gone. Do you understand? I'm not the kind of mother who leaves her child to run rampant in the neighborhood with no parent in sight. Like that baker's daughter. For heaven's sake, does anyone ever give that girl a bath?" Betty pulled her dress on, gave her hair one more definitive pull of the brush, and with a series of reminders to Elise, she clomped down the stairs.

In the middle of the restless night, she'd devised a plan. She was going to march right into that hospital and straight to Claus's room, where she was going to find out the real nature of this setback, this so-called emergency with an ambulance in the middle of the night. She was going to tell him straight away that she planned on taking care of him in the future, that it was ridiculous to think that a flustered little ghost like Tildy could keep him alive in his declining years.

As she walked the three blocks down Fourth Avenue she stacked the deck in her favor and organized the images in her head until she could actually see Claus sitting at her kitchen table, his long legs crossed with elegance and his white shirtsleeves folded neatly to the elbows. He'd be drinking an Old Fashioned or one of those cocktail lounge drinks, a vodka martini maybe, as she sat across from him reading the Duluth newspaper out loud, not the narrow local paper, but the fat and cosmopolitan Duluth paper. And he'd discuss the news with her as they sat together, Elise maybe doing her puzzles on the floor nearby. "Betty," he'd say, "this article is so interesting." That's how life would be. He just wasn't picturing how fine their life together would be. She had to put her foot down and demand action.

She walked in large steps, almost unladylike, her heels hitting the pavement with serious force. When she got to the front of the hospital, she stopped to straighten her stocking seams just as two nuns in white habits swished by on their way into the hospital. "May we help you?" the taller one asked, noticing Betty's nervous fiddling. "Visiting hours are just beginning, you know." They both smiled, waiting to help, waiting to escort her in, waiting for God knew what, maybe the gates of heaven to open.

"Oh, I'm fine," Betty answered. But in that instant she altered her course and dashed away from the two nuns out to the sidewalk, where she turned left and walked straightaway to Woolworth's. Once inside the overly lit store, she hightailed it to the comfort of the cosmetics counter and Roger Vernon's gorgeous redheaded wife.

Sophia stood with perfect posture and perfect makeup and an elegant hairdo of loose strands and curls. "Hi, Mrs. Larsen. You look so nice today. I love that shade of lipstick on you. It's the one you bought here just awhile ago, isn't it?"

For over a week Betty had been hoping someone would compliment her on her lipstick. Now she warmed to the acknowledgment gratefully, even if it was from the woman who had sold it to her. "I love this lipstick," she gushed, and the two of them launched into a lively discussion of the array of colors before them, the experiments of color they'd each tried, the delicious possibilities that makeup unleashed. Betty hadn't had such an easy good time in weeks. Love and intimacy were a compelling pleasure, that was true, but Hot Strawberry lipstick was just plain fun and nobody could convince her that it wasn't.

Plus Sophia Vernon enjoyed the same frivolity, cared about it and continued digging in the drawer under the counter for samples and color charts. "Do you think they're looking for another clerk around here?" Betty asked, dropping a handful of samples into her purse.

Sophia started to laugh. "Mrs. Larsen, can you keep a secret?"

"Tick a lock," Betty answered and leaned against the counter ready for conspiracy.

"Woolworth's might be looking for a new clerk in the next few months." She paused and laughed again, then whispered, "I'm going to have a baby."

"Oh," Betty cried out with excitement. "Good for you, Sophia. Oh my. Isn't that good news."

"Shhhh. Nobody knows. I just saw the doctor this morning. I won't tell Roger until I get home tonight." She did a little dance behind the counter, a dainty cha-cha dance. "I'm so happy."

"And you told me first!" Betty stared at the beautiful woman in wonder. "I'm very honored, Sophia."

"I'll put in a word for you, as soon as I let them know I'll be leaving. I'll tell them what a way you have with makeup." The two of them giggled good-byes until Betty neared the store's side door. Now, she thought, as she pushed out into the sunny morning, what did this mean? She passed the back of the hospital with only a moment's hesitation and continued home, thinking about the future she might have selling makeup behind a shiny store counter where it mattered that she looked good every day and she'd get a paycheck once a week to prove her worth. As she went by Vernon's Grocery, she felt a smug thrill at the secret she knew that Roger had not yet been told.

ii.

At home Elise had painted two very sweet watercolors, one of the curtained kitchen window and the other of the garage apartment with smoke swirling out a brick chimney that, in real life, did not exist. "Those are pretty pictures, Elise," Betty commented on her way to the bathroom to put away her samples of lipstick and rouge. Then in a wild, happy inspiration, she popped back out and said, "Let's bring Claus one of your pretty paintings. People who are sick always need cheering, and you're so imaginative! Look at that pretend chimney."

Though Elise did not jump into her mother's glee, she was at least relieved that she didn't have to sit by herself in the apartment any longer, that she could clatter outside and breathe the summer air, even in her dotted swiss dress and patent leather shoes. As her mother pulled her along, she scanned in all directions for Katie or Sue Too, but saw only Gertrude, too far ahead of them to yell her usual greeting. But maybe when they returned or after lunch, maybe then she would be with her secret club again. She held on to that hope as she held on to her watercolor of the garage apartment that she was bringing to the hospital for Claus, clutched in a sweaty grip.

Only a half hour remained of the morning visiting hours, when Betty and Elise hurried through the double doors and crossed the waxed lobby floor. A different nun gave them the number of Claus's room and the directions to get there. As they waited for the elevator, they saw a doctor, several nurses, and another nun move past, all of them fully committed to their tasks, unhesitating and, to Elise, more terrifying than the loud rain that had pounded her bedroom window in the night. Her mother held her hand too tightly. Her fingers began to poke a hole in her painting and just then, she decided she might have been better off alone in the kitchen after all.

Betty did nothing to reassure her daughter. She told herself that this was the right thing to do, that Claus would most certainly want her to visit and would love Elise's artwork, her off-center, unrealistic painting of the garage apartment with its too big windows and too small doors. That just seeing their cheerful faces would make his day. "Smile now, Elise," she whispered as they approached the door of Claus's room. "Smile big like Momma."

And they went into Claus's room.

iii.

For all her elaborate fantasies, Betty had never really thought about what she would encounter in Claus's hospital room just days after an ambulance had hurried him there in the night. So the sight of his face, still ashen and worn, shocked her. He did not look like her keen and invincible lover, her elegant and elusive lover, but like an old man. Like someone's ailing grandfather. At the sight of him, Elise moved closer to her mother.

Betty also had not considered that both Tildy and one of Claus's daughters might be sitting in chairs at the foot of his bed, their large eyes widening with surprise the minute Betty and Elise came through the door.

Nobody said anything. Betty and Elise stopped moving forward. Tildy and the daughter sat riveted, and Claus stared as if he'd never seen his visitors before. Beyond them the hospital ward bustled. Inside the room, the air remained still.

Then Betty said, "Elise painted you a picture." She didn't say his name, found that it would not come out of her mouth there in the dim light in front of the rest of them. She took the bent paper, its corner sweaty from Elise's grip, and handed it to Claus. "She just did it today, and we thought you'd like it." She spoke loud enough for him to hear her, but she was not her usual sparkly self, and she did not include the two women in her gesture. Elise still clung to Betty's other hand, taking in the rest of the room in a sort of defense—the stark furnishings and bare walls, the older woman with white hair and the other, younger woman who looked familiar to Elise, Claus wearing a nightgown, her mother so tall in the middle of all this, or seeming so tall, so important in the middle of it all.

Claus accepted the painting and set it lightly on the blanket that was tucked around him. He nodded once at Betty and looked down at his hands. His daughter and Tildy still did not speak and he did not look their way.

Betty waited for Claus to say thank you or explain his situation here in this hospital room, but he did not, and Betty could not bring herself to ask. The question of his health suddenly felt too personal, too out of her range. "Well," she said at last. It was an opening. It might trigger one of the others in the room to talk. But they did not. "Well," she said again. "Maybe you can find a spot for the picture." She glanced around, and added, "I hope you feel better soon." Then stiff and humiliated, she turned and left the room.

Behind her Claus studied the simplistic drawing of the garage apartment that he paid for every month so that Betty and her daughter could live respectably, and nodded again to himself. Tildy watched his every breath, too overwhelmed to talk. Because now it was clear, more clear than it had ever been. The little girl holding Betty's hand looked exactly like Tildy's youngest daughter when she was a child. They could have been twins, even to the awkward fidgeting and wide-eyed worry. And that same daughter, sitting next to Tildy at the foot of her ailing father's bed, saw it too. She saw the child version of herself in yellow dotted swiss and the same tight braids she'd always worn. She saw that her father had another child.

Halfway home along Fourth Avenue, Elise asked, "Do you think Claus liked my picture?"

Her mother tugged at her arm. "I'm sure he did."

"He didn't say thank you."

"Well, he's sick, Elise. You can't expect too much from sick people is the truth. You just have to be nice and hope they get better."

"How come that lady in the room looks like me?"

Betty was already too near tears to venture into explanations of any kind, let alone this. She was also too numb to divert Elise with some clever bunch of baloney. So she said, "What do you think?"

Elise pondered this for a half a block as they sped along. "I think it must be magic," she answered at last. Once she said it, she knew it to be true and felt a rush of excitement to tell this bit of wonder to her secret club.

iv.

On her third time around the block, Gertrude passed Betty and Elise on their way home. "How you," she called, taking in the girl's pretty dress and happy face despite the screaming braids, Mrs. Larsen's taut muscles, nothing to say today, nothing to say. "How you," Gertrude called again for good measure and little Elise hopped on one foot in response and made a silly grin, which Gertrude took to be enough for just now. Enough for just now as she slowed to reconsider making her fourth trek around, when she already knew the whole situation, the smirking boy by the store and Mrs. Abelli tying plants again, but no Nicky, no Nicky, no Nicky.

So she kept walking, saw Mrs. Kirshling sweeping debris from the rain, muttering, not seeing, not hearing the weird drenched grass and all its bugs, the ants in a state after the night's ruin.

Gertrude had an idea to cross the street again to the block where Nicky lived and walk only so far, then turn around and go home for lunch, just walk so far and go home for lunch. So she carefully crossed Twenty-Fourth Street and Fourth Avenue, then there she was at his hedge.

And there he was too, coming down his block from the other direction. Bent to the side and limping, lurching along at his angle, his hat low, his shirt white, and then he waved, unmistakable, that Nicky wave, bigger than an old crow flapping, Nicky's wave, and Gertrude, flustered as a girl, yelled, "How you, Nicky," and bolted for her own block, turned at the street to yell it again as Nicky waved again and she knew he was smiling like she was, old Cuckoo Bird Gertie grinning goofy all the way home, where not even Mrs. Wilke's reminders on manners could stop her feet from tapping merrily under the luncheon table.

v.

Betty stood in her kitchen not knowing what to think or do or say. Elise had gone into her room, removed her fancy dress and shoes, put them away and was now making her own peanut butter sandwich lavished with grape jelly, humming the Disney theme song, almost too happy for her mother to bear. "I got to find Katie, Momma. See you," she said, still eating her sandwich, not even sitting down but munching like a wandering gypsy. Even then, Betty had nothing to say.

It might have been the worst moment of her life, possibly worse than the night her father died and she had no date to the dance and her puffy pink dress got put away in favor of a brown serge funeral suit. That night was horrible, and this day was horrible, leaving her with the same desolate abandonment and confusion, the same hollow fear in her stomach.

In these few short days Claus had become a sick old man, frail and uncommunicative, ready to die. She saw it. He'd never be hers. He'd never bound up these stairs into her arms or park his blue sedan in her garage for keeps. He was sick. Something had happened. Better for him to be with little gray-haired Tildy in their house surrounded by flowers. Good for them. Better for them to finish off life the way they'd started, malfunctioning together. What was it to her? Still her legs would not move.

The noon sun came in across the middle of the kitchen, the air remained fresh after the heavy rain and through the windows, she heard vague sounds of the neighborhood. Church bells. A door slamming. Things moving toward an ordinary summer afternoon.

Money. That was the thing now. In a sudden furor, Betty hauled out everything in the apartment related to money—her roll of cash hidden under her nylon stockings, her change from a drawer in the kitchen, their dime bank, even the flowered piggy bank that belonged to Elise. She spread them all on the kitchen table and took a tally. She'd saved some money before Elise was born and she had held on to a few dollars from every payment Claus had given her. Her mother had sent her one hundred dollars when Elise was born asking that Betty buy a bus ticket and come home to live with her family. She'd kept that too.

Counting out loud and adding things up she was surprised to find she had just over $1,200, enough to get her through five months, if it came to that, maybe even six months if she quit buying Oreos and boxes of mixes from Vernon's Grocery. If she stuck to a strict budget. Maybe she could sublet that empty garage downstairs, something she should have done years ago instead of waiting for Claus to move in and park his car there. Maybe she could do some babysitting until the job opened up at Woolworth's. If they hired her. She looked up from her scattered resources to consider why they wouldn't hire her. She'd worked retail before and was a mature woman, and she certainly knew makeup. Clothing too. Maybe she should stop by Nides Fashion and Vera's Smart Shop to see if they needed an experienced and mature sales clerk with an eye for glamour. She had lots of options, she realized. Lots of possibilities.

The planning made her so hungry she scrambled three eggs with Velveeta and toasted two slices of bread. Then she poured herself a glass of brandy to wash it all down. This was going to work for her. Claus wasn't her answer now. She had to block any wisp of her time with him, any hot sweet moment together, his hands and mouth, she had to block all of that. Forever. Bury Claus before he even died. That was what she had to do. She cleared the table, deciding to open an account at First Federal Savings the next day and talk to the Saluccis about renting her garage.

She hadn't changed clothes since the morning and her somber green dress was so wrinkled no one would ever guess that she had ironed it just five hours earlier. To hell with this dress, she thought, pulling it off and tossing it on the bed. She would cut it into squares for hot pads. That was all the dress was good for.

On that thought she poured herself another glass of brandy and sat in her slip and stockings while she slowly sipped it down.

vi.

Feeling more confident than she ever remembered, Elise crossed the street alone, made her way around the expansive Abelli garden and right to Katie's back door, where she finished her last bite of sandwich and knocked, amazed when Katie appeared almost immediately. "It worked," she said.

"You mean knocking on the door?"

The younger girl smiled. "I never did it before."

Katie came outside and the two of them sat on the back steps. "I can't find Sue Too anymore," Katie said. "I guess they don't stay home much."

"I know," Elise replied. "Momma says people come and go all the time in that building. But guess what, Katie?"

"What, Elise? You look so excited. Did your mother let you come over here all by yourself to tell me something?"

"No, she didn't say I could, but I knew I could because it's you. So we went to visit Claus in the hospital and guess what I saw?"

Katie couldn't imagine what Elise was going to say next. The little girl was so unlike her normal self today, so large and lively, so brimming over.

"I saw a grown-up me!" She said this with great pride and lifted herself high and raised her eyebrows high as well.

"A grown-up you?"

Elise lowered her voice and moved her warm, rosy face close to Katie's. "There was a lady in the room who looks just like me, and I know why."

"You do? Really?"

"It's because of magic," Elise answered, still barely audible, still close and confidential.

"Did your mother say the lady looked like you?"

Elise pulled back to think. "She didn't have to say because it was just true." She dug into the back corner of her mouth to loosen some sticky bit of sandwich. "She just did look like me, Katie."

Then they sat, each girl to her thoughts—of magic perhaps or the bouncing sun of the afternoon. Somewhere in their silence, Katie decided to tell Elise that their secret club no longer had a mystery to solve. "I learned something about our old house," she started. "My Aunt Carmella knew the lady who lived there and she said the husband just kind of went crazy and had to be rushed off someplace away from here, so that's why things got left behind and nobody's there."

"He went crazy?"

"She didn't say crazy, I guess, but nervous. He had a breakdown, she said." Even as she spoke, Katie had no idea what she was saying and hoped Elise would not ask for clarification.

Instead, Elise said, "That's magic too. I got good magic and he got bad magic."

"Maybe."

"I'm glad I got good magic anyway. You want to come over and do a puzzle?"

Katie did not want to go to Elise's garage apartment and endure another of Mrs. Larsen's long-winded explanations of whatever was on her mind that day, so she suggested they build a new village in the sandbox. She went inside to get a couple of cookies and they set to work constructing a town of houses, roads, rivers, and small mountains. This took time and only when they were both satisfied with their results did Katie walk Elise back across the street.

At home Katie found her mother reading, her feet up on the ottoman. "Mom, Elise Larsen said they went to the hospital to visit that man Claus who comes around, and she saw a grown-up who looks just like her." She ended this piece of news with a shrug.

Her mother stared at her for such a long time that Katie finally sat on the sofa opposite her mother's chair. "Why are you looking at me like that?" she asked.

"Claus Jacobson is Elise's father. His other three daughters are grown and one of them must look like Elise. I've never seen them, so I can't say."

"He's her father?"

"That's between us, Kate."

"But he hardly talks when he walks by her. He's not married to Mrs. Larsen, is he?"

"He is not."

"Well, how come she's called Mrs. Larsen? Where's Mr. Larsen?"

"There is no Mr. Larsen. There never was."

"So she made it up?"

"She wants to be respectable, Kate. For her daughter's sake. Not everybody knows the whole story, I suppose. But we've seen Claus Jacobson coming and going for years. I can't believe Betty dragged her daughter to the hospital to see him. It's a wonder what people do."

"Elise thinks it's magic that the lady looks like her."

"Good. Let her think that, Kate. Poor thing. How old is she?"

"Six, almost seven, she says. Her birthday's in July."

"Magic," Mrs. Fiori repeated.

"Good magic," Katie clarified.

"Of course," her mother answered and went back to her reading, leaving Katie to sort the complexities of what her mother had told her on her own. Elise had a father married to someone else, who acted like he barely knew Elise. She didn't understand how that could even be true, and once again, she knew some-thing she wished she did not know.

vii.

Julia was the youngest of Claus's three daughters with Tildy. She was the one closest to her father, the one he'd protected the most and read to most often, the daughter he thought most sympathetic to his silences and drive. She had a perfect singing voice, and through the years, whenever he asked her, she'd always stand in the middle of whatever room and belt out a beauty. "Oklahoma" or "The Battle Hymn." While she was singing, she became a force, with a strong voice and the-atrical gestures, and as soon as she finished, she'd melt back into his own dear Julia. Now she was thirty, married to a man Claus thought a bit backward, and they had a baby just two, a waddling, drooling boy not quite at the age that Claus found agreeable.

Julia had watched in shock as Betty Larsen and her daughter stood at his hospital bed. Claus saw it—the appalled, almost horrified look on Julia's face. That look was almost the only thing in the room that he'd seen in those few dreadful moments when two parts of his life collided in front of him and there was nothing he could do about it. When it was over, when Betty and the girl were gone, Julia had asked her mother to wait in the lobby, get coffee, something—she'd said something so that Tildy would go and leave the two of them alone. Then she'd pulled a chair close.

"That little girl is our sister. Anyone seeing her can tell that."

Claus looked at Julia, but he didn't respond.

"What are you going to do, Daddy?"

"Do?" His eyebrows arched. "I'm going to do what the good doctor tells me. Go home. Rest. Walk around the block."

His daughter sat back in her chair. "Do you look out for them?"

He nodded. He did. He had. Now he didn't know what he would do or even what he should do. He wasn't well. He had a wife and three daughters to consider, and this relationship with Betty wasn't all his endeavor, not all his dalliance. Betty had her part too, always willing, always believing, full of her ideas and opinions as the years advanced and the child grew and his eyesight began to blur. Their welfare was not all on him.

"And you see the mother?"

He nodded again, thinking that he'd never once in the ten years he'd known Betty Larsen ever thought of her as a mother.

"So what do we do now, Daddy?"

"What do you suggest?" He said this with an edge she'd heard very seldom in her life.

"Something. An allowance for the little girl. Some protection. We have to do something."

"And that would be at your mother's expense? Or yours? Or your sisters'?"

Julia rested her forehead against the cotton flannel of the hospital blanket. It reminded her of her son's baby blankets, comforting and safe. "Where do they live?"

He told her, then said, "I'm not rich. But I have a decent bank account, Julia. We can look at some modest amount until the girl is eighteen. We could arrange it. But not with the others." He sat straighter as he said this. It was the first real decision in his new life as a man who could die soon.

"You don't even want Mommy to know?"

"Of course not. She's confused enough already. And now she has to worry about me every day. She knows about Betty. For god's sake, the woman called our house last week and told Tildy who she was. Whatever got into her. Your sisters don't need to know either. Getting the whole cluster all in a stir and the husbands counting out their cut of the pie. I'll be dead in a week with all that."

He studied her, her face a bit blurred but lovely and steady, a young woman of such substance. "I'd love to hear 'That Old Black Magic.' You think you could sing that for me?"

"Later, Daddy. I don't want the nurses to throw me out forever."

"Later," he said, as he watched her move her chair farther away and go. "Later," he said one more time to himself and closed his eyes and tried not to think what everything had come to.

viii.

To Nicky, the skinny lady yelling out to him was becoming a bit of a beacon, a sign that his days might get better and the universe might make room for him again. After today's encounter he watched her hike pell-mell down Fourth Avenue, where he remembered seeing her go before.

That afternoon he ventured in the same direction, without purpose really, but with curiosity and even some courage, knowing that he'd had trouble on that block before, boys in front of the store, an old lady with a broom, the sidewalk uneven in places—pushed up at angles from the ice of many winters. There were reasons he hadn't walked the full block over there, reasons why he'd been on alert.

Yet here he was, and step by meditated step he made it to Gertrude's corner, not sure it was her corner and certainly not knowing that inside the white house with the tall backyard fence, his new friend stood drinking a lemonade and thinking about him. He passed her house and the churchyard then, sure enough, there was the old woman with orange hair sweeping grass off her sidewalk, just as she had a decade before. He could not recall her name and walked on hoping for no trouble. Talking under her breath, the old woman headed around the side of her house, words coming with each fierce swish of the broom, so engrossed she did not notice Nicky panting along just like he used to those many years before.

At the next corner an Italian man said, "*Buon giorno*," and this gesture dispelled some of Nicky's worry and helped him balance the small joys of good people against the potential hazards of others. He crossed on the diagonal and went back to sit by himself in the sunshine of his mother's yard.

"Nicky?" he heard her call to him through the kitchen window. "*Sono a casa?*"

"*Ciao*, Mama," he answered, picturing her behind him in the window blessing herself and thanking some saint for keeping him safe one more time.

ix.

Elise never forgot the day she stumbled into magic in her otherwise ordinary life. Her mother was not happy all day, probably because Claus was sick, and so Elise kept her exuberance to herself. Her watercolors were still on the kitchen table where she'd left them when they'd scuttled out the door to the hospital, and after returning from Katie's, she went back to painting objects around the house, while her mother scrubbed everything in sight. "Lift your feet," Betty barked to Elise at one point, but otherwise said nothing until she plopped a bowl of Chef Boyardee raviolis in front of Elise and said, "Eat."

"This is our whole dinner?" It wasn't much to celebrate newly found magic. Her mother hadn't even put cheese on it.

"We have to cut back," Betty said, standing at the kitchen counter chewing one ravioli after another. "We're on a budget now, Elise, which means we can't eat four-course meals and run willy-nilly to Vernon's or—or Bridgeman's either."

"Why, Momma?"

"Because we're running low, that's why. Maybe I'll get a job at Woolworth's. What do you think of that?" Betty still stood with the bowl of ravioli in her hand, imagining herself in this new world of work. "Though where you'll go when I'm working is another story."

"Maybe I could go to Katie's." Elise's heart leaped at the thought.

"Well, I don't know about that. But we'll figure out something."

"Or maybe I could go see the lady who looks like me."

Betty ignored that comment, grabbed both bowls, and washed them with a soapy sponge, not even filling the sink with water and dipping them in. She wiped them with her apron, stuck them back on the shelf and that was the end of the meal. Then she took her bucket and moved on to scrubbing the bathroom.

When her mother was out of sight, Elise rummaged in the cupboard for more to eat and, trying not to make a sound, took a slice of bread and spread it with peanut butter. Then she snuck a handful of chocolate chips out of the Hershey's bag and downed all of these, bent to hide what she was doing.

She was not in the mood for her mother's cleaning. For her, today had been grand and otherworldly. She'd seen another person who looked like her. And not just any other person, but a person who was quite young and seemed nice and knew Claus and came to visit people when they were sick in the hospital. This person might be who Elise would become. She might someday wear her hair like that lady did, loose and wavy, almost like it had not been combed and certainly not like it needed braiding every day of the week. And she might some-day talk in hushed tones in the corner of a room and know the wide world where grown-ups came and went as they pleased. Magic had found her. The possibilities were endless.

x.

Hawk watched television. He observed the world, the restless disagreements and unexpected disasters, the constant harangu-ing. Whenever he could take control of the television, he found programs that let him know the world as it really was, harsh and disturbed and black-and-white. His old man stuck to sports and snored halfway through them anyway. His mother liked soap operas, cheating husbands, dying lovers, fakey dreary crap he couldn't even stand to hear from the next room. But news was something else. Edward R. Murrow was something else. And Westerns, they were something else too. *Maverick. Have Gun-Will Travel. Rawhide.* Just the names said it all.

These shows, the real news and the old cowboys, were what Hawk mulled around when he was biding his time, waiting for night, sitting alone in front of the television or out in the garage or stretched on top of his sunken narrow bed in the back porch they called his bedroom. He thought about wars and power and showdowns on deserted streets. He thought about striking out and getting known and walking away from the scene of some crime without any concern for being caught. Because he was Hawk. No, because he was The Hawk.

Just before dark he left home to meet the guys in front of the Sportsman's Café downtown, but on the way he veered without thinking in the direction of Vernon's Grocery, walked past it, and parked himself against the bricks of the elementary school across the street, where he could study the store from afar. In the ten minutes it took him to smoke two Lucky Strikes, he watched a tall kid go into the store and come out with no visible purchase. He knew that kid, Richard, in the class ahead of him. He watched Richard disappear into the pale green apartment building directly across the street from the store. Then the block fell quiet.

Hawk crossed over to the store without considering what he'd do when he got there. He yanked open the door and as the bell chimed over his head, he found himself face-to-face with the best looking lady he'd ever seen in person. He could hardly believe she was in person, so much did she resemble the famous actresses of the day. Marilyn Monroe with red hair. Or Jane Mansfield. "Hi there," the lady said, friendly as a puppy, her pink lips in a wide, relaxed smile. "Nice night, isn't it?" Her eyes never left him, and they were so easy, so unchallenging that he hung on too, caught in the spell of her mild-mannered goodwill.

"Yeah," he said, "really nice." His head nodded in agreement, but he didn't even notice. "Really nice," he said again.

Sophia Vernon kept smiling. "Can I help you find anything?"

"I could usc cigarettes, I guess."

"Sure, young men always like their cigarettes. What brand do you want?"

"What do you smoke?" he asked before he could stop himself. "I mean, if you smoke. Maybe you don't. Or maybe you do."

Sophia laughed like he'd said something wonderfully funny. "Once in a while," she answered with a wink. "But I just bum whatever I can get."

"Yeah. You want one of mine?" He pulled out his crunched pack of Lucky Strikes and stepped toward her.

"Oh, not while I'm working," she said, still easy, still smiling, like she had nothing better to do than lean on the store counter and chat with him. "But now I see your brand anyway. You want another pack or two?"

Hawk's eyes scanned the rows of cigarettes behind her, thinking he might see something that would impress this lady more than Lucky Strikes. "If you did buy a pack some day, what would you choose?"

She turned and studied the various brands, then she lowered her voice. "You ever hear of Gitanes?"

He shook his head. He wasn't even sure what she'd just said.

"They're French. We order them special for a couple across the alley. You want to try a pack?"

All of a sudden Hawk remembered who he was supposed to be, tough and disinterested, cool. "Sure, why not," he tossed back, above it all, but willing to oblige a shop clerk.

Sophia barely noticed this shift. She loved selling things to people—rouge and eyeliner, cigarettes and candy. Cheerful things that people wanted more than needed and that, she was sure, made their days happier. She dragged a stepstool from the corner and climbed up to reach the opened carton of Gitanes on the top shelf, then climbed carefully back down, all the while unaware that the boy was breathing in every move of every muscle in her entire lovely body. "There," she said and placed the cigarettes on the counter. "In case you want two."

Overwhelmed, Hawk paid for the two packs of Gitanes, nodded abruptly, and left the store, just as Roger Vernon came out from the couple's apartment. "What the hell did he want?"

"That boy? He just bought some cigarettes." Her husband's crankiness never failed to surprise her. He could be so sweet.

Why did customers irk him so much? "Gitanes," she added and laughed. "I wanted to see if I could sell French cigarettes to a little high school hood."

Roger stood at the door watching the boy walk toward downtown. "All we need is his crowd in here buying fancy cigarettes," he grumbled.

But his wife didn't care. She had news for him that night that would change everything. "Oh you," she flirted from her spot behind the counter. "Have a beer."

Two blocks from the Sportsman's, Hawk ripped open a pack of Gitanes and lit one, smoking as he continued on to meet his guys. With each inhale of the dark, strange tobacco his confidence returned. By the time he spotted the hulking shape of Mack up ahead, he was inches taller from his encounter at the store, his exotic cigarettes, and his growing power in the messed-up world. "Hey," he said to his friends as he took his place in the center of their circle. But he didn't meet their eyes. He kept his superior distance. Looking away at nothing in particular, he asked, "Want to try a French cigarette?"

EIGHT

WEDNESDAY, JUNE 15, 1960

i.

Roger opened the store earlier than he ever had in the three years they'd owned it, only because he felt he had to get out of the apartment and away from this news about a baby on the way. He could not let Sophia see that he didn't share her tremulous, almost giddy anticipation. Maybe it was some kind of chemistry. Maybe pregnancy made women feel nutty with excitement just to get them through the whole ordeal. He had no idea. He had absolutely no idea.

Now on top of the store pressing down on him like a ten-ton weight, they'd have a baby to care for and try to do right by, so he wouldn't grow up to be like that Hawk character buying cigarettes and beer before he'd even started shaving. Even if a kid of his own was anything like Roger had been, he and Sophia were in for trouble. Not that she'd think that, his beautiful, hopeful wife. Sophia was all about the baby clothes she knit and a baby's soft sweet skin and all the rest—the baby coos and baby steps and baby giggles when you rolled a ball across the floor. He knew for a fact that Sophia was not thinking for a minute that this baby of hers could grow up to be a boy like Hawk. Then again, maybe they'd have a girl. What the hell was Roger going to do if the baby turned out to be a girl, a knockout, redheaded girl like his wife? He had to stop himself from reaching for a beer.

Instead, he lit a cigarette, not his first that day, and watched the boy from across the street saunter his way. That skinny awkward kid had some kind of antenna as to when the store was open and there he'd be with two bits on the counter buying snacks. He ate like a horse, yet he looked like the pathetic stick of a tree out on the boulevard. "Stand up straight," Roger wanted to holler. "Go home and quit eating so many sweets. Your skinny teeth are going to rot in your head." That's what he wanted to say.

"Hey," the boy greeted Roger, "got any more of those Sno Balls?"

"See for yourself," Roger replied and watched the boy take up two packages of Hostess Sno Balls and set them on the counter with his usual quarter.

"Where you get all these quarters?"

"I earn 'em," the boy answered. "I mow and stuff."

"Really." Roger squinted at the kid trying to imagine him behind a lawn mower.

"Yeah, you got any jobs you want done around here? Stocking shelves or cleaning up out front or anything?"

"What's your name?"

"Richard."

"How old are you, Richard?"

"Sixteen," Richard said with obvious pride, as he pulled open one of the two Sno Ball packages and took a messy big bite, pink coconut flaking to the floor. "Hey, sorry." He bent down trying to pick up the little pieces, juggling the Sno Ball he was eating and the three left wrapped. "Shoot," he muttered.

"Forget it," Roger said.

"No, let me sweep for you, okay? Make it right?" The boy's eyes searched the store for a broom.

"Forget it," Roger said again. "Go eat those pink things outside and forget it." He followed Richard's awkward movements out the door and back across the street to the apartment building where he lived. He wasn't a bad kid. Dopey, but not too bad. Roger snuffed out his cigarette, grabbed the broom, and swept the floor for the first time in weeks.

Maybe he and Sophia could raise a good kid. Not so dopey as Richard, but decent like that. It was something to consider.

ii.

Gertrude felt fresher than the morning dew, that glinting quivering silent dew that hung in suspension ready to become part of the green leaves or green grass or pale early sky. Gertrude felt so good, she put her pedal pushers on backward and had to start over. "Why are these called pedal pushers?" she asked Mrs. Wilke at the breakfast table. "Who's pushing a pedal anyway? Not me," she added before Mrs. could answer, but she said it with great gusto and a willingness to believe whatever the older woman might say.

Mrs. Wilke wrinkled her brow in deep thought at the question and took several sips of her morning tea that she preferred without honey as Gertrude preferred hers with, then said at last that some women wore shortened pants when they rode bicycles and eventually, she said eventually twice, those shortened pants got this name.

"Why do I wear them?" Gertrude continued sipping her thick, sweetened tea like the proud princess of York, and Mrs. Wilke answered only that Gertrude had always preferred them to dresses or long pants, and then the two of them settled snugly into that version and finished breakfast before Gertrude hiked up her pedal pushers at the waist and moseyed outdoors to another sunny day and the full, fat feelings she had about the world.

Nicky's big wave and his loping, crooked walk toward her the day before had changed her gnawing, awful want to a dizzy tumbling love. She didn't wholly know the word love, which had not surfaced at all in her life before Mrs. Wilke or even very much since she'd lived with Mrs. Wilke, except that Mrs. would reference her long-gone husband that way and they'd both say how they loved the Italian mouse on television or how they loved sponge cake when it was warm and Christmas, how they both loved Christmas, and the first robin in spring, and so in these ways Gertrude knew that when you were goofy to grin and bounce and your heart sped along faster than your feet, then it had something to do with love or it even was love and now Cuckoo Bird Gertie herself knew the whole whopping story. She knew the feeling of love.

She took that feeling around her block then and saw the boy Richard sliding into Vernon's and Mrs. Abelli watering her garden and, finally, the red roof of Nicky's house perched up above the bushes like a surprise. You never would have believed that a man in a hat with his tongue hanging sideways would live just there with that color roof and the ripe whiff of tomatoes cooking, you would have never believed.

So she rounded the corner to home thinking what a world, what a loony, loopy red-roofed world.

iii.

Betty hadn't slept well in two nights. First it was the rain, then all her frets and figurings. Now she faced herself in the morning mirror with resolve. Today was the day. She would take all her loose pots of money and put them in a savings account of her own. She'd apply for a job at Woolworth's and Vera's Smart Shop and Nides. Dressing carefully, she called out periodically for Elise to do the same, until they were both ready at the top of the stairs, Betty in her dark blue polka-dot shirtwaist with a red hat and purse and Elise in a blue skirt and white blouse with perky red cherries embroidered on the collar. Details mattered.

At First Federal Savings & Loan Betty was treated with deference. They greeted her as a new friend, actually, which surprised Betty and raised her confidence in herself. The teller got a great kick out of the sack of dimes, because she'd had a dime bank herself when she was a girl. Otherwise the woman happily scooped up Betty's cash without comment. She gave Betty an official booklet with her current balance of $1,203.60 written in black ink, which Betty snapped into her purse like a professional, like a woman of business anyway, someone who had some money and was on her way to get more.

From the bank she trotted Elise to Bridgeman's, bought her a small malted and instructed her to sit and wait while she went to Vera's two doors away to apply for a job. At Vera's Smart Shop the two clerks complimented Betty's sense of style and told her how much they liked working at Vera's, where the everyday woman shopped for clothes more modern and unique than Ward's or JCPenney's down the street. She filled out a one-page application and left in a small storm of cheer. Elise wasn't quite done with her malted when Betty reappeared, large and soaring. "Off we go," she said, and before Elise could think of what to say, her mother had her back out on the sidewalk heading for Woolworth's.

This time Elise sat at the lunch counter drinking a soda while her mother talked to a manager in cosmetics, filled out an application, and chatted with Sophia Vernon just long enough to come back to Elise with two tiny samples of lipstick.

"Nides is just down the block, Elise. You sip that soda and I'll be back in a few minutes. If you let the ice melt, the soda will last longer." Her eyes stayed keenly on the little girl's face, but her mind was a mile away. This was the day she was putting her future into motion. Near the Woolworth's entrance, she saw a rack of comic books, took one called *Little Lulu*, paid for it, and hustled back to Elise. "Read this until Momma comes back."

Nides was possibly the most elite women's clothing store in town, its door a heavy dark wood, its carpeting inside plush and pale. Nobody tracked dirt into Nides, it seemed, or if they did, someone got rid of it in a flash. Betty felt instantly dowdy in Nides. The woman who glided her way wore an elegant two-piece dress, the skirt lean and silky, the top just clingy enough to suggest the woman wearing it, while remaining in utter good taste. Her hair was in a chignon at the nape of her neck, as if she'd been a ballet dancer in another life, and her entire bearing told of ease and grace.

"May I help you today?" Unlike the clerks at Vera's, this woman did not comment on Betty's polka dot dress. She didn't seem to notice it at all.

"I'm interested in applying for a job," Betty answered.

"The owner isn't here today. Might I give her your card?"

Her card. She didn't have a card. Though she remembered hearing of women's calling cards, she had never known anyone who'd used one. She didn't think she had ever seen one.

"Or you might leave me your name and number. I'll give her the information." The woman remained polite, charming even, if she weren't so perfect and so poised, so ready to smooth every wayward particle of air.

"Well, I'm Elizabeth Larsen," Betty said, stretching out her full first name, then giving her phone number.

"Thank you," the woman responded without altering her expression. "Would you like to browse today, Mrs. Larsen?"

"I could browse," Betty answered, thinking immediately of Elise sitting at that lunch counter with an empty glass and a dumb comic book.

"Let me know if I can help you. I'll tell Mrs. Dahl that you stopped." The woman turned with barely a movement, floating on slender ankles to a glass case of accessories, where she bent to organize a display of summer gloves in pastels and laces. Standing in the middle of the store, Betty wondered how the saleswoman would remember her phone number without writing it down, or at least repeating it to make sure she'd heard it right.

Perspiring everywhere, even under her hat, she dragged herself around the displays of beautiful blouses and dresses, clothes made of airy cloth and detailed with tucks and layers, tasteful flounces and cuffs. She'd been in Nides years before with her friend from home. How could she have forgotten the rarefied hush or entertained any notion that she could work in such a place as this?

She left without saying good-bye, rattled and demoralized. She wasn't who she thought she was. Or who she pretended to be. She was an unmarried woman with a daughter to raise on $1,203.60 in an apartment over a garage that belonged, in fact, to Italian immigrants who used garlic in everything they ate. That's who Betty Larsen was. She belonged at Woolworth's selling cheap makeup to high school girls and miners' wives. Not that she'd mind it. But she shouldn't have imagined herself as anything more.

Back at Woolworth's she retrieved Elise, holding on to her hand so tightly that the girl tried to pull it away. Betty walked home in such a sad stupor that she forgot to notice they were passing by the hospital where her longtime lover sat propped on two pillows in his new state of decline. And if she had remembered, it surely would not have eased her despair.

iv.

It was almost noon by the time they climbed the stairs to the apartment. Betty made them bologna sandwiches, and they ate without talking. Then Elise changed clothes and went outside, and Betty sat staring at the four corners of the room, traveling back through her morning and all that she had accomplished, her money in the bank and her applications in at two retail establishments. She opened her purse to take out her new bankbook and saw the lipstick samples from Woolworth's. They were lighter than she tended to wear, but maybe. Leaving the lunch dishes, she went into the bathroom to try out Revlon Raspberry Icing.

Seeing her image in the mirror gave her an unexpected boost, her distinctly unpretty but interesting face and her curls shaped to perfection. To heck with Nides anyway, she thought, then caught herself. Maybe someday. Maybe she could start at Woolworth's or Vera's and work her way up to Nides. She was blotting the pink sample lipstick just as the doorbell rang.

At the foot of the stairs two faces, nearly identical, tipped upward in her direction. Elise and Claus's daughter. She signaled for them to come up, then ran back to the bathroom mirror to check her face once more, fixed a curl, and hurried to meet them.

"I'm Julia, Claus's daughter," the young woman said.

"Nice to meet you," Betty replied, then didn't know what else to say. Was Julia's arrival at their door bad news or good? Betty's muscles felt weak and her mind locked. Elise, meanwhile, had placed herself right next to Julia, their two beautiful faces side by side, Elise grinning at her great good fortune.

"Could we sit for a minute?" Julia asked. "I want to talk just for a minute. Not to trouble you, I promise."

"Oh, of course," Betty exclaimed, coming out of her momentary trance. "Where are my manners? Please, sit down." She gestured toward the sofa, but before Julia had time to move, Elise jumped in front of her to say, "You look just like me," then jumped again, too happy to know what else she should do.

"I think we look alike too. Aren't we lucky?"

"We're magic," Elise added.

"Elise, would you like to run over to Katie's for a minute?"

"Really, Momma?" She leaned in to her look-alike and confided, "Katie Fiore is my best friend." Then she scooted off, her steps sounding lightly until she was out and gone.

"I'm sorry to barge in," Julia started, "but my father is so unwell that I need to speak to you. This morning I helped him set up a trust account for your daughter, so you are secure. No matter what happens, I mean. My father wants to continue to help."

"A trust?"

"It's a bank account for Elise—and for you too, but in her name. For what you need." Julia glanced around her. "Like your apartment and all. Things you need."

"I'm getting a job," Betty said. "I have savings." The young woman seemed kindly, but Betty didn't want Claus's family thinking she was some kind of project, some primitive country to save, or some gold digger, God forbid.

Julia heard Betty's defensive tone. "Anyway, the money is available." She pulled out a bankbook, blue like the one Betty had just filed, and explained how the trust would work, how the money would be available up to a monthly amount until Elise was eighteen. The monthly limit was only slightly less than what Claus had always given her. But now it felt high-handed somehow, even disparaging. Nonetheless, she accepted the bankbook and the daughter's explanations, that her father had had a heart attack, that his heart was permanently damaged, and that there was nothing to be done about it other than for him to take it easy.

Betty listened without comment even though her mind was full of questions. Did this visit mean she would never see Claus again? Did his daughter saying he was so unwell mean he would die soon?

"Only my father and you and I know about this account," Julia said finally. "We'd like it to stay that way, if you don't mind. That's why we did it now and why I came today." She smiled then started to cry, slow and composed, her hands still in her lap as she let the tears cover her face. "I'm sorry," she said. "I'm so sorry." She remained on the sofa awhile more before she stood up to go. She reached out to shake Betty's hand. "You have such a sweet daughter." Then she bowed her head like a solemn dignitary and left.

Betty managed to say thank you from the top of the stairs, too overwhelmed by the entire day to move. In her hand she held the bankbook that would provide for Elise. That's what she had now of Claus—a daughter and survival money. She had never felt so alone in her life, so alone she didn't hear the Fabbros' dog barking or her daughter's voice singing outside on the curb by the door.

v.

When Elise ran outside, she looked both ways twice up and down Twenty-Fourth Street before she crossed over to the fence that enclosed Katie Fiore's house and sandbox and her grandma's house and their garden, borders of flowers all over and everyplace. But Katie was nowhere in sight and the whole property looked too large to navigate. So Elise went back to her safe spot on the curb to wait for something. Certainly things happened lately. Already in this one day she'd had half of a malted and an entire soda, read a comic book her mother bought just for her, and stood in her own apartment listening to the magical woman chat politely as if they'd all been friends for years.

When the woman had come back downstairs to find Elise on the curb, she'd said, "I bet you love living upstairs with a bird's-eye view of the neighborhood, don't you?"

What could Elise answer but yes as she watched her older twin walk away, turn at Sue Too's building, and head in the direction

of the hospital. Even when she could no longer see her, the
woman's voice stayed with Elise like a fairy song.

Gertrude went by across the street and waved twice before she
crossed purposefully to the block kitty corner from Sue Too's
building and marched out of view. Then in a second or two
there was Gertrude again, coming back across the street, her
head forward and arms swinging as she roared along, fast and
forceful. Maybe Gertrude really was going somewhere after all.
Elise considered this, but didn't dwell on the topic. It was just
old Gertrude anyway. Like the sky and the cracked curb where
Elise sat, always there and nothing to ponder.

vi.

After Claus's youngest daughter reported in to him on her
encounter with Betty Larsen, she squeezed his hand and went
home to her baby son. Alone again, Claus worked on breathing
evenly, on keeping his heart steady the way it used to be, whole
and steady and ready to work for him no matter what he chose
to do. He fantasized about when his heart had not expected to
be coddled and ridiculously nurtured in slow walks around the
block, when he had worked a full day in large strides, painted
whole rooms in his house, and waxed his car to a sheen.

In this exercise he did not allow himself to think about Betty
as she was to him once, her wildness barely contained, her
eager mouth, he could not remind himself and risk his heart
racing like the muscular stallion it no longer was. Instead he
thought about Tildy's garden and how she managed every year
to stagger the colors into bold bursts along the sides of the
house. He focused on this, not able to distinguish their exact
petals and leaves, but able to remember the sweeps of yellow,

red, and lavender, the dabs of white, orange, and pink. Now was the time her flowers bloomed. First one, then another—crocuses, tulips, daffodils. Soon the peonies and roses, names he'd learned through the years as she'd fussed over them. This is what he'd come to, he supposed. A sick man daydreaming about peonies.

Betty Larsen had not been his first lover, and at the beginning of their time together, he did not think she'd be his last. Not that he'd ever been indiscreet. And he'd certainly always cared for Tildy and his daughters. It was just that the boundaries of family life had never felt natural to him. He was a tall man with a closely held and intense energy. He knew this about himself. Their little house had held him back, caused him to pace uneasily from room to room while his wife did all her domestic tasks in good cheer around him and his daughters played with their few toys for hours on end. He'd almost always needed somewhere else.

He met Betty when she sold him chocolates at the drugstore where she worked and though she was not flirtatious, she was aware. That's what he'd call Betty's interaction with him over the Whitman's Samplers that day a decade ago. She was aware of his height, his face, the angle of his hat, perhaps, his polished shoes and sense of personal power.

And he took to that awareness as a match to the flint. He couldn't get enough of Betty Larsen then, even stealing away from work once or twice to meet up with her. Within months he'd rented the garage apartment on Twenty-Fourth Street for her, which gave him a sure place of escape. He held a key. He came and went, and Betty was always there for him, the apartment neat, her lips red, the bed made so that it could be undone.

So it continued. When she had her baby, she rearranged her life some, but he was still the center of her world and he knew it. Even now he suspected she was waiting for him to get through this hospital business, put on his summer suit, and drive over to see her.

But his time with Betty Larsen had come to this abrupt end. Not because his eyes could not be trusted to drive over to the garage apartment or because her constant worries and questions had exhausted him, but because he was the focus of his family's attentions. They watched his every move to see if he was following all the doctor's recommendations and if he felt comfortable or needed something to eat or more light in the room or less. And they now had seen Betty. And Elise. Their watch of him would not allow a midafternoon tryst even if he wanted that.

Maybe he had been ready to let Betty go soon. Or maybe not. He couldn't let himself think about it.

When Dr. Milton had made his rounds that morning, he'd said, "Ready to go home to your wife's good cooking, Claus? Let's shoot for tomorrow." The doctor had patted Claus's arm, as he tended to do, made some comment about the weather, then moved on in his hale and hardy manner. Claus didn't have time to say that his wife had never been much of a cook overall. Anyway, what was the point?

A week earlier Claus Jacobson had been a man with options and a sufficient future, however blurry. Now Betty's little girl had a trust and his heart had its permanent damage and he lay in a bed delineating flowers to keep himself calm.

vii.

Katie woke up that day just after sunrise, ate quickly, and left for the old green house with a plan. This was no longer the scene of a crime, but the remnant of tragedy and someone needed to intervene. For adult reasons she did not know and could not conceive, nobody had returned to the young minister's house to organize his things or clean the kitchen mess. Nobody had dusted or washed the floors like Katie's mother and grandmother did every spring of every year, scrubbing and airing and shoving furniture into different spaces in the rooms to catch the summer breezes. The house needed her. The nervous minister and his blonde wife needed her.

She found a broom and a mop in the kitchen closet of the old house, as well as dishcloths and soap. She washed the coffee pot and cups, put them in the cupboard and wiped off the table and the sink. She pretended she was her mother on a mission, as her mother often was, to create order where it was required. Without thinking, she started singing one of her songs—"catch a falling star and put it in your pocket, never let it fade away." She swept the floor and pulled the chairs in closely around the table. She considered throwing the calendar away, but after facing the one lonesome kitten in its basket for a long while, she decided to leave it alone.

The living room posed a greater challenge. Before addressing the floors, she had to move all those boxes of books and piles of newspapers out of her way, which took time and tired her out. A low, wide table left in the corner of the room gave her the idea to rearrange the space altogether. She swept the dusty living room and washed it with a towel she took from the bathroom upstairs, a thin towel with frayed ends that she hoped nobody would miss. The brown stain on the floor might not be blood, but Katie held her breath as she wiped over it anyway. Then she pushed the low table in front of the sofa to hide the stain and began stacking the religious books in careful rows on top of it until all the boxes were empty and the stacks piled beautifully high. The room took on a friendly comfort that it did not have before.

She straightened the other two chairs in the room so that they too faced the table of books and this pleased her even more. She sang more songs as she worked—"He's Got the Whole World in His Hands" and "Don't Fence Me In"—losing herself to the magnitude of her task.

Finally, she made a dozen trips to the back porch to pile the newspapers so they could be toted out to the trash someday. By then she felt tired and hungry and the morning heat began to move in on her. With a glance back at the work she had done, she left the old house and all the stories it might hold.

Back at home she ate a few cookies and fell asleep on the sofa, where she remained all afternoon. Her mother woke her up for dinner at five, but after dinner she flopped back on the sofa. Comfortable on the velveteen cushions, she watched out the window as the sun went down and the streetlights came on. If she'd gone outside to the porch, she would have seen the moon carved into the deep sky and the sky beginning to crowd with its myriad of stars, brightly scattered and endless.

viii.

The moon that rose over Lake Bemidji in Beltrami County that night might have been the same moon that rose over Katie Fiore's porch, but it didn't feel that way to Sue Too. The moon over Lake Bemidji hung high and strange to her, not the angle she wanted that night, not the moon she wanted to see. There was no secret club at her sister Diane's and no mystery that called to her, even if only a people mystery, even if only figuring out why nobody ever locked the door of an abandoned house.

She'd been gone two long days. She'd painted a bedroom wall some ugly green using a fleecy roller that splattered the paint in her face. She hated green walls. Diane had the dumbest ideas anyway and everyone just went along with them. Not even her father could bring himself to say, "Diane, this room looks like something you eat in a salad." Diane was appreciative though. She bought Sue Too a sack of marshmallows to eat all herself. But even that wasn't enough to keep Sue Too from missing the life she'd almost had with a couple of kids willing to knock around their wacky neighborhood and whisper secret codes.

"When we going home?" she asked her mother, who seemed happier working on her daughter's unsettled house than returning to deal with her own.

"Oh, soon enough," she answered.

It would not be soon enough, Sue Too knew, because with every passing hour her friends and secrets drifted farther away, like those wisps of white clouds trailing after the remote and indifferent moon.

ix.

The guys had never seen Hawk as agitated as he was that night, but he didn't say why. He cursed and pulled out those French cigarettes of his and kicked the grass and snarled at them as if they were to blame.

"Heh, Hawk, maybe we should rock a car," Mack suggested, figuring that the effort of pushing on a 3,000-pound vehicle might do the trick. Hawk didn't answer. He walked head down and the others followed. At the edge of the town's park he wheeled on them and said, "Don't you guys ever want nothing?" His eyes roamed fiercely from face to face.

"You mean something or nothing?" one of the more thoughtful boys asked, believing that Hawk actually cared to hear an answer.

"Nothing," Hawk spit back. "You guys don't want nothing, do you?"

Mack shrugged. "Suppose."

"You mean you think we want nothing?" the thoughtful boy continued to clarify. His name was Larry, but they called him Shiner for the genetically dark shadows around his eyes. "I want something," he went on. "Everyone wants something, Hawk."

"Balls."

"Yeah, he wants those for sure," one of the others quipped, and the group had a laugh. Except for Hawk, who had climbed onto a picnic table and sat staring away from them into the black night.

"Fuck you guys. You don't know want from a dead cat."

None of them knew what to say to that. Mack wondered how Hawk's mind could draw a dead cat into the conversation. He wasn't about to kill cats, that was for sure. Not even for Hawk. He raised his eyebrows at a kid named Joey who raised his back with a shrug.

"Don't you want to make a mark, assholes?"

Again they stared, each in his own way dreading whatever kind of mark Hawk was thinking about.

"Let's rock a car," Mack said again and the group rumbled in concurrence.

"What the hell," Joey said.

"Long as it don't rock over on me," Shiner joked in the tense air surrounding them.

Hawk tossed his cigarette butt. "Why?" He glared at them all. "How's that make a mark? Tell me that." He waited for a response but nobody said a thing.

Then Hawk said, "We're going to rob Mooney's."

"The liquor warehouse?"

Hawk went on. "We're going to plan it tonight and hit it tomorrow as soon as the sun goes down." His voice had risen to a level of strength that the others could not ignore.

"That place's pretty tight, though," Shiner said. He couldn't imagine how they'd get through those windowless wide doors. The whole idea was crazy. "Easier to hit one of the stores, if you're looking for free booze."

The rest of the group held silent as Hawk breathed in deeply and lit another cigarette. "Ever heard of an axe?"

"You want me to bring my dad's axe, Hawk?" Mack was trying to keep peace. "I can do that."

"Let's take a look," Hawk said, starting for Third Avenue and Mooney's liquor warehouse. Mooney's stood like a fortress near the railroad tracks that ran across the northern perimeter of the downtown. Owned by three Irish cousins, the warehouse supplied spirits for every retail and restaurant establishment on that side of the Iron Range. The Mooneys were all three jolly, shrewd men, beloved and respected. Nobody in his right mind would want to bump up against them. But Hawk didn't know that. None of the boys knew the subtleties of the business climate in town. Their dads didn't run in those circles and their moms worked too hard to care. So they circled the warehouse as if it were the enemy's encampment.

"No way you hack them mothers down," Shiner said after they'd assessed the twenty-foot-high doors. "Can't be done."

Mack slammed his fists against the doors, as if testing their resistance, but really just showing Hawk how he was on his side.

Hawk said nothing. Every impenetrable wall or door or situation in his life ignited such rage, he could not call up words. Shiner's comment that it couldn't be done hit Hawk like every other no in his life, every glare of disapproval, slight, or disregard. His chest and fists tightened. But he said nothing. Hawk's eyes darted from boy to boy, watching each movement, Mack's fists hammering at the door, Shiner walking back and forth to study the problem like a goddamned city inspector, Joey shaking his head, the other two goofing around in the dark, punching at each other, loud and irreverent.

"What'd you think, Hawk?" Mack asked finally. "Want me to bring an axe tomorrow? Maybe two? Give it a try?" His heavy shoulders lifted and fell.

Hawk waited to answer until all of the others focused on him entirely, the way the shop teacher waited, looming over the class until they shut up and faced forward. When Hawk spoke, his voice came to them low and level. "You think this town cares if you live or die, you dumb assholes? Or me or any of us? We got nothing. We got to want something. We got to show this town we're going to get what we want or else." He let that sink in. "We're going to break down these motherfucking doors and howl like those coyotes out on the dumps. By tomorrow night people will know we're not nothing. We're something."

His ferocity was such that they did not argue. Mack got scared, though, every time Hawk started talking about cats or coyotes or stuff like that, and Shiner knew Hawk was wrong, and they'd never break through Mooney's doors, axe or no axe. The other three didn't know what to think. Hawk was nuts, but he gave them a good time most nights, so they stuck around.

"Meet at my house at seven tomorrow night. And be ready." With that he left them. They watched the light of his cigarette as he slouched into darkness toward downtown.

"I guess we go along with him," Joey said, but he was shifting from foot to foot as if looking for a middle ground.

Shiner looked over at Mack. "You think you can hack through that door?"

"Naw. Never. But what the hell."

"Mack, your grandma still make those pigs in the blankets with sauerkraut?"

The big kid nodded and grinned. "Those are something, eh?"

Shiner socked Mack's arm. "They sure ain't nothing."

x.

The hospital did not sleep. Nurses moved about, lights remained on in the hallways, occasionally some noise alarmed Claus with its urgent unfamiliarity. It was a world unto itself, and though he'd been there five nights, he still found the low-level hubbub unnerving and the fact of his being there difficult to accept.

Tomorrow night he'd be in his own bed in a still house with only the whispers of Tildy floating from room to room. And then what? This new life he was to lead. He closed his eyes, his blurry eyes, blue though not bright like Tildy's. Dark blue, his blurry dark blue eyes.

His father had died in this hospital, older than Claus was now, but not so old. Claus couldn't remember the exact age or year, sometime when his own daughters were teenagers large in every room and long before Betty, but at the time of some other woman in his life surely, the very young widow of one of his friends maybe, or the girl who answered phones in the office back when. His strapping, silent father had worked every day of his life and landed in the hospital only when he had no strength left to hoist, haul, dig, or make another thing. Not even to carve a salt spoon. Nothing. He'd lay stretched in bed with these crisp hospital sheets pulled around him, eyes shut refusing to acknowledge anything that was happening to him.

Claus had come to visit, sat in one of these same hospital chairs to regard the stranger in the bed who used to be his father. Claus had asked how the old man was feeling, but received no answer. His father wouldn't open his eyes, those blue eyes as dark as Claus's or darker, the color of a deep lake in fall when a gray sky hangs low. As a child Claus had not wanted his father's scrutiny ever, for it had always tended to the critical, his eyes stern and unreadable. So Claus had sat in the hospital chair, his hat on his lap, coat still buttoned, and he'd watched the old man refuse him again. The sun went down. Nurses came and went. The food tray sat untouched on the bedside table, a cheery, wiggly Jell-O in a cup, Claus remembered, and some kind of soup steaming for a while, the only movement in the room except for his father's slow breath and Claus's own keeping pace.

Claus had been the only son. He'd never understood his father's cool assessment of him, his unwillingness to let his son lean against him now and then. Claus left home at fifteen. It seemed expected. Now he was the man in the hospital bed.

For more than an hour in the middle of the June night Claus returned to those harsh years before he was a man on his own, when he was a gawky boy ever on the watch, nose to the grindstone as they used to say, evolving but always on his own. Even after fifty years of achievement and respect, a family and many loves, a certain stature he'd grown into and maintained, he squirmed on the hospital's unforgiving mattress as he thought of the man who would not ever offer him praise.

Claus felt his heart begin to race, even leap, as his mind furrowed around in the past, but he couldn't stop. His father's glances, turned shoulder, the hard exact movements, the steel gray hair clipped to a bristle, and the dark eyes terrified him in his thoughts as if he were once again a boy waiting for a sign that he never got. He couldn't stop himself. He saw it all the way it was then, the chickens whose necks he couldn't snap clean enough, the water sloshing out of the pail and wasted, his own hair hacked and untidy, his father seeing every move, every error and inept slip, Claus's arms too long for his shirts and his eyes watering in constant defeat and fear.

These rampant and awful thoughts of Claus's did not stop until his heart did. He didn't see his moment coming or resist when it did. His long fingers gripped the edge of the sheet, his mouth opened for air and in a staggering heartbeat, all the anguish of his dreams left him.

NINE

Thursday, June 16, 1960

i.

Clouds had moved in during the night, low and thick, threatening rain that came only as mist, wet and dreary enough so that Godfrey and Edna delayed their midday travels through town. After a late lingering breakfast, they put on a Tommy Dorsey record saved from years back and danced in a fashion around their pink kitchen. Godfrey had never learned how to dance, nobody had taught him and he had difficulty breaking it down into specific steps and pauses, heel to toe and all of that, slides and glides. But he'd figured out young that if his arms went around and he pressed close, the actual leg and footwork might not matter. He held on tightly to Edna and did whatever felt good, rubbing his hips into her round stomach and his cheek against her cheek, his right hand roaming her backside and under her flimsy nightdress until they could hardly stumble back into bed fast enough.

They rolled together for hours as the mist hovered, Godfrey in his buttoned shirt and Edna in her pale strappy gown, and Thursday morning passed along to Thursday afternoon.

Only then did they finish dressing and get themselves outside for their daily spree. On the way to the downtown stores they did not see Gertrude or the girls on the curb or Kaka Roo. Nobody seemed to be in Vernon's Grocery. That little bit of rain had kept everyone inside. "Quiet," Edna remarked at the corner by the church.

"Not us," Godfrey answered and chuckled his innuendo and pinched her once before she could see it coming.

ii.

Betty got the call from Claus's daughter after breakfast, just as she'd finished dabbing at her hair with a Miss Clairol dark brown. She'd busied Elise with her watercolor paints, turned on the radio for amusement, and sat down with a second cup of coffee to let the hair color sink in or set or whatever it was supposed to do to keep her looking young and attractive. Claus's daughter's voice wavered so much that Betty could almost not understand the message. "He's gone," Julia cried, "he's gone, Mrs. Larsen."

Juggling the phone so that it wouldn't get stained by the hair dye and caught off guard, Betty stood at her kitchen counter shaking her head back and forth in disagreement. Claus was not gone. He was three blocks away in the hospital, sick but alive, remote perhaps as she'd known him to be, but surely not gone. "I'm so sorry to tell you, Mrs. Larsen." Claus's daughter gasped a sob and hung up, leaving Betty in shock, a tiny stream of brown dye trickling along her hairline.

Somewhere in that brief exchange, Elise had stopped painting an orange cat she wished was real to listen. "What's the matter, Momma?"

Betty hung up the phone. "Claus's gone."

"Where'd he go?"

"I think she meant he died. Gone from the world, I think she meant." Betty frowned, not meeting her daughter's eyes.

"Who's she?" Elise held her paintbrush in midair.

"His daughter Julia who was here yesterday." Betty's head kept shaking in denial, a reflex she didn't notice and couldn't stop.

Elise beamed at this answer, happy to know her look-alike had called and not at all concerned about the message.

"Don't smile, Elise," Betty barked. "Your magic twin just lost her father and I just lost my—my only friend." Saying this broke the tears loose, wild, noisy tears that made her choke. She grabbed the edge of a kitchen chair to keep from sliding to the floor, then folded over the top of the chair and cried and cried.

Elise, brush still poised, watched her mother in amazement, as if she were witnessing a marvel of nature, an exploding star trailing to earth, or the hard concrete of her curb outside cracking to reveal the center of the universe. "Momma?" she whispered without moving. "Momma?"

Her sweet, soft voice poked into Betty's pain like that bit of light parting the dense clouds outside the window. Betty straightened to her full height and wiped at her eyes with her hand. "I'm going to rinse my hair," she said, "before I start to look like one of those Italians." Then she went into the bathroom and closed the door.

iii.

On her corner of the block Gertrude spent the drizzly day help-ing Mrs. Wilke organize. First they organized the bathroom medicine cabinet and then their two sparsely filled closets. They stopped at lunchtime to heat a can of tomato soup, which they ate with Saltines and thin slices of yellow cheese. "Don't slurp, dear," Mrs. commented twice during lunch, because as soon as Gertrude got excited about the creamy flavor, she forgot her manners. After lunch they continued organizing the kitchen utensil drawer and the inside of the refrigerator. Mrs. Wilke kept the radio on to hear popular tunes of the day, though neither woman knew the words to any of them.

Gertrude's mind pushed against these tasks, her heart so full of Nicky she could barely think straight. She could help organize a closet, but she surely could not organize herself. She didn't think he'd be out on a day like today, when besides the dreary rain, the air had become cool, more like early April than June. Nonetheless, she kept an eye on the clock as it click-clicked past two and two twenty, past three and nearing four. That's when Mrs. Wilke decided they should make a stew to ward off the chill of the day and set Gertrude to work chopping carrots and potatoes, which took a very long time and made Gertrude nervous with containment. But they finished the vegetables and Mrs. chopped the meat and then while the stew bubbled on the stove they organized more cupboards, as if this were some type of entertainment for a dreary day.

"Maybe I'll try the block now," Gertrude declared the very second she'd finished eating the stew, which didn't turn out to taste as good as she hoped it would when they were waiting for it to cook that long hour. "Get some air," she added.

"Suit yourself, Gertie. It's a miserable day out there and we're cozy here inside, us two."

But Gertrude pulled on her sweater and her raincoat and grabbed that stupid rain scarf just in case and went out to walk.

Like Godfrey and Edna before her, she saw that the neighborhood was quiet after the rain. Even the birds were quiet and the fast grass sprouting and the busy ants. All quiet. Across from Nicky's corner, she stopped for a minute to study his unruly hedge and high-pitched roof, wondering if they were in there cooking again, surrounded by the sweet smell of tomatoes, instead of homely old carrots in a stew.

iv.

Mack and the boys showed up at Hawk's house at seven that night already in lousy humor before their impossible rampage even began. Shiner hated rain in general, Mack had given up a chance to eat lemon meringue pie at his grandmother's, and Joey's dad had whacked him into a wall for forgetting to close the upstairs windows against the drizzle. Dressed in dark jackets, they clustered by Hawk's garage listening to him pump them up with more of his rebellious talk, how they were going to be something now, fuck the world and so on. Today Joey tended to agree with him. The others nodded, whether they agreed or not. Mack, clutching his dad's axe wrapped in newspaper, kept saying, "Sure, Hawk," again and again, as if to convince himself.

The walk to Mooney's would take half an hour, maybe less, and Hawk wanted to get there before sunset so they'd have time to strategize. Shiner loved that word, strategize. "Like a chess match, eh, Hawk?"

"Yeah, right," Hawk answered.

"You play chess?" Joey asked Hawk, but he got no reply.

They were on the move. When they came to the edge of the Greenhaven neighborhood with its new ramblers and attached garages, Hawk encouraged them to spit into a yard or two, goading them into a test of who could project the farthest. Out of Greenhaven they turned onto Third Avenue, now just a mile from Mooney's. "Let's hit that grocery store on our way downtown," Hawk called to the rest of them as he pushed ahead, a general leading his troop.

"With my dad's axe?" Mack really didn't like the idea. That Vernon guy knew his name and where he lived.

"No, asshole. I mean grab supplies. Give old man Vernon a scare."

The boys who had seen Roger Vernon did not for a minute think this was a guy to scare. One shoo from him and they'd all run sideways last time. But they kept those thoughts to themselves. Maybe the store would be closed, Mack prayed, and, without realizing it, began to drag his feet to slow himself down, like a plane reversing engines. Two boys stayed at Mack's side and Joey took out his penknife to clean his fingernails as they walked, as if being groomed could keep him out of trouble. Only Hawk strode out, with Shiner more or less keeping pace. At the corner of Twenty-Seventh Street, Hawk wheeled around to yell, "What the hell?"

"Charley horse," Mack answered, giving them all a chance to sock each other a few times before continuing on their mission.

v.

Mrs. Marodi didn't cook tomato sauce that damp day, but minestrone soup with cannellini beans and dandelion greens. She put a pint of her canned tomatoes into the broth, though, so the house had that tangy, sweet aroma, just as Gertrude had imagined. Nicky sat at the kitchen table and watched his mother, shuffling a deck of cards to master a technique he'd seen when he was in Moose Lake, a way one of the other patients had of lifting the cards in formation and letting them fall back like water over falls, steady and graceful. As the light rain hit the window and his mother's soup steamed in the pot, Nicky shuffled and dropped, lifted and dropped, mostly failing but persisting nonetheless.

"*Mangiare formaggio, Nicolo,*" his mother said at one point, setting a plate of asiago in front of him. His dedication to the cards made her nervous, the sound of the cards, the repetition, his unnatural focus on it. "*Mangiare formaggio,*" she repeated and cut herself a slice, which she chewed standing there in front of him. But he didn't eat the cheese and he didn't master the shuffling technique and the rain didn't stop its small steady rhythm until late in the long day.

When he left after dinner to walk a bit, his mother took up her embroidery with relief that the dark, edgy day was almost done. What was to become of her grown son, she could not think. He was home and he was safe. They were together again. He ate well, shaved every morning, liked his clean white shirts and new socks. There were worse occupations than card tricks, she considered, as her deft fingers poked the needle in and out of the fabric. Maybe she should encourage him to take care of their lawn. Plant flowers out front perhaps. Nicky had always resonated to beauty. Maybe he could become a gardener here and there about town. Her hope ran ahead of her in large leaps, all that might be, all the good ahead, just there like her scrappy tomato plants ready to burst forth into fruit.

Meanwhile Nicky made his way south for a block before remembering skinny Gertrude and her funny pants, then he turned around toward her block instead, believing that he'd see her rounding some corner over there, catching up to herself after the slow wet day. He picked up his pace, lurching back past his mother's house on his way to Gertrude's busy dangerous block, thinking only of the good humor he'd feel when he saw that skinny bird loping along again.

vi.

The boys pulled up to Vernon's like a swaggering beast with wayward arms and slick hair, belching out bad air as they came through the door to face Roger, who was two beers in and ornery at the mere sight of them. "Get out," he stormed and came quickly around the counter to face off with this herd of losers, coming so close to Hawk that the boy stood eye to eye with Roger's shirt buttons. "Get!"

Hawk glanced at the gang behind him. "Don't move," he commanded, "this guy's an asshole bluff." But the boys moved anyway, a jumble of body parts rolling toward the door, tugging a raging Hawk out too just as Nicky Marodi lurched down the sidewalk toward them, tongue unwittingly loose and eyes wild.

"What the fuck?" one of the boys called out as the others instinctively blocked Nicky from getting past them.

Inside the store Roger returned to his counter for a cigarette and another chug of beer, which took just long enough to give the boys traction. Hawk and Shiner jeered at the peculiar-looking stranger, then Mack, who really never meant harm to anyone, pushed the man a bit just to test him out, and with that push Nicky's knees collapsed beneath him and he toppled, hat flying and fingers groping.

That was when Godfrey and Edna toddled in a hurry from across the street urgently calling, "Kaka Roo, Kaka Roo," as if to save him, instead giving Hawk just the ammunition he needed. "A Kaka Roo, that's what we got here, no wonder—" he started, but was stopped as Nicky began to shriek and shriek, anguished and uncontrolled, the horrible cry of an animal caught in the hunt.

Roger flew out the door, but the scene was now beyond his control, for there were the boys laughing "Kaka Roo" and the cross-eyed Godfrey waving his arms and the man on the sidewalk flailing as though unable to get up, and if that weren't enough, the oddball named Gertrude was barreling down the street as if not realizing she was walking right into the fire. And sure enough, Hawk yelled, "If it ain't the Cuckoo Bird come to see her boyfriend. Kaka Roo your boyfriend, Cuckoo Bird?" as the other boys laughed even louder, long as it wasn't them writhing around on the ground and all this better than trying to bust down a warehouse door at Mooney's.

Gertrude stopped and stood deaf to their names, her eyes wholly on Nicky, poor Nicky, like a beetle on its back trying to right itself and his hat off, his hair thinning, fingers reaching, poor Nicky. Gertrude felt a bolt of summer lightning strike her heart and split it in two. "Nicky, Nicky," she cried, and would not stop no matter how much Edna shushed her, she would not stop.

Unable to bear it, Roger pushed himself through the barrier the boys had made, giving a hard shove to the twerp laughing the loudest, and reached down to guide Nicky to his feet. But as soon as Nicky felt Roger's hand on him, his instinct to survive topped everything else, his shame and horror, his belief in a future, and even his mother's prayers. He attacked Roger with every muscle he had and bit his hand and kicked his groin and shrieked and shrieked until Roger had to let go and step back.

Next door, Katie Fiore's pop slammed through their screen door, took one look at the gathering, and went back inside to call the police. When the boys heard the police siren from blocks away, they scattered in so many directions, none of the witnesses could attest to where they had gone. Two cops restrained Nicky, and against the protests of Roger and Vince Fiore, they took him to the police station and locked him in a jail cell.

Only then, when he was alone behind bars with his hat on the bunk beside him, did Nicky stop shrieking. His breathing slowed, and his hands quit shaking. He heard the low hum of the police talking and the occasional ringing of their telephones. Not remembering his home or his old mother waiting, he collapsed on the saggy bunk and fell asleep.

vii.

Watching him go, Gertrude cried harder, her arms flapping in miserable confusion, as if she might fly off, follow Nicky, escape anywhere, if only her shoes were not so heavy. "We'll walk her home," Edna announced, and with her hand on Gertrude's elbow, she turned her around and began to make slow steps back the way Gertrude had come.

With pride in his wife's resourcefulness, Godfrey chuckled and nudged Roger's arm. "They got old Kaka Roo again, that's for sure. Throw him back in Moose Lake, I guess, poor fellow."

"What's he talking about?" Roger said to Katie's pop, Vince Fiori.

"The man they took away had that nickname years ago, when he got sick. You know, he used to be so smart people thought he was a genius."

"Lot of good that did him," Roger remarked. "He wouldn't let me help him up. Son of a bitch bit me."

"Well, you tried," Vince said, as the two of them watched the Godfrey group inch away. He'd never liked Roger Vernon before, but here he felt the big man meant well. "At least you tried."

Gertrude let the Godfreys lead her home backward, as it were, south to north on the wrong side of the block, because all order had been lost anyway and maybe would never be brought to right again. They went so slowly, the Godfreys, as if the sun would never set and the shooting stars of night never appear.

"There now, dear," Edna kept saying until, at last, they were at the gate to Mrs. Wilke's yard. Edna helped Gertrude open the gate, then reached into her market basket and pulled out a small bottle of Shalimar perfume, the prize of her day's work. "Here you go, dear. Dab a spot of this under your ears and see how much better you'll feel." She turned to her husband. "Right?"

"Somebody'll feel better," he remarked and moved forward thinking of what might happen when he and Edna were back home alone again.

Clutching the bottle without an idea of what it was, Gertrude lifted one foot after another until she was inside Mrs. Wilke's kitchen, where she hung up her coat, letting the plastic rain scarf flutter to the floor like a wounded bird.

"That you, Gertie," she heard Mrs. call from the living room. "Come watch this Zane Grey show with me, just about to start. A good Western, Gertie, that's the thing for us."

But Gertrude did not go into the living room. She dragged herself upstairs to her bedroom, put the strange bottle from Edna on her dresser, and took off her thick tie shoes, which she placed side by side, soles touching with the symmetry of lovers. She hung her shirt and pedal pushers on the back of her door and pulled on the seersucker pajamas that Mrs. had bought to keep her cool. Then she got into bed, her eyes fixed on the shadows flickering in all the room's corners. She had come to someplace different again, someplace dangerous again. That's all she could think. The world no longer sang to her. Try as she would, she could barely hear the throngs of grasshoppers screeching loudly in the night. Far on the edge of the mines she heard the train whistle, though, tons of steel charging through town at top speed, with nothing imaginable to stop it.

viii.

Minutes after Roger turned off the outside light, he saw the boy Richard's face looking in the window. "You open, Mr. Vernon?"

The boy was already inside the door, so what could Roger say. "Some big doings here tonight, eh? Some kind of trouble, eh?"

Roger sunk onto his stool behind the counter. "Yeah. Some kind of trouble. You want a Twinkie or something?"

"Maybe," Richard said, but he didn't scramble to grab one like he usually did.

Roger regarded him. "You know those boys that come around here once in a while? One calls himself Hawk. You know that kid?"

Richard nodded.

"You know the big kid Mack too? From Kelly Lake."

Richard wasn't so sure about Mack, and Roger wasn't so sure why he was even talking to the boy when what he really wanted was to close up shop and go curl around sweet Sophia. "Still looking to earn quarters?"

Richard nodded again.

"You come by around nine at night, clean up out front, and I'll give you a quarter."

"Tonight?"

"If you want. Come every night until I say not to. Take it out in trade if you want." Roger laughed at the thought of it. Skinny Richard and his goddamned Sno Balls. He handed Richard the broom and a quarter all at one time. Then he sat back down and lit a cigarette, the best he'd had all night.

ix.

As soon as the police car taillights disappeared down Third
Avenue, Vince Fiore went next door to tell his mother-in-law
the story. Then the two of them, armed with wine from the
Abellis' barrels and a chunk of orange cake, walked straight to
Mrs. Marodi's door, where Nicky's mother was already standing
watch, waiting for her son. He'd been gone too long. When she
heard the sirens, she pulled out her rosary beads and started
to pray and now stood in the door clenching her beads, eyes
searching the fading light outside. The minute she saw the two
visitors, her hand flew to her mouth, as if to contain the fear
within her.

"I'll get the car," Vince Fiori said, sprinting off, as Mrs. Abelli
let herself inside, murmuring in Italian to her neighbor, consol-
ing her not with the words she used, but the hushed rhythm,
the steady soft beat of syllables not intended to mean anything,
only to soothe. She poured Mrs. Marodi a glass of the wine
she'd brought and drank one herself as she continued her talk,
the low sweet talk of women who'd known loss and hardship
and whose eyes, on different nights in their long lives, had
searched the bedroom ceiling for answers.

When Mrs. Abelli heard Vincent pull up in front with his
car, she wrapped a shawl around Mrs. Marodi's shoulders and
escorted her out of her yard and into the front seat. They drove
three blocks to the City Hall in silence and entered the police
station offices, the women moving with caution as Vince hurried ahead to talk to the cops on duty.

The policemen were polite. They told Mrs. Marodi that her
son had fallen asleep in his cell and was safe for the night. She

asked Vincent to explain and, in Italian, he told her that the police would not release Nicky that night.

"Go home," one of the policemen said and signaled Vince Fiori to take the women away. Back in the car, Mrs. Abelli concluded that her friend should not be alone that night. She let her son-in-law drive them back and walk them into Mrs. Marodi's house, then she herself settled into her neighbor's velvet chair for the duration. She watched Mrs. Marodi shuffle past into her bedroom and heard her continuing to utter prayers.

Alone in her room, Nicky's mother dropped to her knees against the bed. Again her dear Mary Mother of God had not spared her, but had drawn her into the tight weary circle of mothers who mourn. Like Mary herself. "*Maria Madre di Dio aiuti,*" she whispered. Help me, she prayed over and over, until she had no words or sounds left. She pulled herself onto the bed, seeing only her son in the strange jail cell, out of her range, and returned to a world that was not his and did not love him.

A pair of pigeons had found their way to the peak of the Marodis' roof, where they began to coo just as the two women inside the house closed their eyes. The birds' round peculiar moans steadied Mrs. Abelli sitting alone in her neighbor's living room. She hadn't heard pigeons in years and here they were on the night of trouble. Pigeons off their course. Like Nicky, another poor odd pigeon off his course.

x.

None of the boys in Hawk's motley gang had ever been arrested, not even Hawk, so the siren coming their way sent a new kind of panic into each of them. Mack took off for the nearest exit, which happened to be the narrow sidewalk leading to the alley behind Vernon's. Not taking even a second to check with his friends, he chugged away at full speed, lugging his axe still hidden in yesterday's newspaper, and crossed the backyard and alley until he was in the shadows of a three-story apartment building with a thicket of raspberries out back. He dove into that thicket and pulled himself along so that he was in the deep center and invisible.

The sun set completely, the whole block grew silent, and still Mack stayed there. Then at some hour in the dead of night, he brushed himself off and headed home, choosing the darkest streets until he was past the center of town and out on the country road to Kelly Lake. He'd never been so scared in his life walking that lone road toting his father's axe and his own piercing guilt. If the cops didn't get him, the coyotes would. And if not them, then his mother waiting at the end of the line.

Shiner ran past Katie Fiore's house and her grandma's and pell-mell into the yards kitty-corner from there. After two blocks, he slowed to a comfortable pace, a boy out for a stroll after the rain. His breath caught up to him so that by the time he turned onto the sidewalk in front of his own house, he'd defeated most of the fear within him. Even so, he stayed outside on guard until every light had gone dark. Only then did he creep inside to bed.

Joey and two of the others scattered like wild rabbits, zigzagging all over the place. One of them lost track of where he was and which direction he needed to walk to get himself home, wandering desperately as he looked for some marker to guide him. Joey knew where he was all right, but he couldn't stop his legs from bounding all over town. He understood, in an instinctive way, that this crazy running might actually draw attention, but he couldn't stop, he just couldn't stop. It was as if his legs had been fueled beyond his control, keeping him going and going until, by some miracle of destiny, he landed in his own yard on the west side of town, where he collapsed on his back with no concern for the wet ground.

Hawk was the fastest. He shot off across the street into the high grasses of the vacant lot next to the elementary school then ran around the school and down the street on the other side. Like Shiner, his wits kicked in and he slowed to look like anyone else out walking, like any teenage boy on his way to the downtown two blocks ahead. But he didn't stay downtown. He kept going until he stood in front of Mooney's liquor warehouse, dark and brooding at this hour, its wide doors locked and impenetrable.

TEN

Friday, June 17, 1960

i.

Claus had died without saying good-bye. After the ambulance had carried him away, he'd said almost nothing to Tildy, not hello when she showed up at his hospital room every day or how are you as she sat by his side. He didn't ask after the lawn or her flowers. He raised an eyebrow whenever he wanted her to give him something off his food tray and he waved her away when she tried to rearrange the pillows he sat propped against in bed. Once he asked her how long they all expected him to stay in the godforsaken hospital, but when she had no answer, he shook his head in dismissal. That was all.

Now Tildy sat in her living room in her favorite chair facing Claus's favorite chair. She was dressed in black for his funeral and waiting for her oldest daughter, Grace, to pick her up, but she wasn't thinking about that. She'd sat through Claus's visitation for two hours the night before trying not to think. All their neighbors and family friends took her hand and told her of their shock at the news, they had no idea, he was such a vigorous man. So tall, the lady who lived down the street had remarked, as if that were an attribute that could have kept him alive. Such a presence, so tall.

Tildy had tried hard to act as though she could feel the grief that everyone expected. But she understood little and felt even less. Claus may not have even liked her, though she suspected that he did in some way. He surely liked her meatloaf. He'd always liked her pies, the edges crimped almost as evenly as those from the bakery. In summertime, he seemed to like her flowers too. "What are those pink ones?" she remembered him asking not long ago, maybe just a year or two ago. "Snapdragons," she'd answered, which made him laugh. "Quite a name, Tildy," he'd said then, as though she herself had come up with it, and she remembered that she'd laughed too. So Claus must have liked her flowers.

Once, of course, he'd liked far more—her eyes, her figure, her merriment. On his own Claus was not a cheerful man. He was dignified and purposeful, magnetic and handsome. But not easy. Not merry or playful. He'd looked to her for that. He'd loved that in her. And then, after a while, he hadn't, she supposed, though she never knew why or how to change it. Pretty soon she had nothing to say to him.

Tildy looked around her and wondered what would be different. She still had to cook and clean and do a weekly laundry, even for herself. She had to mow and tend her flowers. Bake for her daughters and grandchildren. Open windows every morning and draw the drapes at night. She'd leave Claus's room alone for a time, she concluded, because it was his. She'd leave his car in the garage and his chair facing her chair and his magazines by the chair and his hat at the door.

She'd made up her face for the funeral, a dab of pink on her cheeks and mouth, her hair pinned in some order. She wore a small black hat that she'd bought years ago when those things mattered to her, and she sat straight with her knees together watching the silent air swirl dust particles all around her. "Oh well then," she sighed out loud. "Good-bye, Claus."

ii.

Betty read Claus's obituary that had no mention of her, which made sense, but was still startling. As though she hadn't existed alongside his beloved wife, Mathilda, and their three daughters, sons-in-law, grandchildren. As though he had no other beloved and no other daughter. Betty had not gone to the visitation, but today was Claus's funeral. Didn't she have to go to Claus's funeral?

"What, Momma?" Elise exclaimed when Betty bumped up out of her chair after breakfast, slammed the dishes into the sink, and pulled Elise with her to the bathroom.

"We're going someplace, so wash your face and let Momma braid your hair."

A half hour later Elise found herself dressed in her blue skirt and white blouse, her braids formed so tightly that they made her eyes wide. Mother and daughter forged down Third Avenue to the First Lutheran Church where a black hearse waited for Claus's trip to the cemetery.

"Where are we going?" Elise whispered, holding onto Betty's hand.

Betty stopped at the corner across the street from First Lutheran and said nothing. She didn't recognize the people straggling into the church, had probably never seen them before, so distant was Claus's day-to-day life from her own. They meandered from their cars to the church steps, talking to one another as if this were another regular event, somber and dutiful, but not harrowing, not the sort of event that would break their hearts and leave them awash in loneliness on a sidewalk corner across the street.

"Are we going into the church?" Elise said, still whispering.

"I don't know. We'll see."

The girl wanted to ask if her mother was figuring this out the way that Katie and the club figured things out, weighing clues that might lead them to some kind of truth. But Betty's firm grip on Elise's hand signaled the need for silence. So they watched. At last a man closed the church doors and a bell rang in the narrow steeple. Elise balanced from one patent leather shoe to the other, wishing to jump around a bit if she could.

Betty wanted to be inside the church. Claus would surely want her there in his last moments above ground, possibly laid out in a tie she had bought for him one Christmas or another. She pictured herself and Elise entering the church together and sitting in a back pew, heads bowed as they offered last respects to a man who had visited their apartment not even two weeks before. She would sing the funeral hymns for Claus. Light a candle possibly. Her mind took her inside the church the entire time that she stood rigidly on the cracked sidewalk across the street holding Elise's hand, desiring another time, another ending, another chance.

Instead she turned and steered them back toward home. Elise immediately sensed the change in purpose and let go of her mother's hand to skip ahead, a radio song in her head, the bright June day still before her. Betty followed, letting Elise hop all about like some kind of bird in the grass. As they crossed the street they saw Mrs. Kirshling sweeping bits of twigs off her sidewalk, bent into it and uninterested in who was passing by or why. She didn't even glance their way.

But at Vernon's the door had been propped open and without thinking, Betty stepped inside, catching Roger just as he was slicing open a carton of canned soups. She stopped in the doorway, confused as to what she should do next.

"Hi," Roger called, continuing to unpack the box and arrange cans on a shelf. "On your way downtown?" He'd noticed her navy blue printed dress and dark veiled hat.

"I thought I was going to a funeral."

"Sorry to hear."

"Well, then I didn't go, as it turned out."

He stood up and wiped the packing dust from his hands onto his shirt. "Don't blame you. Never cared for funerals myself. My wife's family, they take to them, weeping and moaning. You ever hear those old Italian ladies at a funeral? Honest to god, those ladies can wail."

Betty nodded, but she couldn't find anything to say. She didn't want to leave either. Roger Vernon's observations on life were exactly what she needed right now, uncomplicated and clear. She tried a smile.

"Some friend of the family die? Say you want something to drink? Root beer or something? On the house." He took her silence as a sort of grief and shook his head sympathetically as he handed her a bottle of root beer. "Better in a glass, but what can you do." He opened a second bottle for himself. "Your little girl out there want something?"

Betty whirled around to see Elise in some happy game of her own making, leaping about from step to step, outside Vernon's door. "Kids," she said, then remembered that Roger's wife was pregnant. "Kids know how to have a good time. I'll give her a sip of mine. Thank you though, Roger."

"Good, good," he answered, feeling as though he'd navigated this woman out of an ordeal. "Nice dress, by the way. My wife, Sophia, you know her, she likes that kind of dress too, with a belt like that."

"Shirtwaists they're called," Betty clarified. "Sophia always dresses so well."

Then they both smiled, as Elise flitted back and forth, humming a song. "Thank you for the soda," Betty said.

"You bet." Roger went back to his boxes and Betty left the store, root beer in hand.

"Mr. Vernon gave us a soda, Elise. For free. You see how nice people can be?"

"I know, Momma," Elise replied as they passed in front of Katie Fiore's house. "Like Katie," she added, thinking she could hardly wait to sit out on her curb and see what might happen next.

iii.

Katie Fiore woke to the voices of her mother and Aunt Carmella in the kitchen discussing Nicky Marodi and his mother, his poor mother, as Katie heard the women say. Katie had played by herself in the basement the evening before, so completely involved in her own elaborate story of a girl detective solving crimes, that she had missed the real-life drama in front of Vernon's. "What happened?" she said as she barged into the kitchen, still in her pajamas, hair on end.

The two women looked at each other uncomfortably before her mother answered. "Some boys pushed Nicky Marodi around last night outside Vernon's and he had a kind of fit. They put him in jail."

"He got pushed and they put *him* in jail? What happened to the boys?"

"They ran away," Aunt Carmella said. "That's how it goes, Katie. The bullies run and the victims suffer." She sniffed. "That's just how it goes."

"So was this a fit like the minister across the street had?"

Again her mother and aunt exchanged looks.

"I think the minister was more the sensitive type, Katie," her aunt said. "I think life just got to be too much for him—it happens to those sensitive types. Deep thinkers, they struggle. But Nicky, he's got an illness. He was such a good son, wasn't he?" She directed this to Katie's mother. "Remember him when he was an altar boy, speaking Latin, so intelligent and sweet."

"He's probably still sweet if people would just leave him alone," Katie's mother remarked.

"Anyway," her aunt continued, "Nicky's got that kind of illness where people see things, they imagine things that aren't real and then get all upset about it." Aunt Carmella took a long drink of her coffee.

"How do you know this?" Katie's mother asked, almost annoyed at the older woman's insight.

"I read," Aunt Carmella answered. "Well, I better go home. I'm going to cook up a ham for Mrs. Marodi, I think."

"You better get dressed, Kate," her mother admonished. "It's late to be lounging around." She got up from the table and walked out onto the porch with Aunt Carmella.

Left alone in the kitchen, Katie found herself nearly para-lyzed by the stories of the minister and Nicky Marodi, whose lives had started out with such promise, better than her own, really. One sensitive and well-read, married to a pretty blonde who wore nice gloves and kept scented handkerchiefs in her bedroom drawer and Nicky with his devout intelligence now thrown in jail for having a fit on the sidewalk. How did such things happen? How could luck be so bad and lives so out of control?

She was still standing there when her mother returned. "What will happen next?" Katie asked her.

"You mean about Nicky? He'll go home and his mother will take care of him."

"Then what?"

"Then what," her mother repeated, as she thought about her daughter's question. "Then we go on, Kate." She lifted her shoulders in apology. "You better get dressed."

Katie went back to her room. She took out the black-and-white photo Elise had found in the old house, the tiny couple beneath the towering pines, smiling and sure, not knowing what she now knew. This was something she really did not want to know, something without borders or facts, more like a cloud that might shift and reshape and drift and disappear. Like the dark shadows above those towering pines. That things could happen inside someone's head. Tornadoes and earthquakes and avalanches in someone's head. Tongues hanging. Coffee grounds molding. Fits of nerves or fears or anything. It could even happen to her and nobody could stop it or even say why. And if it did happen, she'd just have to go on, like her mother said. She'd have to tie on her tenners just as she was doing this very minute and walk outside into a perfectly normal June day and go on.

iv.

Sue Too's family pulled up in front of their apartment building to a changed neighborhood that day. Though Elise still sat on the curb and the boulevard trees still bloomed their same new green, a suspense loomed that had not been there before. Mrs. Larsen was not talking through the screen to her daughter, Gertrude did not round the block calling "How you" at every turn. The Abelli garden had been left to inch skyward unattended and the June birds had taken a noonday rest in the limbs of the elms.

Sue Too took one long look and blurted, "Where is everybody?"

"Well, it's Friday," her mother responded, another of her polite responses that Sue Too never quite understood.

"Looks busy enough to me," her father muttered as he slid out of the truck and reached into the back for a couple of the grocery bags stuffed with their belongings. Anyplace in any town looked busy enough to him.

"Heh, kid," Sue Too yelled across the street to Elise. "What's shakin'?" She strode closer, then saw immediately that little Elise had changed too. Her whole face beamed in self-satisfaction as she waved one hand back and forth like a homecoming queen on her float.

"Claus had a funeral but we didn't go in," Elise stated. "Hi, Sue Too."

"Claus died?" Sue Too scrunched her forehead trying to remember who he was. Elise nodded, but offered nothing more. "So how's the secret club?"

"It's still a secret."

Sue Too scanned Katie's yard across the street. "Any more exploring?"

Just then they saw Katie emerge from the other side of her grandparents' garden, walking slowly as though carrying something too heavy on her back. Her friends called out and watched her coming toward them. "Hey, Kate the great," Sue Too greeted.

Seeing the two girls over on the curb, Katie picked up her pace. "Where've you been?" she asked Sue Too.

"You guys don't want to know what goes on at my sister Diane's." She rolled her eyes. "Be glad you're an only child, Kate, that's all I've got to say. And you too," she added to Elise.

They sat on the curb, each of them relishing the familiarity of it for their various reasons. They let the hush of the neighborhood settle around them, Elise picked up little pinches of street sand and sprinkled it on the toes of her shoes, and Sue Too sighed in satisfaction. Katie sat safely between them. "So," she said finally, "I've already told Elise this, but the guy in our mystery house for sure didn't kill his wife."

"She killed him?" Sue Too was all on it.

"No. My Aunt Carmella knew his wife from sewing circle and she says the man's life got to be too much for him and he—he just broke down. He was a deep thinker." Elise nodded as if she truly understood and Sue Too listened with her mouth half open. "Anyway, his family took him away in a hurry I guess. Anyway, I went into the house and cleaned it up a little for them."

Sue Too exploded, "You cleaned?"

"I did. I went in there a couple of days ago and made the living room and kitchen look nice in case they come back. If things were too much for him before, think how he'd feel looking at that sink full of dishes and old coffee grounds. I brought all the newspapers from the living room and piled them on top of the ones already out on the porch too."

Sue Too shook her head. "How could you do that without us? What kind of secret club is this? Not that I'd want to clean," she added. "But we're supposed to be a team."

"You weren't here," Katie said. "I hardly even saw Elise."

"I've been busy," Elise threw in. "Claus died."

"He died? I didn't know he died." Katie stared at Elise in a kind of awe, then lowered her voice to ask, "How?"

"Just in the hospital. I painted a picture for him though." The two older girls were not sure what to say to Elise about Claus's death, and after a few uncomfortable minutes, Sue Too stood up. "Well, let's go see how Katie fixed up the old house."

"I didn't fix the upstairs, if you want to do that together," Katie offered. "Long as we're in there."

Sue Too shuddered. "That's all I need," she grumbled, but they went off together nonetheless, with Katie in the lead and Elise trailing behind.

At the back gate they ducked down and snuck along fast and low across the overgrown lawn to the warped old door, which they opened into the hot and musty back porch now stacked with newspapers halfway up the windows. Katie turned the knob to the kitchen and shoved hard against the inside door. She didn't remember that it had ever been shut before, and it did not budge when she rattled the knob and banged on the wood.

Sue Too moved Katie out of the way. "Let me try. Farm girls know about these things." Elise giggled because she didn't know what else to do. The heavy old air was strangling her to death. "It's locked," Sue Too announced.

"How can it be? I just left it two days ago."

"It's locked now," Sue Too said again.

"I can't breathe," Elise whispered barely, not wanting to bother her friends, but believing she might die like Claus if she stayed in that slanting, jam-packed, and overheated porch.

Disgusted with the whole situation—the uncooperative door, heat, dust, and their gasping friend—Katie and Sue Too gathered themselves and they all left the house, running for the alley as low to the ground as tomcats in the night.

"I can't believe it," Katie said over and over.

"Oh well." Sue Too sunk back onto the curb in front of Elise's. "I guess it didn't turn out to be much of a mystery anyway."

"But why do you think it's locked?" Katie did not want to let go.

Elise took large, exaggerated breaths. "Maybe somebody's home. Maybe we should have knocked."

Katie shook her head. "Some church owns the house, my aunt said. I bet they locked the doors. I bet that neighbor saw us coming and going and told."

"What if those people came back though, Katie?" Elise liked the idea of the tiny couple in the photograph returning to read their books and newspapers. She dropped her voice. "Maybe they're in there now."

"He might kill her yet," Sue Too offered and, lost in their particular story lines, neither of her friends disagreed.

v.

Sue Too could close her eyes and just see her name in the evening newspaper, heralded for solving some crime. Without that what would her life amount to? Just a series of insignificant tasks lined up one after another in a messy apartment in another new town with a new school not even three months in the future. "There's gotta be some other mystery around here," she said.

As they sat side by side keeping watch on the block for some idea of crime, a brown station wagon parked close by and a thin woman in a black suit got out and waved in their direction.

"Who's that?" Sue Too said out of the corner of her mouth, her eyes fixed on the newcomer.

"My twin!" Elise exclaimed, jumping to her feet.

"There you are," the woman said. "I was hoping to find you out and about." In her hand she held a thick, irregularly shaped rock in a ruddy brown. "I wanted to bring this to you. From Claus. It was one of his favorite things. He kept it on his desk where he worked at home." She kept smiling at Elise who hopped on and off the curb in excitement. "Here, Elise. Please take it as a treasure. From Claus to you. And from me to you."

Elise opened both hands to the rock. "Thank you," she replied, damp and fuzzy.

"Tell your mother hello. Bye-bye." The woman walked to her car, but turned to say "Bye-bye" once more before she slid inside, adjusted the visor, and drove off waving as she passed them.

Sue Too waited until the brown station wagon was a block away before she said, "So is she a relative or something? She sure looks like you."

Clutching the rock to her chest, Elise wiggled back down on the curb between her two friends. "It's magic," she confided. "We have magic."

"She sure looks like you," Sue Too said again.

"That's hematite," Katie explained.

"What is?"

"Elise's rock. It's what they mine for iron ore."

Sue Too looked interested. "So is it worth something? Like money?"

Katie had no idea. "It's a treasure," Elise boasted.

"So why did this guy Claus want you to have a hunk of hematite anyway?"

Elise didn't answer right away and the other two remained silent in the equally silent afternoon. "It's a mystery," Elise whispered at last.

Sue Too yanked a weed and put it into her mouth. "That's for sure," she said, but Katie knew different. The lady had given Elise the rock because Claus was her father and someday Elise would know that too. But a hunk of hematite didn't seem much to give a sweet little daughter like Elise Larsen, even from a dead man.

"Maybe everything is a mystery," she said to her friends, as they sat side by side in their reveries of life.

And for the second time that afternoon none of them could disagree.

vi.

Holding her rock as if it were something fragile, Elise came into the apartment to find her mother sitting at the table with her sewing machine making something out of red flowered cloth. "Look what I got, Momma," she said.

Betty stopped sewing and scowled. "I don't like you in the alley, Elise."

"This isn't from the alley, it's from the lady, you know, whose face is like mine."

Betty stiffened. "When did she give you that?"

Elise told her mother about the car pulling up and how her twin said Claus loved the rock and how Katie said it was mined for iron ore. "It's my treasure, Momma," she concluded.

Betty didn't know what to say. In one week her world had changed from a set routine with Claus and Elise to this strange mix of death and bankbooks and job interviews. Sophia Vernon telling her secrets and Roger Vernon giving her free root beer. Now Claus's lump of rock like a booby prize at the fair. An hour ago she'd felt such a fervor she'd dragged out her portable sewing machine and started making a skirt out of a bedroom curtain she replaced years ago because Claus found the big red flowers too showy. Now looking across at Elise holding that rock, she lost any energy to even comment.

"I'll put it by my bed, Momma," the little girl said, shining like the summer sun, her life more purposeful and interesting than she'd ever thought possible, brimming with good will and mystery and magic.

Betty stopped sewing and opened a can of chili she'd bought in one of her sprees at Vernon's Grocery. The two had a quick meal and afterward Elise took out a puzzle, bent her head in concentration, and was lost in making something out of the pieces spread before her.

All day Betty had thought about Claus, not the Claus who had come to her for more than ten years, calmly magnetic like a cool fire, and not the sick old man she'd seen propped in his hospital bed, but the Claus she'd never known, who'd gone to work in his pressed suits and raised three daughters and shopped at the drugstore for chocolates to give to his wife, the Claus that those people at the funeral must have known, the everyday man she hadn't known and now never would.

With Elise outside playing, Betty had moved around her small apartment that afternoon not sure what to do next or what to plan for herself. She kept returning to the bathroom mirror again and again as if her own reflection held some answer. But each time her plain face told her the same story. If life was a ladder, then she was back to the first rung. Well, she had a daughter, so maybe she was on the second rung. Not far though. Not far enough. She was middle-aged and alone, not beautiful like Sophia Vernon over there or surrounded by family like those Italians. She didn't own anything much or drive a car or have friends who dropped by just to talk about their seven-layer bars or the shoe sale at Kinney's.

What did she have, that was the question. After almost two hours of hapless melancholy she began to tally what she had—a daughter, yes, and a beautiful daughter at that, and some money, not a lot, but enough, plus this new trust for Elise, her applications in for work. Once on this track, she kept going. She had decent furniture and a good view over Twenty-Fourth Street. She had manners, wavy hair, and some style.

That's when she thought about her Singer sewing machine and began rummaging through her closet and drawers to find something she could make. Something new. That was the thing she needed on the day they buried Claus. Just something new.

vii.

All day Hawk expected to see the police at his door. He figured old man Vernon would remember Mack was from Kelly Lake so that's where they'd start and Mack would spill because he was basically scared of his own shadow. He'd rattle off their names faster than Hawk could light a match to one of those French cigarettes, and then the cops would come calling, stirring up all their parents, bringing down curfews and threats, clucking and scolding like those hens out at Mack's grandma's.

But that didn't happen. The cops had more to do than chase down a petty gang of boys making fun of Nicky Marodi. One cop swung by Vernon's, smoked a cigarette with Roger, and heard what he had to say, concluding in the end that it was all a disaster waiting to happen. Kaka Roo, Gertrude, the pathetic delinquents, and cross-eyed Godfrey thrown in for good measure. By the time the two men had finished their collegial smoke, they'd agreed that no real harm had been done. Nicky had slept well all night. Doc Murray had come by in the morning with something to keep Nicky calm.

"If those boys come back and bust a window, give me a call," the cop said with a laugh as he left the store.

"I breathe on those guys and they run six ways to Jesus," Roger said, and he laughed too.

Roger and the cop had no idea what molten rage roiled inside the boy called Hawk. They weren't men of imagination. They saw what they saw and that was a baby-faced punk with a scowl and an overblown notion of what he was in the world. Nothing they hadn't seen before. So they let it go, while Hawk sat in his dad's garage waiting for them to come for him. As the hours wore on and nobody came, he veered off to his next idea. Maybe it would be broken windows, maybe some girl looking for trouble, maybe Mooney's. He still had the challenge of

Mooney's. Just thinking of the news splash on that made him grin. Maybe he'd call Mack later and see if he'd hung on to that axe in the scurry of bodies the night before.

He couldn't know that in the terrifying hour when Mack walked home to Kelly Lake, he'd made a hard covenant with God to never get caught up in Hawk's mischief again. In return, he begged for a pass on shoving the crazy man whose tongue hung out of his mouth. While Hawk plotted his next game of fury, Mack scrubbed his mother's floors in silent prayer, thinking only of what he could do in atonement.

viii.

Old Dr. Murray didn't have any experience treating mental illness, though he'd be ready to tell anyone that he'd seen enough kooks in his career and enough tragedy as well. When he got the call from Mrs. Marodi that her son had been jailed for causing a ruckus in front of a neighborhood store, he might have reached out to any of several psychiatrists he knew about in Duluth and Minneapolis. But it was a Friday in June, and he didn't think he'd reach anyone soon enough to help poor Nicky anyway. So he gave the man a heavy dose of sedatives and signed him out of the jail.

He personally drove him home to his mother, got him situated on the living room sofa, and left Mrs. Marodi with pills and the instructions on when to administer them. He patted the old woman's arm, a beautiful woman, this Mrs. Marodi, with the face of a Madonna and the soul of a saint.

"You keep him quiet and he'll be just fine," he said reassuringly and left.

But within an hour Mrs. Marodi knew Nicky was not just fine. His head lolled loosely to the left, as though barely attached to his neck, and his eyes looked glazed to her, veiled in a watery film. She sat beside him and took his hand. "Nicky—*come ti senti*, Nicky?" She was asking him how he felt, though she already knew the answer. Her son was sick. "*Sei malato?*" He raised his eyes to hers and held her there. "You want a glass of wine, Nicky?" His eyes closed and he leaned toward her until his head lay heavy against her arm.

They sat through the afternoon that way, Nicky in a dark, unnatural sleep and his mother sitting still to not disturb him. The arm holding Nicky's weight numbed and her foot fell asleep, but she didn't move from her position. She flexed her toes inside her shoes trying to stop the tingling. She could see outside to the street and the high bushes in front of the house full and green. She'd left her screens open just enough to feel the air move in, fresh and still like the day.

When Nicky began to flail, climbing the steep angle out of his stupor, his hands reached out and his head shook left and right, like a man in battle. Mrs. Marodi carefully pulled herself away and tucked pillows around him to hold him upright. Then she went into the kitchen to heat her minestrone soup, soup she'd made only one day before as Nicky shuffled cards and a light rain pattered at the windows. Now look. Lucky if he could hold a deck of cards without dropping them, let alone shuffle them in a cascading flow.

Nicky barely heard her in the kitchen. Whatever had happened— he did not remember—it had made him so tired. He did not want to move. He did not want to sleep either, for his dreams offered no peace. His dreams demanded a great effort on his part to defend himself from horror and hopelessness. It wasn't sleep he craved or being awake either, but someplace in between. A place like his mother's garden in the sun or a country far away, where he could sit and breathe and be and not be.

If he caught the aroma of his mother's soup, it did not bring him to the place he sought, but with all the drugged desire within him, he tried to get there. He wandered his senses, stumbling into the warm sun, the green shrubs outside and fat cushions tucked around him, the vague noises of birds in the boulevard trees and tomatoes steaming in a pot, which might all together lead him to the place where he wanted to be. Though he couldn't be sure. His mind dulled and his limbs nearly deadened, it was hard for Nicky to be sure really of anything.

ix.

Luisa Abelli came home from her night with Nicky's mother, tired and nervous. Whatever would happen to Nicky, none of them knew. They'd come to this country to get away from trouble, from infertile ground or villainous gangs or unwanted love. Luisa had sat in a cold cramped corner on a ship for two weeks, refusing to eat any food but what she'd brought with her, just to escape an engagement she didn't choose. She'd left her brothers and father, whom she loved, and tiled floors and ornate doors to come to this mining town of wilderness and ore dust. Her first baby was born without breath until her friend, Mrs. Romani, grabbed the infant and dunked him in hot and cold water to force his first fierce cry. Now that first son lived in a city and ran a company, her other son as well, and her daughter lived next door. The Abellis owned property on both sides of their street. That's what it had come to for them. Not so for the Marodis.

Back at home she washed her face and splashed it with rose water. She combed her hair back into a neat bun and pinned on her hairnet. Then she went outside to her garden, where just the smell of the dirt might still her agitation. She had planted five rows of tomatoes with six plants in each row. She had half as many bean plants in just two rows at the back of the garden and a border of head lettuces surrounding these. She counted the sprouting lettuces as they appeared, eight of them already inches above the soil. She also had cucumbers and beets, carrots, leaf lettuce, and strawberries. She had asparagus climbing the side fence and her raspberries in their separate patch, four rows of ten plants each.

Luisa's knack for numbers kept her ahead of any configuration. She remembered who drew which card and what they'd thrown away, how many one-dollar bills she'd rolled into her coin purse, the number of eggs she needed per person for any cake, castagnole, or macaroni. She calculated each month's earnings minus their expenses without pencil or paper. Her husband thought she could tell him the number for anything. "How many stars in the sky, Luisa?" he'd ask her now and then, maybe joking, maybe not.

Weeds loved a June garden. All that good soil and no big plants to squeeze them out. Luisa bent to pull them, holding a bunch in her left hand as she continued to yank them out with her right. She didn't count weeds. That was the thing, to not count trouble. Not to buy trouble and not to count trouble. Better to count the stars. After much thought on many nights, she estimated 2,000 stars in the midnight sky.

And those were just the ones she could see.

x.

Mrs. Wilke fretted all morning over Gertrude's unwillingness to get out of bed. Every twenty minutes or so she popped into Gertrude's doorway to see her stretched straight as a stick under her covers, the sheet folded over the blanket just so, and Gertrude's nose pointed right to the ceiling. "Do you need a doctor, Gertie?" she asked each time, though she never got an answer. "Gertie?" By noon Mrs. Wilke, now nearly beside herself with worry, began scuttling about the kitchen to make a chicken salad, which she knew Gertrude loved and peanut butter cookies too, though Mrs. Wilke had never been the best at baking, as she lacked the instinct to take things out of the oven when they were exactly done and so typically tacked on an extra five minutes for good measure.

Even so, just after she'd plunged into this fury of endeavor, Gertrude appeared, dressed as crisp as ever, but with unmistakable dark circles under her tired eyes. "Mixing up a bit of lunch for us, Gertie," Mrs. Wilke greeted, delighted that her charge was not dying and had emerged without further effort into the sweet light of day. "You want to sugar and smash the cookies here, dear?" She could not hide her solicitousness. At this point she would have done anything to keep Gertrude out of bed and functioning. She might even have walked her to Woolworth's for a sack of candy.

But that wasn't necessary. Gertrude felt a real hunger, a gurgling, faint, and woozy hunger that had drawn her out of bed and into her clothes in spite of her other debilitating hunger for poor Nicky. She sugared the peanut butter cookies and smashed them flat, a bit too flat Mrs. Wilke thought, but who was she to say, then helped the salad along by stirring great globs of mayonnaise into the bowl. The one o'clock whistle blew down at the Water & Light just as the two women settled together at the table to eat their salad. The overly browned cookies cooled on the counter and Mrs. Wilke gave Gertrude two paper napkins because Gertie loved them so.

"Well, there's the day," Mrs. exclaimed, taking in a pleased breath. "Glad to have you up and about."

Gertrude didn't answer. She quickly ate all the salad Mrs. had delicately arranged on a leaf of iceberg and scooped more out of the bowl, hardly hearing anything Mrs. Wilke had to say. Something about dew after rain, summer lunches, all thin as the two tissue napkins rustling on Gertrude's lap. Instead her mind twitched and jumped around like those little black spiders that knew no bounds. How to save Nicky, how to save Nicky.

"You been to the jail," she blurted in the short pause between the chicken salad and the cookies. "You been there?"

"Well, good heavens no, Gertie. Why on earth? I think it's downstairs of City Hall. Why my dear?"

"How many blocks?"

"City Hall? Gracious, Gertie, do you plan to land in jail on me?"

Gertrude didn't even crack a smile at that; she was too intent on her answer.

"Two blocks down Fourth Avenue," Mrs. Wilke said, but she didn't like saying it. She didn't like how simple the route sounded.

Gertrude stuck out her thumb in the direction of downtown. "That way?"

"Yes, Gertie. Do you want me to walk you to the jail then? Just to see what's what?"

Gertrude chewed on her lip for a beat, then shook her head.

"Well, tell me if you do, Gertie. We could go to Woolworth's then for a bag of candy. You've never been to Woolworth's before."

Gertrude shrugged it off. She didn't want candy or care about Woolworth's, and she didn't want Mrs. Wilke leading her to City Hall either. Together they washed the dishes and munched on the dry cookies and went outside to sit in the lawn chairs.

Such a sleepy day, Mrs. Wilke said, crossing her thick ankles and drifting off into an afternoon nap, her left hand twitching as Gertrude knew that it would. Only then did she head out in her usual way toward the churchyard, its grass still wet and sparkling, bugs hysterical as they were, ants rebuilding, a whole merriment calling out to her and so, at the churchyard corner, she busied herself too. She turned on the spot, a soldier on parade, and crossed that street.

Eyes front and arms swinging widely, Gertrude walked two blocks until she could see the high flying flag of the United States of America in front of City Hall. She followed it to the low double doors where City Jail was etched into the concrete overhead. Refusing to think, refusing fear, she took those few steps down and through another door to stand at the jail's broad wooden desk.

"Nicky here?" She was leaning to one side a bit she knew, but could not fix it and her eyes moved back and forth to all corners of everywhere in that room, desks and windows, blinds and doors, two cops with shining hair. "You got Nicky?"

The policemen stared in wonder.

"He's home with his mother," the one with the most hair answered at last, and smiled, maybe wanting to laugh, but Gertrude took it as it was. A good answer. She'd forgotten to say "How you."

She'd forgotten all her manners, but now she had her answer anyway. "How you," she hollered out as she left, an eagerness mounting in her and propelling her ahead down Fourth Avenue, Nicky's own street and her own street too. She roared along those two blocks right by Mrs. Wilke's house and the Dominechettis's and Mrs. Kern's, the two apartment buildings, right to Nicky's block where she finally stopped to consider.

Should she go past the bushes and into his yard? Should she knock? She inched toward the house with the red roof and sure enough, she could smell the sweet tomatoes. She stood by the bushes and closed her eyes to hear the tomatoes boiling and their bubbles and steam, the whole Nicky concoction reaching her way. "How you, Nicky," she whispered.

Then she did something new that she'd never thought to do; she blew a kiss like the opera singer on *Ed Sullivan* and then again, before she turned and walked the right direction home.